KEEPING
THE
Peace

Linda Cunningham

OMNIFIC PUBLISHING
LOS ANGELES

Omnific Publishing
1901 Avenue of the Stars, 2nd floor
Los Angeles, CA 90067
www.omnificpublishing.com

First Omnific eBook edition, May 2014
First Omnific trade paperback edition, May 2014

The characters and events in this book are fictitious.
Any similarity to real persons, living or dead,
is coincidental and not intended by the author.

Library of Congress Cataloguing-in-Publication Data

Cunningham, Linda.
   Keeping the Peace / Linda Cunningham – 1st ed.
   ISBN: 978-1-623421-35-2
   1. Romance — Fiction. 2. Vermont — Fiction.
   3. Murder — Fiction. 4. Marriage — Fiction. I. Title

10 9 8 7 6 5 4 3 2 1

Cover Design by Micha Stone and Amy Brokaw
Interior Book Design by Coreen Montagna

Printed in the United States of America

*Since their personalities figure so prominently in this story,
I dedicate this book with my whole heart to my three children,
Ian, Megan, and Colin.
Many thanks to Makayla Smith,
whose creative judgment and talent with a computer
has helped me so much.*

Chapter One

It was February and the dead of winter in Clark's Corner, Vermont. John Giamo stood naked, towel in hand, watching the blizzard from his bedroom window. Somehow, he felt older than forty-six this morning. Maybe it was just the weather. Another Vermont winter. He glanced at his reflection in the mirror on the wall. He still weighed the same as he had for years, his stomach muscles still tight. Peering closer, he could see that his light brown hair was just beginning to show a little gray around the edges of his high forehead, highlighting his slightly swarthy complexion. Was it making him look older, or more distinguished, he wondered. He knew that upon first impression, he gave the appearance of being the same khaki color all over, but Melanie always said it was his eyes that changed the whole equation. No matter how ordinary John Giamo appeared at first glance, his wife insisted, those eyes betrayed a unique and intense intelligence. They were light brown, too, but flecks of green danced in the irises. People who might judge him as phlegmatic, unassuming, or even depressed, she told him, were forced to reevaluate their opinions when they looked into those eyes. It was this trait, she said, that made him particularly effective as police chief of this small Vermont town where he had grown up.

He turned away from the mirror with a sigh and stood in front of the window awhile longer, enjoying the slight chill on his skin as the moisture from his recent shower evaporated into the dry air of the room. It was quarter past six. The morning light was struggling to penetrate the thick, blowing snow. John watched as the wind gusted and little swirls of white blew against the window like tiny ghosts trying to get in. He heard the familiar clunking sounds in the kitchen and knew that Melanie was stirring up the wood stove as she did every winter morning, building the wall of warmth between her family and the elements outside.

John began to dress. As the chief of police in such a small town, he spent very little time in one place. Sometimes he was traversing the streets downtown; sometimes he was cruising the back roads to make a general check on things. He knew he should spend more time at his desk, but he was pulled in so many directions that he relied heavily on his dispatcher/secretary, Becky, to keep most of the paperwork in order. Thank heavens for Becky. Today, the weather was so extreme that he was careful to dress accordingly. More than likely, before the day was out, he thought ruefully, he would find himself at the scene of some traffic accident, if not multiple ones. He pulled on his long underwear, his uniform blues, and the standard-issue wool sweater, then opened the bedroom door. The smell of coffee wafted up the stairwell. Happily, he meandered down into the kitchen, anticipating the first swallow of the hot liquid.

The large room where John's wife and coffee awaited him was bright and warm. She was always up an hour before him. Although they'd moved to Maine when their children were small, allowing John to start his career in law enforcement, they'd come back to Clark's Corner ten years ago to a home that had been in the Giamo family for generations. John and Melanie had done some renovations, opening the old kitchen ell into the woodshed to expand the space to fit their family of five. It was now a combination kitchen and family room, where the fireplace crackled most evenings of the year. There was also a wood-burning stove that they, like most local families, kept blazing all winter long. It cut their fuel oil bills considerably, and the wood heat made the house extra warm and cozy. The walls were lined with bookshelves, and there were comfortable couches where the kids curled up to watch TV or do their homework on winter evenings. Two dogs, a German shepherd and a brown-and-white Jack Russell terrier, occupied the couches now. The German shepherd flopped his tail when John came into the room, but didn't raise his head. Melanie Giamo set a big white mug of coffee on the table as John crossed the room and sat down. Then she poured herself the same and pulled up a chair to sit next to him. They looked out the window together. The winter sun had succeeded in penetrating the blowing snow, dragging the day into action. The chickadees were swarming the bird feeders in the garden, hanging on with their tiny claws, gobbling up the sunflower seeds.

"Look at them go," said John between sips of coffee. "That's a sign of heavy snow."

"They look like ornaments on a Christmas tree, don't they? I never get tired of watching them. I filled the feeders first thing this morning," Melanie said. "There was almost six inches out there then. I bet there's eight, now. They're predicting eighteen inches to two feet."

"At least they'll have snow for the Winter Carnival this year. It rained last year. I take it there's a snow day?"

"Yes. I delivered the news upstairs just before you came down. Everybody rolled over and went back to sleep."

"Everybody" was their seventeen-year-old daughter, Mia, and their fifteen-year-old son, Peter.

"How about Michael?" asked John, just as her cell phone rang.

"I bet that's him." Melanie dug the device out of her pocket. "They said on the radio that Dartmouth was closing for the day." John listened to the one-sided conversation. "No," his wife said. "No, Michael. Just stay where you are. You've got plenty of clothes. You don't need to bring your laundry home on a day like today. I don't want you driving. Okay, well, that's better. I'll call you later. Bye-bye." Melanie stuffed the phone back into her pocket and turned to her husband. "Can you believe that? Michael wanted to come home today to do his laundry."

"Hmph," grunted John. "I think he wanted to come home to eat. If he'd gone to school in California, it wouldn't be an option, would it? What would he do with his laundry then? Mail it home?"

Melanie laughed. "You know he always wanted to go to Dartmouth. And he *is* a homebody, John. He takes after you."

"I went away to school, not down the road."

"You went to Boston. You could almost walk there from here. Your mother said you came home every weekend."

"That's because you were here."

"You still know what to say to a girl." She flashed him a smile as she rose and took his mug to refill it.

He watched her as she turned away from him. It seemed to him that she had not changed since he first saw her, when she was fifteen, except she wore her blond hair shorter now. It curled around her face in thick, feathery, sexy disarray. He watched her small trim figure in jeans and turtleneck sweater, pouring them each a second cup of coffee. The same familiar desire he had felt for her all these years rose up in him again. She was irresistible. He never could fully understand what she saw in him, why she'd married him. He stood and walked up behind her, encircling her waist with his big hands.

Bending his head, he nuzzled her hair. "Do we have time to go back to bed? It's a snow day."

"What's gotten into you?" she said. "You haven't touched me in two weeks!"

"You look pretty sexy in that sweater. I guess it *has* been a while."

"Well, we're going to have to wait a little longer. You're too late. You should have gotten up half an hour sooner." She feigned impatience, but she pressed back against him as she said it. He kissed her neck and sat down again, sipping his coffee silently and watching the birds at the feeder. Melanie set a bowl of steaming cereal before him, along with two small pitchers, one with milk and the other with maple syrup. He stared down into the bowl.

"What's this?" He snorted. He knew very well what it was, but he didn't like oatmeal. He liked pancakes and sausage drowned in maple syrup.

"It's oatmeal," answered his wife from over his shoulder. "It'll keep you going. You don't know what you're going to face today, John. Besides, it lowers cholesterol, and we've got to start watching things like that now. We're not getting any younger."

It was not something he wanted to be reminded of. "You don't look any different to me than the day we got married."

This made her smile. "Very sweet, but eat your oatmeal anyway."

"Are you going into the paper today?" He stirred the milk into the steaming bowl pensively.

She joined him at the table with her own bowl of breakfast, shaking her head at his question. "No. We've got all the stories we need, and I can cut and paste here all day as long as we don't lose power. Lisa's got this issue pretty much ready for print."

John was glad to hear her decision. Melanie and two employees published a small community newspaper, *The Town Crier*. They worked out of office space in a big brick Federal house in the center of town, property that had been left to Melanie by her grandfather. The newspaper was circulated for free and reported local marriages, births and deaths, college and high school honor roll students, municipal awards, and the area school lunch programs, as well as posting notices of items for sale, help wanted ads, and weekend tag sales. The office wasn't more than three miles from the Giamo home, but Lisa and Roger, her two cohorts, both had to travel more than ten miles to get there. John knew the blizzard was only beautiful from a safe vantage point, that it could turn deadly in a heartbeat, and he gave thanks for this age of computers, cell phones, and fax machines. Still, there would be people out and about. Out-of-state skiers would abound, speeding along the highways in little cars or huge SUVs, oblivious to black ice, snow drifts, or sudden white-outs. And the locals weren't much better. They would fight their way through the blizzard today in beat-up pickup trucks with studded tires or four-wheel-drive SUVs, thinking that the ability to drive safely in hazardous winter weather was theirs by birthright. He nodded his approval as he finished his breakfast and rose from the table. He wanted to get into town early and mobilize his officers in an attempt to get the jump on whatever was coming his way.

Melanie stood, and they kissed each other lightly on the lips. She touched his face softly with her fingers. "Please be careful today," she said.

Reluctantly, he let her go and pulled on his overcoat, jamming a blue wool hat over his ears. "I'll call you later," he said. Then he went out the door.

Outside, he felt the full force of the blizzard. As with the most powerful nor'easters, it wasn't terribly cold, just above twenty degrees Fahrenheit, but the snowfall was dense. The small, dry snowflakes fell quickly. John judged it to be over an inch an hour. Wind gusts created total white-outs as he trudged around the house and heaved up the garage door. He backed the police SUV out into the weather and popped it into four-wheel drive low. The vehicle made the trek down the narrow hilltop road through a foot of snow; the town plows had not been on the back roads yet. If it hadn't been for the previously plowed snow banks, he wouldn't have been able to distinguish the road. Still, the specially modified Suburban crawled solidly onward. At least it was all snow, the police chief reflected gratefully. There had been no rain or sleet, and there was no ice underneath.

As he turned out of his driveway onto the road, John glanced back over his shoulder at his house. It looked like a postcard. No matter the season, it always looked like a postcard, and depending upon his stress level, the sight of it could bring tears to his eyes.

The house sat surrounded by a hundred acres of high pasture and forest, snuggled into the protective lee of the hill that rose up behind it. Made of native granite quarried only a mile away, the house was two full stories, with the traditional New England single-story white clapboard kitchen ell. It had been built in the mid-nineteenth century. At that time, the great barn that stood behind the house was home to a team of draft horses, three saddle horses, ten dairy cattle, two oxen, laying hens, and a flock of thirty-two ewes. The floor above the animals burgeoned with carefully cured and stacked loose hay and ear corn. The floor below was given over to farming equipment and a manure pit. These days, the barn sheltered the Giamo family's array of pet livestock: two horses, three sheep, a three-legged goat, and myriad assorted poultry and barn cats. And instead of using the damp below-ground level for machinery, John had built a separate shed that housed his beloved tractor and the various implements that kept him happy when he wasn't on duty.

Under the snow, the lawns spread out gracefully around the house to the stone walls that separated the manicured yard and garden from the wilder meadow and pastures. Over the years, John and Melanie had added to the perennial borders planted by his grandmother. There were several varieties of lilacs, peonies, daylilies, and coreopsis, so there was always something in bloom from early May until November. The vegetable garden took up the lower portion of the back lawn and was surrounded by a white picket fence. In the tradition of the old world, the previous Giamos had planted a small fruit orchard as well as grape trellises. Melanie's kitchen garden hugged the back porch, where they sat on summer evenings to watch the sunsets. As often as not, the cats would be stalking something among the herbs, and their movements released the sweet smells of basil, rosemary, tarragon, or mint. At the bottom of the property, where the land sloped south, there was a small pond. In the spring, the noise from the peepers could be almost deafening.

John loved the house for more than the obvious reason that it sheltered those dearest to him. The homestead had belonged to his paternal grandparents. John's father, Joe Giamo, was born there, in the very bedroom he now shared with Melanie. As he drove toward town, his mind drifted back to the familiar family stories and the rich history of this home and this land.

Chapter Two

Paulo and Mia

Paulo Giamo had been a stone-cutter by trade. When he decided to come to America in 1937, he settled in Vermont, where some of the finest granites and fanciest marble in the world were quarried. There was money to be made, and although Paulo Giamo had come to work, he had also come for something else: land. Besides the granite and marble, there was land in Vermont, and it was Paulo's dream to own some of it. By living with his sister and brother-in-law, who had moved to America before him, the young quarry worker was able to save most of his money, and in a lucky break that he could only attribute to divine intervention, Paulo acquired the beautiful stone house, its barn and, most importantly, the land.

In old country tradition, Paulo was now ready to marry. He was late getting around to it. At nearly thirty, he knew his sister had given up hope, but Paulo had an agenda, which he pursued ardently. For some time, he had watched a young girl who appealed to him. Her name was Mia Maronetti. He saw her in church, and sometimes he met her coming in or out of the grocery or drug store where she did bookkeeping.

"She's too young for you," chided his sister when he asked about her. "Too young and too pretty. She'll never have you."

"How old is she?" persisted Paulo.

"I don't know," his sister said, but of course she did. It was her duty to know these things.

In the end, she prodded her husband to make the introductions. He knew the Maronetti family. The old man was always up for a whiskey, so the men met in the bar. The next Sunday, Paulo was invited to dinner after church.

Mia did agree to have Paulo. She was twenty when they married a year later, and though she was young, she was more woman than girl. She loved the stone house, and they were happy together there for ten years. Then Paulo died, killed in a fall into the quarry. Mia Maronetti Giamo found herself alone on a hilltop far from town, with three young children and winter coming on.

Always resourceful, she swallowed her grief and went back to her former employers to do bookkeeping jobs, but it was hard to get in and out of town. She didn't drive, so she depended on her brother for transportation. She had a cow and some chickens, and she canned plenty of food from her fertile vegetable garden. Mia's young family would not starve, but the children were left alone every day until she made it home after dark. The money wasn't that good either. The young widow lay awake nights thinking of something else she could do to add to her income. The answer came quite innocuously one evening as she was preparing to lock up the pharmacy office and meet her brother for her ride home. Roger Barrett, the pharmacist, appeared at the door, smiling awkwardly.

Mia blinked. "I thought you had gone home."

"I was waiting to talk to you about something," he said shyly.

Mia waited. Roger stared at the floor until she said, "Well, what is it?"

"My daughter is getting married soon. The man she's marrying comes from a wealthy family from Boston. They are used to the best of everything."

"How does this involve me?"

He shifted on his feet. "Well, I," he stammered, "I have been told, that is, my wife wanted me to ask you this…"

"Well, ask," Mia replied in her direct fashion.

"You see, what with the war and all, things are very expensive now. All manner of things are hard to get. I cannot afford the wedding dress my daughter wants, and she does not want any of the ones I can afford. My daughter is in tears, and my wife is beside herself with frustration. My wife says that you are a wonderful seamstress. She says you made the wedding dress for your cousin and that everybody who saw it was impressed. She…she thought that perhaps you could look at the dress my daughter wants and perhaps sew one like it for her. Would you do that, Mia? It would mean so much to me, and I would…I would pay you a fair price. I can get the fabrics and lace you would need."

Mia blinked at him. People had complimented her on her sewing before. She had done wedding dresses and other projects for her relatives, but she had never thought it of any importance. It was just something any good housewife was trained to do.

Roger shifted uncomfortably on his feet again.

"Your wife does not sew?" she asked.

"No. No, she doesn't."

Poor man, she thought as she considered his predicament. Sometimes in their quest for the good life, they overlooked where it was actually to be found. "Okay," she said simply. "I will do it."

And so, as Mia was particularly talented at what she considered to be just a household chore, her new business took off. She made and sold wedding dresses, bridesmaids' dresses, and other fancy formal women's wear. People came from all over the state, sometimes with designs they wanted copied, sometimes to order a custom design from the beautiful Italian dressmaker. Mia prospered, buying a car and learning to drive. She kept her little farm. Her children were all able to finish high school. However, her children never felt the pull to the land as their father had. They married, took jobs at the marble companies, and built brand new houses in nearby Barre, becoming steadfast members of the comfortable, post-war middle class. Grandchildren came, and Mia loved them all, but there was something different about Joe's youngest son John. He reminded her of Paulo, and she had a special bond with him. He spent as much time with her on the farm as he could, never seeming to tire of her stories of "the old days." In him, she saw the legacy she and Paulo had hoped to create. It pleased her that he promised to raise his family someday on the homestead Paulo had bought all those years ago.

The blinding snow snapped John out of his reverie. He slowed the big vehicle and crept down the hill. He could just make out his in-laws' house as he passed. His father-in-law, Tom Dearborne, the seventh Thomas Dearborne in a direct line to own Dearborne Farm, was crossing the road to the big dairy barn. He waved as John chugged past, and John waved back. *This weather should make the old man happy*, John thought. The Dearbornes loved the cold. Sunshine made them nervous and giddy, and giddiness for any reason made them uncomfortable. They were Yankees, after all, and they were nothing if they could not control their emotions. John remembered with a sardonic smile the staid Dearbornes forced into friendliness when he had married their daughter. The Dearbornes could literally trace their lineage back to the Mayflower, and the marriage of their beautiful only daughter to the son of Roman Catholic Italian stone cutters was hard for them to swallow. The fact that John went to Boston College appeased them somewhat, as they had a begrudging respect for the Jesuits, but his career choice was beneath them. He did not join the family dairy business when they offered him a place. Medicine would have been acceptable, or education, or law itself. The Dearbornes respected lawyers and had been known to use them cleverly here and there over the years, but in their eyes, law enforcement was something not quite acceptable.

Still, although reserved and austere, they remained a close family. They would rather tolerate John Giamo than lose their daughter or the grandchildren, so for the most part, they kept any irritation they felt well under control. John watched in the rearview mirror as his father-in-law disappeared, like a snow-cloaked phantom, into the blizzard. He was inclined to think that if Tom cut himself, he would bleed ice water. The police chief shook his head as he peered through the snow, wondering from whence his sexy, lusty wife came. Perhaps she was a throwback to her great-grandfather, who, according to rumors in both families, might have been warmer than anyone imagined. It had been whispered around town for three generations that old Tom Dearborne was the reason the young and very beautiful widow Mia Giamo had never remarried.

John's mind seemed stuck on his wife's family this morning. Perhaps it was the cold and the snow. In this new world, the Dearbornes were seven generations on the same plot of land. The Giamos were only three. However, the new world was a great equalizer, and though the Dearbornes privately considered themselves to be several rungs up the socio-economic ladder from the Giamo family, the defining parameters of their assumption were blurred by a capitalist society that rewarded hard work and independent thinking. Although the Dearbornes would have vehemently denied it, they still held to a certain caste system that had put them on top, and they were loath to share the spot. For generations, everything from town politics to family dynamics had pretty much gone their way. They were ill-prepared when faced with the fact that their only daughter had fallen in love with a handsome Italian boy from a family only two generations born in America, and Catholic at that. It was frustrating for them to not be in control of their daughter's life.

To add to their disgruntlement, they had to share another of their lifelines—their water, the life's blood of their farm—and guilt didn't shadow the somewhat perverse pleasure John felt about him and Melanie owning it. It had been the sore tooth the Dearbornes had been forced to bite on since the first Thomas Dearborne had signed the deed in 1790. For, although the Dearbornes could be rigid and elitist, they were nonetheless honest, and each generation following on the other knew the secret to the spring would eventually come out.

The Dearbornes

The Dearborne farm water had flowed copiously from a spring on the hillside a quarter of a mile from the farm buildings. It was not until the property lines were re-surveyed when the stone house was built that the Dearbornes discovered their spring lay nearly five hundred feet inside their neighbor's land. Years passed, and each generation of Dearbornes inherited the duty of trying to acquire the hundred acres that held their secret and plentiful water supply. Acquiring the land would absolve them of the sin of stolen water for every previous generation. They tried everything, legal and sometimes barely so. Once, the spring was hidden with a carefully placed "blowdown." Another time, the survey team was spied upon and the pins quietly moved after dark. When their neighbor finally died in 1939 without issue and the will was contested, the Dearbornes waited, money in hand and confident, for the lawyers to approach them. Rumors began to circulate that the place was being sold for a song to a newly landed Italian stone cutter, but the Dearbornes scoffed. No Italian stone cutter would ever want a place so far out of town. Most of them lived in Barre, but there were a few Italian families in Clark's Corner. The Dearbornes didn't know any of them. They worked in the local quarry owned by the Barre stone company. They lived down by the railroad tracks and seemed to be related to each other. The Dearbornes' cold dismissal of the more common aspects of the world around them proved to be fatal for their plans.

The truth of the matter was that the foreman of the local quarry knew the banker who held the mortgage on the contested property. The foreman knew that one of his most talented workers, Paulo Giamo, was looking for land. The foreman wanted Paulo to stay with the company, preferably in his local quarry in Clark's Corner. He was afraid that Paulo would be offered a better position in the headstone factory in Barre and leave his employ. So he approached the banker, the lawyers, and Paulo and brought them together one day in the bank. Paulo put his money—cash—down on the big desk, signed the proper papers, and walked out onto the street a landowner. When the Dearbornes learned about the sale, they were furious. They ranted and raved. They threatened. They cajoled. They almost begged. They tried to litigate, but Paulo Giamo had made an impression on the bank president, who, like many other people, secretly felt that it wouldn't hurt the Dearbornes to be taken down a peg or two. The litigation was dropped.

During his lifetime, Paulo Giamo had cause to speak to the Dearbornes perhaps once or twice, but after his death, his widow came calling one Sunday afternoon asking to speak to Tom. Instantly curious, Mrs. Dearborne invited Mia Giamo into the big drafty kitchen and called her husband in from the woodshed, where he was chopping kindling. Mia Giamo sat at the kitchen table, hands folded, facing the Dearbornes. She was still very young, only thirty, and her olive skin was unlined and touched with a rosy glow. She was undeniably beautiful. With her dark hair curling out from under her bright kerchief, she would have been an exotic enough figure to the tall, pale Dearbornes, but it was the small gold hoops in her pierced ears and the gold bracelets on her wrist that made her so unspeakably foreign and somewhat frightening to them. They were uncomfortable in her presence, but they were well-mannered, after all, and listened to what she had to say.

"You may have heard that my husband was killed in an accident in the quarry," Mia Maronetti Giamo said.

"Yes, I heard that. I am sorry for you," Tom replied. He had never seen her up close.

Mrs. Dearborne made a noise. Mia Giamo thought she might say something, but when she didn't, Mia continued. "Yes, well. In settling his estate, it has been necessary to account for certain taxes paid on certain acreage, and a survey of the property was ordered." If Mia noticed the flicker of eye contact between the man and his wife, she ignored it and went on. "The survey has been completed." She looked up at both of them then. "Here it is," she said. "There is a spring on my property, from which a pipe runs to your property. Do you know this?" She noticed Tom's jaw muscle flex. She waited.

"Our water does come from a spring on the hillside that abuts your property," he said.

"It turns out that the spring is actually on my property, quite a ways in, actually," said Mia with a little smile. No one spoke for a few moments. Then she said, "I have a proposal. I am a poor widow. I have three children. I am always in need of money."

The Dearbornes' hearts leaped as one. *At last*, they thought.

"I propose," said Mia carefully, "I propose a lease. I lease you the water rights, a lifetime lease, renewable the next time the deed changes hands."

It was not what the Dearbornes had been expecting to hear. Tom leaned forward, smiling in his most friendly way, but as he was not accustomed to smiling much, it appeared as more of a grimace.

"I have a proposal," he said. "A counter proposal. I will buy the farm from you. Tomorrow. Name your price. I will pay cash. That will give you plenty of money, and your children will be safe."

They were shocked when she laughed. She laughed suddenly and out loud, and her laughter was honest and beautiful. Mia's full lips parted, and the sound cut through that somber household so dramatically that the beagle in the backyard bayed. The Dearbornes had never heard such a magical sound, although they were incapable of labeling it as such. Tom was moved by unfamiliar feelings.

"No, no, you misunderstand me," she said. Her gold bracelets tinkled as she raised her arms playfully. "Let me explain. My farm is not for sale. If I sell my farm, I could only buy some house in Barre or in Clark's Corner. I would spend my money on food, on fuel. I have a cow here for milk. I have wood for my fires. I have gardens and chickens. I have planted grapes and apples. I have security for my children. They will not go hungry. I would rather have a little money and a lot of land. No, the land is not for sale, but the lease… the lease is available to you. Pay the lease. I will have some money, and you will have your water." She leaned forward, smiling.

Tom would not give up so easily. He cleared his throat. "Mrs. Giamo, I will buy just the acre of land that surrounds the spring, the water supply. Surely we can come to a price for an acre of land that is agreeable to us both."

Mia blinked. She sighed, as if explaining something to a dull child. "Thank you for your offer, Mr. Dearborne. Normally, I might not be opposed to selling one acre of my land. However, the acre of which you speak has on it a spring. A spring that has fed this farm for over one hundred years. That's a lot of water, and that makes that particular acre very valuable. Now, I have another spring, near my house. It gives me plenty of water, too, but we never know about these things. Certainly I know that unplanned things can happen at any moment. A husband can slip. A rock could slip, too. The earth could tremble. And there would be no more water for Mia and her children. That is why I must keep both springs. Just in case. However, since these events of which I speak may not ever come to pass, I agree to lease you the water rights. As I said before, it will give me a little cash and secure the water supply for you."

Mia left that day with cash and a signed agreement for the lease of the water rights from her spring to the Dearborne Farm. The Dearbornes sat, unsettled, at their kitchen table long after she had left, each nursing their personal interpretation of what had just happened. Tom in particular felt warm around his ears. They had achieved their goal, but not in the way they had hoped. They had what they needed, but not what they wanted. The cool Yankee ingenuity that had made them wealthy and held them steady against countless Vermont winters had melted before the warm beauty of the Italian widow with the magical laugh.

Dark shapes in the middle of the road interrupted John's pleasant daydreams. He slowed to a stop. He would have to wait. About thirty wild turkeys, spectacular in their bronze plumage, were crossing the road, single file, probably headed for shelter in the hemlock stand at the southeast corner of Dearborne's lower woodlot. They were a common sight, but John never tired of watching them. As he waited for the big birds to cross, he glanced at his watch. It was nearly seven o'clock, and the snow seemed to be swirling faster and more densely than ever.

Chapter Three

In the stone house, Melanie continued to stare out the window after she had watched the billowing snow swallow the tail lights of her husband's car. She let the storm mesmerize her. Recently, she had been on such a treadmill, her days running into one another. She juggled her household, her children, and her business automatically, changing hats as needed almost unconsciously. Sometimes she felt her life was a dizzying carousel, or a Ferris wheel, spinning round and round in concentric circles reaching such a crescendo lately that she felt if it stopped and she looked up, she wouldn't know where, or even who, she was. So she appreciated the blizzard that now raged outside. It would ground her. It would give her a chance to look up. The storm would hold the rest of the world at bay. Suddenly, she wished that John had been stranded with her. She wished she had gone back upstairs with him this morning. He hadn't shown much interest lately, and she had let an opportunity slip away.

She heard the creaking of the stairs. Somebody was awake. Melanie turned away from the window to see her daughter Mia shuffle sleepily into the room, still dressed in the T-shirt and yoga pants she'd slept in.

"Good morning, baby," said Melanie as the girl plopped down on the couch and pulled a puffy blanket over her legs. "What are you doing up so early?"

Mia yawned audibly. "Emmie texted me. She wants to get together today. She wants to come up here. It would be a perfect day to work on our project. You know, I told you about it. We have to do a comprehensive talk on politics, the media, and the consumer. I said I'd go pick her up."

Melanie handed her daughter a cup of coffee. "Honestly, Mia! Sometimes your lack of judgment just baffles me! You are absolutely not going anywhere in this weather. Just look at it outside!"

"Mom! Come on! Debbie won't drive anywhere in weather like this, and she won't let Emmie take the car. I'm a good driver. The Jeep has four-wheel drive. What am I supposed to do all day?"

"Work on your project over the phone or the computer. I'm telling you once and for all, you are not driving anywhere."

The girl didn't reply. Melanie rolled her eyes to the ceiling, glad that the issue had been put to rest so quickly.

Mia seemed to change the subject as she scrolled through the television channels, landing on the local weather report. "Mom, do you think this will mess up Winter Carnival? Emmie and I are still trying to get tickets to the Ragged Rainbow concert Saturday night. I really, really want to go."

"I should think they would have the roads cleaned up by then," Melanie said as she put the dirty breakfast dishes into the dishwasher. "These storms only last two days at the most. It's just not wise to drive during the height of it."

"I told Emmie I would pick her up at nine thirty."

"Mia, did you not hear me? Call her back and tell her no, you can't."

"Mom! Please! Come on. Why don't you call Dad and ask him how the roads are?"

"Your father has a whole town to worry about. I'm not going to bother him about two bored teenagers."

"You don't have to be nasty about it."

"I'm not being nasty. I don't tell you or your brothers no because I want to be nasty. I tell you no for your own safety!" Melanie ran her fingers through her hair in exasperation. She hoped the whole day would not be one of carping back and forth with her daughter.

"Mom. Listen to me. Emmie keeps texting me. What am I going to tell her? How would you like to be locked up in a house all day with Debbie?"

Melanie laughed. "Debbie is an adoring mother. Emmie is spoiled. You're all spoiled. Tell her you can't pick her up."

"Can you drive us? Can you go pick her up? Please? Please, Mom?"

Melanie slammed the dishwasher closed. "Okay. Okay. You broke me. You really did. Tell Emmie I'll come to pick her up when I can."

Mia jumped off the couch. "Oh, thank you, Mom! Thank you! I'll go with you." She ran out of the room. Melanie heard her running up the stairs to her room to get dressed.

Sighing, she stared out the window, feeling the sting of defeat. She had never been a very good disciplinarian, but maybe this was a good way to compromise. After all, she'd driven in worse.

Twenty minutes later, Melanie was peering through the blowing snow at the base of the dirt road. "Can you see anything your way?" she asked Mia. Mia's face was pressed to the window.

"I think you're clear, Mom," she said.

Melanie pulled out onto the main road into town, hoping that if anybody was coming, they would see the lights of her car. She felt the car's jolt as the tires first slid and then caught some traction in the sand that had been spread. Warily, she proceeded into the village.

When John finally arrived at the big brick building in the middle of town that housed the police station and the town offices, the weather had not abated in the least. He was grateful to see Becky's small four-wheel drive vehicle in the parking lot. At least he had a dispatcher. Now he would see how many of his officers showed. His footsteps echoed through the high-ceilinged old building as he opened the main door, stomping the snow off his boots as he went. He headed to the police station, which was actually a block of small rooms cramped together at the back of the building.

Becky sat at her desk in the reception area. She was a large, pleasant-looking woman with wide eyes in a flat face. She wore her shoulder-length light brown hair pulled back from her face with two barrettes. She was dressed in jeans, a turtleneck, and sweatshirt, and in the same way her gruffness belied a soft heart, her slightly sloppy appearance did not translate to her job. She was deadly efficient. John didn't know what the police department would do without her. He had known her since their teenage years when they had attended the same high school. They had something else in common, too. Becky's husband was Melanie's cousin Jim Dearborne, who worked for Melanie's father, managing the Dearborne dairy. The familial connection had created a bond between them that served as a comfort to whichever of them was in need at the time. It was their own two-person support group.

"What's happening?" asked John, walking past her. His office was a small room off the reception area.

"It's snowing," she answered over her shoulder.

"That's a lovely shade of sarcasm you're wearing today. I see you got down off the hill." John punched a key on the computer on his desk and waited. The tinkle of chimes announced that he had mail, and he brought up the page. Every morning, he checked the log, the roster of incidents that had taken place the night before. The overnight dispatcher at the state police barracks kept it updated and sent it, at six every morning, to all the surrounding local police departments. All the on-duty police officers had to file immediate reports with the state dispatcher. If something had occurred in his town during the night, John would likely always know about it even before his officer could fill him in.

"I like my little car. It goes," Becky said. "Have you heard from Cully or Jason or Steve?"

"I have not," answered John.

Steve Bruno had been on duty overnight, but the log reflected no activity in Clark's Corner. Giamo wondered where Bruno was now. Probably feeding his face at the diner. Steve was the best of his three regulars, but it was still dismal to think that the ages of his three officers only added up to eighty-five years. He and Becky often felt like mother and father to the Clark's Corner PD.

"Well" — and this time, Becky sounded exasperated — "I just got here. I know I'm early, but you'd think they'd get their asses in gear and get here on time, especially on a day like today."

As if in answer to her crabbing, the door swung open and a young man in uniform stamped into the room, all the while whacking at himself with his hat and sending snow flying in all directions.

Becky set up a howl. "Cully! Stop that! You're making a mess! It's all over my desk!"

The young man stopped shedding snow. John came back through his office door carrying two cups of coffee. The coffee machine was in his office because it housed the only free outlet in the suite of old rooms. The younger man reached out his hand, but John scowled and set the cup down in front of Becky. Nonplussed, the chastised officer took off his jacket and hat and hung them on the pegs behind the door.

"They say we're going to get twenty-four inches," he exclaimed. Tim Cully was twenty-one years old, with curly dark hair and equally dark brows over snapping eyes. He was of average height, but powerfully built and particularly handsome. What he lacked in experience, he made up for in enthusiasm, honesty, and energy, although this was sometimes to his own detriment.

"What's that to you?" huffed Becky. "You're on duty, snow or no snow."

John interrupted her grousing. "Are the plows out anywhere?"

Cully nodded vigorously. "Yeah. The main road through town is plowed, and they're getting to the side streets. Patterson called my brother out at four this morning. He's plowing up your way."

"I didn't see him," Giamo said into his coffee cup. He could picture Woody Patterson, head of Town Maintenance, running around, self-important. Woody went crazy in weather like this, calling in independent plow trucks, zipping around in his town pickup with the yellow flashers piercing the snowfall, "checking on" his drivers, measuring the salt and sand piles. In the end, he mostly succeeded in irritating everyone, with the police department absorbing the majority of the complaint calls.

Steve's voice crackled over the dispatch mike.

John leaned over Becky's shoulder and pushed the button. "Yeah, Steve, what's up?"

"Hey, I'm on the south side of River Street Bridge. There's a rig jackknifed across the whole bridge. The tractor's hanging over the side."

"Son of a bitch. Driver?"

"He's okay. Crawled out the window. We gotta move this thing. The side of the bridge is punched out. What're we going to do about that?"

"Reroute the traffic around River Street."

"I'm trying to do that now."

John could hear an angry voice in the background and said, "I'll get Woody down there with some flashers. We'll call Larry and get the wrecker down there. I'm on my way."

He stabbed at the button again and turned to Becky, but she was already on the phone to Larry Sample. It was so early, John reflected, and she would know that the garage wouldn't be open. But only she would actually track him down at the diner and order him and his wrecker to the accident on the bridge.

John opened his mouth to say something, but Becky waved him impatiently toward the door. "Go, go," she urged, covering the phone with her hand. "I've got things here. I'll call Woody as soon as I'm sure Larry's on his way."

He thanked her silently with a smile, shut the door behind him, and hurried down the hall. John was a little surprised when he pulled out of his parking place at the town hall and fishtailed into the road. What traffic there was had turned the slush made by passing plows into a shining coat of slick icing, like the glaze on a doughnut. The SUV responded sluggishly to his skillful twist of the steering wheel, and he proceeded up and over the hill.

The scene of the accident was chaotic. John parked in the driveway of one of the River Street homes and left his lights flashing. He could see Steve Bruno in the midst of it as he approached. Thank the Lord it was Steve, thought John. If it had been Cully at the scene, fistfights would have broken out. Steve was trying to talk to Larry, who, contrary to usual behavior, had already arrived. He was shouting over the dieseling of the wrecker engine and waving his arms towards the bridge. A small man with a cigarette hanging from his lips, obviously the irritated driver of the rig, hopped up and down at Steve's elbow, also shouting. John could hear broken English mixed with angry French. At the same time, Steve was frantically motioning the creeping line of morning traffic to detour through River Street, trying to keep it moving.

"Got your hands full, Steve?" asked John.

"I'm glad to see you," his young officer responded candidly. He gestured toward the skinny little man who stood at his side. "This is Joe Boulanger, the driver."

John reached out to shake the man's hand. The exasperated driver politely took the cigarette out of his mouth and dashed it to the ground before he shook the chief's hand. "You sure you're all right, sir?"

"Fine, fine." The driver nodded vigorously. "Not my rig, though. Damn bridge! Damn bridge. I been coming this way for years. Every time, I say, one day somebody's gonna fall off this bridge. Then, it gotta be me. When somebody gonna do something about that bridge?"

"We'll get your truck out, sir. Just be patient," said John, but he had to agree that the man had a point.

The bridge had been built in 1941. It was narrow, made of reinforced concrete. It wasn't high above the water, just fifteen feet, but the road curved coming off it at each end, and the bridge itself was improperly banked. Apparently, the driver had skidded just as he came onto the bridge. He'd fought to regain his control as, in maddeningly slow motion, the rig continued to slide forward, twisting until the rear wheels of the tractor smashed into the far abutment. The ancient, cracked cement, already swollen with ice, crumbled under the blow. The driver found himself at a standstill, jackknifed on the narrow bridge, with the rear wheels of the tractor and the front wheels of the box perched precariously over the river. Now, as John could see, the little man was literally hopping mad.

"John," called Larry from the wrecker.

John raised his head in acknowledgment.

"Where the hell is Woody? It's gonna take me some time here. We need them flashers."

"Becky has him on the way," the chief shouted back.

Larry Sample spat tobacco juice out the open window of the wrecker. Untrimmed gray hair frizzled out from under his frayed and greasy Red Sox ball cap. He wore a full beard, and there were icicles hanging from under his nose. The icicles were slightly brown, tinged by perpetual flying tobacco juice. He was not a pretty sight, but every man there was glad to see him.

"Hey, you, Bub," called Larry again, pointing at the little driver.

"You mean me?" the driver shouted, puffing out his chest. "My name ain't Bub. It's Boulanger."

"Whatever," said Larry good-naturedly. "Climb up here with me. We gotta go round, and you gotta help me hook on."

The driver nodded and leaped nimbly into Larry's battered wrecker. Steve was scrambling to clear the traffic. Larry was especially famous for going where he wanted to go when he wanted to go there without looking in his rearview mirror first. John helped Bruno hold the traffic at bay until the wrecker had made its way via River Street to the other side of the bridge. He heard the gears crunch as Larry backed up to the crippled tractor.

John could now see flashing yellow lights coming through the snow. "Looks like Woody made it," he said. "Steve, you've been on all night. You better get home and catch some sleep. The power might go, and then we'll need everybody on."

John could see the young man's eyes were heavy with fatigue. He clapped Bruno's shoulder with his right hand and physically propelled him toward the cruiser. Bruno stumbled off, climbed into the car, and drove away. John gave a short, sharp sigh and trudged back to talk to the maintenance chief, Woody Patterson, who was placing detour signs with flashing yellow lights in front of the bridge abutments.

"We didn't need this, John," the man shouted to John. "We didn't need this now. This thing won't get fixed before spring now. No way. No way we can do it. I hope you soaked him good with a ticket. Was he legal on that bridge? What'd ya wanna bet he wasn't legal."

John sighed. "The bridge wasn't plowed or sanded, Woody. It wasn't the driver's fault. Better make sure those flashers are good. This snow is blinding. I haven't seen it like this in years, even when we were in Maine."

"It's heavy, too, John. I'm saying we'll lose power."

"I wish people would just stay off the roads," muttered John, more to himself than anyone. "Keep in touch with me today, Woody. I'm going to make a pass through town. If there's nothing going on, I'll be back at my office."

Both men looked up as an earsplitting, metal on metal screeching sound filled the air. Through the snow, they could see the tractor slowly being winched back up onto solid ground. There was a huge *pop*, and what was left of the bridge abutment shattered, as though it had been dynamited. The truck cab bounced on its own tires and settled back on the roadway.

"Ah, Larry!" Woody said, agonized and stamping his foot in the snow.

"I think he did you a favor," John remarked, heading back toward his vehicle. "Now you can start from scratch. A good project for next summer. You better start hammering the finance committee now."

Woody shook his head, wiped his nose on the sleeve of his jacket, and turned away.

The beleaguered police chief climbed into the Suburban and backed out onto the street. He was glad to note that most of the traffic had cleared. It looked as though those who were going to work had finally arrived there and everyone else had thankfully elected to stay home. He decided to swing over Poplar Road, which looped halfway around the western border of the town. He would make a quick check at that end for any trouble and then return to the station over the back road.

Chapter Four

Poplar Road was like so many roads that traverse small Vermont towns. It was a dirt road, wider than most, and due to municipal growth that had taken place over the last ten years, it had become one of the major roads in town, even though it hadn't been originally designed for the traffic it now handled. Poplar Road extended from the state highway, back into the hills where new houses were being built or old houses, like John's, were being reclaimed. It continued up one side of the ridge of the small mountain that made the western border of Clark's Corner and down the other. John had just reached the top when his cell phone went off. He grabbed it out of the console where he had thrown it that morning and spoke into it.

"Hello? Hello?" There was nothing. Melanie's number was showing on the screen, but the storm must have knocked out reception. He put the phone back in the console, opting to call her when he got back to the station. He continued to crawl along through the storm. On top of the hill, the wind was whipping the snow into a white-out, and he had to be careful. Suddenly, the radio called out to him. He picked it up.

"Yeah," he said.

"John, there's an accident," Becky's voice crackled over the radio.

"Look, get Cully on it. He's a first responder. I'm way the hell up Poplar Road."

"The ambulance is deployed. Cully's already there."

"Well, I'll be—"

"John! John, listen to me. It's Melanie and Mia."

Her comment didn't register at first. He thought she was saying it was Melanie and Mia on the radio. "What? What did you say?"

"Melanie and Mia got hit, John. They got broadsided."

"Becky?"

"I don't know anything except Cully got called out. Melanie called in on nine-one-one. It's right down in the middle of town. Please drive carefully."

Now he understood. His mouth went dry, and he could barely see where he was going, but it had nothing to do with the driving snow.

"They hurt? Are they hurt, Becky?" He was having difficulty controlling the encroaching panic.

"Well, Melanie called in, so...oh, John, I don't know. It happened right down in the middle of town, at the intersection. Cully just left. Please be careful. I'll take care of things here."

He clipped the radio back in its holder and shook his head, confused. Melanie and Mia were home. They had to be. But apparently, they weren't. What were they doing out? He tried to push the Suburban faster, but he dared not slip off the road. Wild thoughts raced through his head. To calm himself, he concentrated on the facts: Melanie had called in, so she had at least been able to use her cell. Mia. Mia would have been riding in the passenger seat. They couldn't have been going very fast, but they had been hit on the side, Becky said. Fighting his way down the mountain road, John felt weak with fear. He found himself thinking of his daughter, thinking back to when she was born. She had been born fast. They almost hadn't made it to the hospital before the eight-pound baby girl burst into the world, wailing for her first meal. They'd named her Mia after John's grandmother.

Melanie's mother had been nasty about the name. She'd laughed when she heard it and said sarcastically, "So Mia, is it? Mama Mia. Did you name her after the song or the spaghetti sauce?"

Melanie had been furious, but John had only laughed back, saying, "No, we named her in honor of my grandmother." He'd said "in honor of" on purpose.

He thought of his pet name for her. Mouse. He had called her that since her mother had dressed her as a tiny mouse, complete with a pink-eared headband and a long tail, for her first Halloween. Born in August, Mia was too tiny to walk across the stage at the town hall for the annual Halloween pageant, but Melanie had dressed her up anyway, and John carried her across the stage, holding her high for all to see. Mia had continued to live in the same manner as she had been born. She was fast and fearless, dashing ahead, sometimes rashly. John couldn't count the times he had plucked her out of one danger or another. Still, she continued to thrive in spite of herself, growing tall and lean, with long, dark blond hair and light brown, almost green, eyes. Naturally athletic, she rode the endurance trail riding circuit in the summer and led the school ski team in the winter. To John, his wife's rosy skin, blond hair, and blue eyes were beautiful enough, but their daughter was possessed of a more arresting, mercurial beauty, as though the exotic, mysterious magnetism of the first Mia shone through, softening and illuminating the icy, northern Yankee beauty with an inner fire.

When he'd left their home this morning, his daughter had been sleeping safe in her bed under the eaves of the warm stone house. But now? He stifled the horrible, random thoughts playing in his head, giving an involuntary, sharp hiccup, almost a dry sob, as he bent closer and closer over the steering wheel.

At last, he could make out the main street in front of him. He swung out of the steep road, blasting through a large snow drift left by the plows, and made for the intersection. He could see flashing blue lights alongside the red lights of the ambulance. He felt as though he were running through water. The world seemed altogether silent. The snow seemed to have muffled everything, even the swish of the wiper blades. Finally, he was there. He shut the Suburban off in the middle of the street and jumped out. He saw his wife. She was standing near the passenger side of her Jeep Grand Cherokee. The side was crumpled and the door was popped open. He could see that the window had been shattered.

John strained every sense in his body as he ran forward. A gust of blowing snow blinded him, and he brought his hand up to wipe his eyes.

"John!" Melanie cried out.

Now he could see her, running toward him, holding out her arms. They clasped hands and held on, each seeking a life preserver in the other.

"Is she hurt bad?" he made himself ask.

"No, no, I don't think so. She's conscious and talking. Cully's putting the collar on her, though. Come quickly."

He let her lead him to the side of the crumpled vehicle. He fell on his knees beside the stretcher, his blood thundering in his ears.

"Daddy," said the girl, reaching out.

Cully was tightening the straps on the stretcher.

"Mouse," John said, willing himself to stay calm. He looked into her eyes. They were equal and reactive. He began to relax a little. Her color was good.

"I'm sorry, Daddy," she whined. "I made Mom go out because I wanted to pick up Emmie. We wanted to spend the day together, and her mother wouldn't drive or let her take the car."

"Shh," John quieted the girl. "Mouse, are you okay? Anything feel broken or hurt bad?"

"No, Daddy. I'm fine. I think my shoulder hurts. I'm not sure."

"Well, we'll get you looked at." He put his hand on her forehead and smoothed back her hair.

"Where's Mom?"

Melanie stepped up. "Right here, baby. Let Cully finish tying you in."

"I'm fine, really, Cully." Mia's eyes turned toward to the young man fussing over the clamps on the straps that held her to the stretcher. She had known Tim Cully all her life and treated him more like a sibling than anything else. "Let me up. I can sit all right."

"Can't do that Mia," said Cully, posturing importantly. "You might have some kind of injury we don't know about and —"

It was then that an anxious voice suddenly spoke from behind them. "Let me through, please. I just want to know if the girl's all right!"

John and Melanie turned and peered through the blowing snow. Someone was pushing through the small crowd of bystanders.

Even in the confusion surrounding the accident and her obvious concern for Mia, John noticed that his wife seemed intently focused on the stranger. He was handsome, almost pretty, a little older than Cully, perhaps, with wavy brown hair. He was rail thin and ridiculously dressed for the present weather in cowboy boots, black jeans, and a long black leather coat. His hands were stuffed in his pockets, and he was hunched against the wind. He extended his black gloved hand to Melanie. John was not surprised. Melanie had that effect on every man.

"I'm Gabriel Strand," he said. "I skidded and hit you. I'm so sorry. Is she all right?"

Still kneeling beside his daughter, John felt the girl tremble. Alarmed, he turned away from the stranger and gripped her hand.

"Mouse — Mia," he said urgently, "are you okay?"

"Daddy! Daddy!" she said in an almost hysterical whisper. "What did he say his name was? Is it Gabriel Strand? Daddy! Listen to me!"

John knelt there, confused. He turned to look again at the young man who was still holding Melanie's hand and talking to her intently. Then, Cully and the other EMT were raising Mia on her stretcher off the ground, preparing to load her into the ambulance. The stranger, apparently loath to let go of Melanie's hand, stepped up and bent over Mia.

"Look," he said, "I'm really sorry. I really am. I hope you're okay."

"Excuse us, please," said Cully. "You're interfering, sir."

They carried Mia to the back of the ambulance and hoisted her in, John in attendance. Out of the corner of his eye, he saw Melanie put both arms around the young man in a reassuring hug. Then he saw her step slowly free of him and flash one of her brilliant smiles. Melanie had always been friendly and free with her smiles to the point where an undercurrent of gossip centering around their marriage was always present on the lips of certain local individuals who enjoyed speculating on those things. Usually, John laughed it off, or they laughed together about the latest rumor that filtered back to them, but this time, an uneasy feeling settled over him. Well, maybe she knew who he was, he thought, or more likely, he was overreacting due to the stress of the situation. He shrugged it off and turned back to his daughter.

Through the blowing snow, he saw the stranger step back and heard him call out to Mia, "I'll check on you later. Please, I'm really sorry."

Steve Bruno strode through the crowd and spoke sharply to the young man. "Mr. Strand. Mr. Strand, you can't leave the police officer in the middle of interrogation. Mr. Strand? You'll have to finish this report for me."

John lifted his foot to get in the ambulance, but Melanie's hand was on his arm. "John, you take the Suburban and follow. I'll ride with Mia. We'll meet you at the hospital."

"Who was that guy? Do you know him?"

"Not exactly, I guess," Melanie answered as she climbed into the ambulance.

"Mom! Mom!" Mia was calling from inside the ambulance.

Melanie puckered her lips at her husband as Cully slammed the door shut. The ambulance moved away.

John turned around. Steve Bruno and Gabriel Strand were facing each other. Strand was blatantly shivering. He was hatless, and his thick hair was covered with snow. His lips were blue. Steve was bundled against the elements. He was obviously enjoying himself.

John said, "What are you doing here, Steve?"

"I heard it on the scanner as soon as I walked into my house. I didn't know where you'd gone, so I turned around and came back."

A thought flashed through John's mind about how he might magically fire Cully and clone Steve. "I'm going to the hospital," he said. "I'll check with you in a while. You might take Mr. Strand here back to the station to finish the report. He looks cold." He winked at Bruno.

Steve nodded back and took the young man by the arm. The chief couldn't help but overhear Steve's remarks as he guided the man back toward the cruiser.

"You can come with me back to the station, Mr. Strand, and then we can finish the report. I see you've got a lot of snow piling up on your head. Ya know, in Vermont, we take that as a good sign. When the snow stays on the backs of the cows in a snowstorm, it means their winter coat is heavy enough to insulate them and all their warmth is staying on the inside. The rest of us just have to wear hats."

John smiled to himself, fishing for the keys to the Suburban in his pocket. He was beginning to feel the cold himself. Behind him, he heard the grind of a big engine. Larry Sample's wrecker was pulling up to the battered vehicles, still stalled in the street. Becky was on it today. The wrecker ground to a stop in the road beside him, like some giant prehistoric animal, idling and lurching in place, as if champing at the bit.

Larry, the dubious knight in shining armor, held his mount steady with greasy hands and rolled down the window. Truly concerned, he asked, "Everything all right with your daughter, John?"

John nodded. "Yeah. She might have hurt her shoulder. They're checking her out at the hospital. I'm going there now."

"Becky said to take these wrecks to Rick's?"

"Yeah," John affirmed, "that's as good a plan as any right now."

"What'd you do with that rock star?"

"Rock star?"

"Yeah, the guy that hit your daughter."

"Rock star?" John repeated.

"Yeah, man." Larry stained the snow with a random spit of tobacco juice. "The guy's some sort of rock star. They're supposed to be playing Winter Carnival up at Dartmouth this weekend."

The beleaguered chief gave one of his short, sharp sighs. He was beginning to understand.

Larry snorted. "I can't believe you didn't know that, man. You gotta keep up with things. Your kid'll know. Ask her. Apparently, he's quite the heartthrob. From California. Can't imagine what made him think he could drive in a blizzard like this, especially in that Mercedes. Stupid, I guess. Now, you wouldn't see Toby Keith doing something like that."

"Hmm," said John. "Thanks, Larry. I gotta get to the hospital."

The wrecker driver waved his hand. The wrecker-beast bounded forward into position. The newly enlightened police chief got into his Suburban and drove off.

Chapter Five

John could see Melanie waiting for him just inside as the hospital's automatic doors slid open. They reached out and clasped hands in the gesture that was a habitual communication between them ever since they'd become a couple. It meant that everything was okay now because they're together.

Melanie said, "She's over here, in the ER. They're getting ready to X-ray that shoulder."

"So it might be broken?" he asked as she took his arm and guided him through the reception area. Ahead, past the curtain of one of the little cubicles, he could see his daughter lying on the bed. She wore a foam collar around her neck and her eyes were closed.

"I don't think so," said Melanie. "She moved it around pretty good for the doctor. They just want to X-ray and make sure." Gently, she pulled back the curtain. "Baby," she said, "Daddy's here."

Mia opened her eyes, then closed them again.

"How're you feeling, Mouse?" John approached slowly and sat on the edge of the bed.

Mia's eyes flashed open, and she raised herself on her pillow, grimacing a little with pain. Then she spoke with conviction and authority. "Daddy," she said, "tell me you did not give Gabriel Strand a ticket or an injunction or whatever it is you give for this. I really hope not. It's Gabriel Strand, Dad. What was Steve Bruno grilling him like that for? You should be handling this, Dad. Really. This is huge."

John's first response was indignation, but he retained his passive expression and looked back over his shoulder at Melanie, who was standing behind him, a small smile on her lips. "Am I the only one who doesn't know this person?" he said, trying to appear nonchalant. "Who the hell is this guy? What's he doing here? And why the hell am I supposed to be impressed?"

"Mom, you tell him," said the girl with exasperation, falling back against her pillow.

Melanie walked around and sat in the chair near the head of the bed.

"It appears that we were lucky enough to have our car wrecked by one of the hottest pop stars of the day," she said.

"There's no reason to be sarcastic." Mia pouted, fluffing her thin hospital blanket peevishly.

"And that matters why?" John persisted.

This time, Melanie shrugged and wiggled her eyebrows.

"Daddy, listen, I know you don't know, but Gabriel Strand is the lead singer of Ragged Rainbow. It's the hottest group out there. I love their stuff. I know you've heard it."

"Not that I know of," said the chief. "Have you?" He looked at Melanie.

"Yes, I've heard it. It's pretty good."

"Pretty good!" exclaimed the teenager. "I *guess* it's pretty good. It's the best! And they're going to be at Winter Carnival at Dartmouth."

"So Larry told me when he came to drag your mother's car away," John said with a snort.

"Larry! Larry Sample, the spitty wrecker guy? Oh, Daddy!" Mia was obviously disgusted with his ignorance. "Emmie and I were trying and trying to think of a way to get tickets. I guess they've been sold out for months. He's so adorable! Isn't he, Mom?"

Melanie gave a wry smile. "He's pretty cute."

John looked at her very carefully, trying to interpret the expression that played on her face as he spoke to Mia. "He doesn't seem very bright, though."

"He's from California, Daddy. He doesn't know about stupid Vermont's stupid winters."

At that moment, two more people walked into Mia's little curtained cubby: Emmie Cohen and her mother, Debbie. Emmie was Mia's best friend. She was tall and athletic, like Mia, with thick, dark hair. When the girls were anywhere together, they looked like a pair of gazelles. Debbie was a small, pretty, pudgy woman whose lack of common sense was compensated for by her unfathomable good nature. Melanie maintained it was this good nature that kept Debbie looking at least ten years younger than she was. John always countered that it was her lack of worry resulting from a parallel lack of any sense whatsoever. That and the fact that her husband was head of surgery at Dartmouth Medical Center. Debbie never had to worry about money. Such a person, John had postulated to his wife privately, was never in danger of developing any wrinkles.

Debbie entered the cubicle whooping. Whooping was her way of expressing any strong emotion. She threw her arms around Melanie. "Ooh," she whooped. "Melanie, Melanie, I'm *so, so* sorry!" She threw her hands in the air. "Ooh, if I had only known! I never would have let you drive down! Oh, this is my fault. My fault!" She turned to Mia and clucked like a mother hen. "Are you okay, darling? Oh, you're hurt. Is it bad?"

Mia smiled. "I'm fine, Debbie, really."

"I'll call Jim immediately if you want me to," she said.

"Oh, you don't need to bother him. I think they can handle this here, Deb," said Melanie, "but thanks a lot." Despite Debbie's silly nature, her offer was sincere.

"Well, I heard you were hit by a star, at least. How exciting!" The plump woman giggled and giggled.

John sat silently, his face totally bland. He and his wife exchanged glances. Melanie was keeping her lips taut, smothering her amusement. He didn't feel entirely amused.

Emmie was on the bed next to Mia, holding her by both hands. "If I had known what was going to happen, I would have made Mother drive me! You're so lucky! Did you see him?"

"Yes, I saw him," Mia answered. "He talked to me, Emmie. Gabriel Strand talked to me!"

"Oh crap! I can't believe I wasn't there! Is he just as adorable in person?"

"More!"

"No!"

"Yes! I'm not kidding!"

Just then, a nurse's aide and a radiology technician entered the cubicle with a wheelchair. John heaved a sigh of relief. He wasn't sure how much more of the current conversation he could stand. "We're going to take you for your X-ray now, dear," said the nursing assistant. "Can you get in the wheelchair?"

Mia obliged and was soon being wheeled down the hallway, accompanied by her mother and father.

"We'll wait here," trilled Debbie Cohen, waving after them.

Following the wheelchair, John felt his stomach rumbling. "I thought you said the oatmeal would stick to my ribs."

"It's only ten o'clock, John. Are you hungry already?"

"I'm starving."

"I don't think so," said Melanie. "I think it's just a reaction to the stress."

"After this X-ray is over, I've got to get something to eat somewhere. They must have a cafeteria here."

"You've got to make it till noon," hissed his wife as they went through the door to the radiology department. "You've been complaining about your weight lately, so I thought we agreed no more snacking for a while."

"Hmph."

They both settled in chairs to wait for their daughter's return and the results of the X-ray.

Melanie pulled out her cell phone. "I haven't called Peter yet to tell him. He was still asleep when we left. Would you call him and tell him what's going on? Ask him to run out to the barn and give the horses more hay. They're going to be in all day. Also check the dogs' water."

"Why don't you call him?"

"That kid has been obnoxious lately, and frankly, I'm just as happy to have you tell him the news. He's going to flip out anyway and somehow turn it around to be about him."

John nodded. Peter, now fifteen, had always been intense and self-centered. It was the extended family's opinion that Melanie, knowing he was her last baby, had spoiled him. If he didn't like what they were having for dinner, she would fix him something special. If he wanted a specific toy, she would scour the greater Northeast until she found it. He possessed a fierce energy; once fixated on something, nothing could divert his attention until he had accomplished his goal. He was going through a particularly surly time now, however, and John had had to step on him more than once recently.

"Peter," he said into the phone, "we're at the hospital. Your mother and Mia got in an accident."

"Are they all right?" John could hear the real fear in his son's voice.

"Yeah, Mia's getting her shoulder X-rayed, but Mom's fine. Mia's just shook up. We'll be home as soon as we can. Can you give the horses more hay and check the dogs' water? Keep the fire going, too."

"Hey. Come on!" The boy's voice thundered through the phone.

This was why she made me call him. Melanie wanted to avoid the inevitable argument. Well, the thought flitted through his mind as he listened to his son sputter, she did have to handle things most of the time, and he hadn't been around much lately.

"Why is it always me?" Peter continued. "What were they doing out today anyway? Are they crazy? Mia just wanted Emmie here. Mom should have told her no. She always tells me no. Is the car wrecked? Who's going to take me to the gym? I have to miss my workout because Mia is spoiled and stupid and Mom's too afraid of her to say no?"

"Peter," John said sharply, "you watch your voice. Maybe you didn't hear me. We've got a problem here. You've got to help out at home. We'll be there as soon as possible. And you just try to think about somebody other than yourself, okay? Peter? Are you listening to me?"

"Yeah, I'm listening. I still think they were stupid."

"You and I are going to have a long talk when I get home unless you have an attitude adjustment in about two seconds."

"Okay, okay," the boy said, acquiescing. "When are you coming home?"

"As soon as Mia gets her X-rays read," John answered with a sigh. "I'll see you then."

He clicked off the phone and looked at Melanie. "What's wrong with that kid?"

"I don't know. He's going through a stage."

"I'm inclined to think your mother's right. You spoiled him."

"He's your kid, too."

"Let's just hope he snaps out of it soon." John leaned his head back in the chair and closed his eyes.

It was nearly two o'clock in the afternoon by the time Mia was discharged. Her shoulder showed no break. The doctor examined her carefully again and determined that her neck and shoulder probably snapped to the side upon impact and she would suffer some pain for a time. He put her arm in a sling with directions to wear it and the collar for at least a week. He wrote her a prescription for Vicodin for the pain.

"Vicodin?" The teenager scrunched her nose at the doctor. "I won't be able to maneuver the halls at school if I take that stuff. I'll just take the pain, thank you."

"She's pretty serious," Melanie explained. "She doesn't like medicine."

"Well," said the doctor, "take Tylenol, then, if you're bothered, but take the prescription in case you need it. You don't have to fill it, but it's best to keep ahead of the pain."

Melanie bundled Mia's coat around her the best she could as John pulled out his keys. Debbie and Emmie fussed around until Melanie said, "Debbie, why don't you run along? It was really sweet of you to come and check on us. I really appreciate it. Let Emmie come with us. It'll help keep Mia down and quiet if they can be together. I promise I won't run into anything on the way home!"

"Yeah, Dad's driving," Mia said.

Debbie whooped with happiness. "As long as you guys are fine, I'll go home, but remember, I'm there if you need me for anything. Anything." She kissed her daughter and hurried down the hall.

John winked at Melanie. "I'll go get the Suburban and meet you at the emergency room door."

He drove his family home through the continuing blizzard. Even though the plow had gone up through that morning, there was almost as much snow down again as when he'd come in to the station. He pulled into the driveway, and the girls got out of the car.

"Bye, Daddy," shouted Mia. "See you tonight."

He waved and watched them push their way through the un-shoveled walkway into the house. Apparently, Peter hadn't gotten to it yet. Melanie, still inside the car, turned toward him.

"This is a pickle," she said. "I have no car now. Can you call me before you leave to come home in case I need something for supper? I think we should fill this prescription, too. I have a feeling Mia's going to be pretty sore in the morning."

"Just let me pick up something. I'll make dinner tonight. Are you feeling all right?"

"Yes, why?" she asked.

"Well, it's been a long day. I was worried you might be hurt and not even know it. That happens sometimes."

"The doctor checked me out. I was feeling a bit shaky there for a while, but I think I was just worried about Mia."

"I'll just pick up some groceries and the prescription. You take care of Mia. Make that lazy son of ours shovel some snow. It'll change his perspective on things, at least temporarily."

Melanie smiled, leaned over the console, and kissed him. "I'm going to fill some buckets and kettles with water and fill up the animal troughs. I bet the power goes out, especially when the wind starts blowing tonight."

He nodded in agreement.

"Be careful today. I'll see you when you get home."

She jumped out of the Suburban, and he watched her until she was safely inside. Then he started back down the hill.

She had kissed him in the same familiar way, her lips soft and warm and just a little bit parted. Why did he feel so insecure all of sudden?

Chapter Six

"Hey, Chief," Becky said sympathetically as he walked in the door. He gave her one of his wry smiles, walking around her to his office in the back.

"No breaks, slight whiplash, she'll be a little sore. Melanie's fine," he said. He poured himself a cup of the coffee that had been brewed early that morning. It was syrupy thick, so he dumped in the last of the half-and-half and up-ended the sugar bowl into it. It tasted like melted coffee ice cream. He stood in the doorway of his office, leaning on the door jamb.

"Give me an update," he said.

"Steve Bruno's gone home." Becky swiveled in her chair to face him. "He was exhausted. He finished the report from Melanie's accident and then left." Giamo nodded, and she continued, "Cully's up at the inn. There was some trouble with some overzealous fans or paparazzi with this Ragged Rainbow group. I guess everyone had heard about the accident. Everybody's got a scanner these days. Anyway, there were about six or seven of them waiting in the lobby for Mr. Gabriel Strand. Bill Noyes got nervous and told them all to book rooms or buy dinner or leave, then he called Cully."

"Nervous is Noyes's middle name," John said with a snort. "Cully still up there?"

"Yes. Frankly, I think he's enjoying himself. He's as much a fan as all those girls."

"Well, he's only twenty-one. He's a kid himself." John shook his head. "And Jason?"

"Jason got called by the state police dispatcher. There was an accident down on the exit ramp, and the officer down there needed backup. Larry Sample's going nuts. He had to call the guys in from White River to help out."

John swallowed the last of the tepid coffee as anger stirred in him. "I hate to have one of my guys on an accident on the ramp. That's really dangerous. Why don't people just stay home? The state's gotta learn to take care of itself!"

Becky brought his tirade up short. "Easy, John," she said, speaking softly. "You're still upset about Mia."

The chief gave one of his sharp sighs. "Well, I never heard of this guy Gabriel Strand. Have you? What do you know about him?"

"Not much, I guess. I've seen him on videos and TV. My kids like the group. Strand is pretty cute. He's the hottest heartthrob around right now."

"Is he married?"

"I don't think so. He's pretty young."

"How old is he?"

Before she could answer, they heard stamping in the outer hallway and Cully came through the door.

"Jeez, it's still snowing just as hard as it was this morning!" he exclaimed.

John asked, "Any power outages yet?"

"Naw, I don't think so, but it's hard to believe. I bet we get 'em tonight."

"What's happening with that rock group?"

Cully instantly assumed an air of importance. "I had a long talk with Gabriel Strand and the group's promoter—I forget his name. They're the only ones here. The rest of the group's coming in for the weekend concert. In the first place, no one was supposed to know they were here. They thought if they just quietly crept into town, they'd be able to keep a low profile until Winter Carnival. They had some contract issues to sort out, I guess. They thought it would be easier to hide here. Anyway, it really leaked out after he hit Mia—I mean, after he hit Melanie. People started to collect at the inn, mostly kids, but there were a few guys with cameras. Pappa-whatchamacallits."

"Paparazzi," said Becky, not looking up. There was no point in encouraging Cully.

Cully ignored her. "Did Mia check out okay?" he asked.

Now it was John's turn to ignore Cully. "Is Bill calm now?"

"Yeah, most everybody's gone. There was one girl who really gave me a hard time. She was going to camp out right there until Strand made an entrance. She even gave me this letter to give to him." Cully waved a crumpled envelope in the air and then stuffed it back into his pocket. "A couple of people did book rooms at the inn, but I told Gabe to just stay in his room for a while and I'd clear the crowds. Poor guy can't get a deep breath without girls all over the place."

Becky did look up now. She arched her eyebrows. "Gabe? Who is he? Your best friend?"

Cully was ignorant of her sarcasm. "That's what he told me to call him. He's a nice guy, and we got to talking about a lot of things. You know, he wanted to be a cop once?"

"Really?" said Becky skeptically. "Cully, go back to your desk and fill out the report. I don't want to be here all night, and we've got to get this e-mailed to the state dispatcher for distribution."

Cully made a face, but did as he was told, asking again as he disappeared into the tiny office across from her desk, "Hey, is Mia okay?"

"Yes, she just wrenched her shoulder," John assured him as he turned to Becky. "How come we weren't told about this guy?"

Becky shrugged. "He's a private citizen. It's a free country. He can do as he likes, I guess, and I guess he didn't want anyone to know where he was."

"For an anonymous guy, he sure has been a pain in the ass."

Becky smiled. "He gave the girls quite a thrill, though."

"Hmph," the chief replied, snorting. "What time is it, Beck?"

She glanced at the clock on her desk. "It's just about five," she said. "Why don't you go home, John? I'll just wait for Cully's report, and then I'm outta here."

John set his mug down on her desk and heaved another habitual sigh. "You know, that's what I'm going to do. I think I'm having adrenalin withdrawal. I'm feeling exhausted. Let the state dispatcher—who is it tonight?"

"I think it's Gerry Ryan."

"Let Gerry know I'm home, and make sure she's got all the numbers. See you tomorrow, Becky."

"Good night, John."

Chapter Seven

John Giamo had three passions. In order, they were his wife, his food, and his garden. The second one had been giving him trouble lately. He'd been eating a little too much, exercising a little too infrequently. He had promised Melanie he would try to watch his intake, try to push himself to more physical activity. Certainly, he didn't want the second passion to compromise his first passion. Tonight, however, was an exception. He'd been through the wringer today, and he wasn't going to hold himself to any parameters. He was going to decompress. He tried consciously to turn off the police business in his head and think about food. Yes, he was hungry. This diet he was on was annoying him and making him crabby. Even though he wanted to lose the weight in a last-ditch effort to recapture at least part of the physique he had always taken for granted, he couldn't think straight when he was hungry. Tonight, he would make a real comfort food meal. Something his grandmother might have made for dinner on a cold, snowy winter night, something to warm a body from the inside out.

He pulled the Suburban up to the small grocery store in town and went in. It was dark outside, but as always, the store was warm and inviting. Chandler's Grocery had been in business since 1894 and had been run by the same Chandler family, father to son, for all those years. There was a Chandler's Grocery in three other neighboring towns, each run by a brother — peers of John's — and their spouses and half-grown children. In Clark's Corner, the store occupied a one-hundred-and-fifty-year-old Victorian house. The downstairs had been modified a hundred years before to accommodate the merchant's business. The upstairs had been living quarters and still was. Brad Chandler's two sons lived there, opening and closing the store every day.

Chandler's Grocery was a comforting fixture in town. The ancient floor creaked when walked upon. It was decorated along the tops of the high shelves with dry goods-related soap boxes, cheese containers, and colorfully labeled fruit crates left by generations past. The store smelled good. You could buy anything you really needed there, and they sold the best meat in the whole southern end of the state. It was a place to make brief contact with neighbors, to glean little snippets of gossip, to come in out of the cold or the heat.

Marsha was at the check-out, where she had been for twenty years with her ever-present platinum hair piled high and her immaculately done fake scarlet fingernails. "Hi, Chief," she said as he came through the door. "How are Melanie and Mia?"

"They're fine. Mia's got some whiplash, that's all."

"Oh, my brother-in-law got hit from behind, and he got whiplash bad. He suffers to this day. He gets terrible headaches, just awful," Marsha rambled on, caught up in her own words.

John nodded politely and proceeded down the aisle. It wasn't the first time he had heard a brother-in-law story. There was a brother-in-law story for just about any scenario anyone could think up. Marsha probably had the most entertaining brother-in-law in the state of Vermont, or at least her tales about him were entertaining, regardless of whether the stories were true or not. It stood to reason, the chief thought, that standing behind the cash register for twenty years couldn't be easy. At least she had something to talk to the customers about. John picked up a small grocery basket and strode up and down the aisles, picking his purchases with care. Twenty minutes later, he was on his way back up the hill to the stone house.

Plowing his way past the Dearborne farm, he glanced toward the big yellow house. A single pale light shone from the kitchen, but on the other side of the road, the barns were lit, looking warm and inviting. Becky's car was parked in the barnyard. John knew she had stopped to help her husband finish the evening chores. It was the Dearbornes' good fortune that their nephew/farm manager had married a girl who liked cows. In fact, John thought, if Becky had been born an animal, she probably would have been bovine. Warm and maternal with her large dark brown eyes, she prodded her husband and two sons along the cow path of life with gentle bullying and an occasional swift kick.

John smiled and drove on. He looked up the hill and saw the lights of his own home glowing through the still thickly falling snow. The windows were golden with light, and some of that gold spilled out through the windows onto the undisturbed snow, making it glittery gold, too. The Christmas wreath was still up, illuminated by the lanterns on either side of the door. As he turned into the driveway, he saw his mother-in-law's pickup truck parked there. She would be checking on Mia, he figured. He backed the Suburban into the garage as quickly as possible, gathered up his groceries, and went into the house.

The warmth of the room surrounded him as he entered. The dogs crowded around him, begging for attention. His mother-in-law, who had been sitting in the big chair, rose to meet him.

"Hello, John," she said. "Can I take one of those bags for you?"

"No, thanks, Catherine. I can manage."

She was a handsome woman, taller than her daughter, and lean. She kept her hair blond and wore it in a classic pageboy. Had there been any spontaneity in her laugh or flush to her cheek, she might have resembled Melanie more closely, but Catherine Dearborne was cool and precise in everything she did or said. John often thought of the emotional effort it must have taken her to decide to have the one child. And then to have a child as warm and earthy as Melanie. It was as though the Ice Queen had given birth to spring.

"Hi, Daddy!" Mia called out to him. She was lying on the couch, her neck in a foam collar and her arm in a sling. Her bare feet were in Emmie's lap. Emmie was painting her toenails.

"Hey, Mouse," he answered. "How're you feeling?"

Emmie spoke first. "She's fine, Chief. She was going to get up, but I made her stay down." Emmie looked fondly at her friend. "Did you get the prescription?"

John hid his amusement at her matter-of-fact intimacy. "Yes, Emmie, I got it." He humored her. "Do you think she needs one?"

"Well," said Emmie with authority, "I would say no, she doesn't."

"Hey, I'm the patient," howled Mia. "Somebody ask me!"

"Do you need a Vicodin, Mia?" Emmie asked.

"No, I don't, thank you."

Catherine said, "Oh my word! Of course you don't need a Vicodin! We don't take things like that." It was one of her favorite personal declarations: *we* don't do this, or *we* don't do that.

John finally managed to wade through the dogs and set his burden down on the kitchen counter. "The house smells like bread," he said. "Did Mom make bread?"

"Yes, she did," Mia said, not turning away from the television. They were watching music videos.

"Where is she?" John asked.

"She and Peter are out bringing in wood. They went out just as you were coming in," answered Mia. "Hey, Dad, look, quick. This is Ragged Rainbow. It's their new video. Look, there's Gabriel Strand. Look, Daddy!"

He squinted, and then, honestly curious, he crossed the room to look at the television. It was the visiting rock star, all right, complete with band members, singing a rock ballad unfamiliar to John. The sound was good, though, and he stood there watching.

"Isn't he gorgeous!" breathed Emmie.

"He's adorable. Ha! And he spoke to me! And he *touched* me, Em. He *touched* me," Mia said, lording it over her friend. "You're so jealous."

"Oh, yes I am," said Emmie, "but if I had been there, he would have liked me better. Then what? You'd get stuck with the manager!"

They both squealed, and Emmie, forgetting she was armed with a nail polish brush, accidentally painted a plum-colored streak across Mia's bare foot. They both squealed again.

"Argh! Get it off me, Em. Get it off me!" Mia continued to giggle as she waved her foot in the air.

At that moment, Melanie and Peter came into the room, each dumping a huge load of wood into the wood box. John was surprised to see a third person, also carrying an armload of wood, with them: Michael, his oldest son.

"Mike! What are you doing here?"

"Power's out at school. Classes canceled for tomorrow, maybe longer. I didn't want to stay there and freeze."

John asked, "Did you drive here?"

"Yes."

John rubbed his hand across his face. "Doesn't anybody in this family do what I tell them? Mike, you see your sister. We've had one accident. You turn my hair gray!"

Except for his coloring, Michael looked more like a Dearborne than anyone else in the family. His hair was longish, wavy, and dark brown. His eyes were nearly black. His coloring may have been Mediterranean, but he was built more like the Dearbornes, taller and thinner than his sister or brother. He was unlike them in personality as well, more reserved and cautious with his emotions than his sister or brother. "Look, I made it, didn't I? I just went slow. It wasn't that bad. Calm down."

Melanie pulled off her gloves and walked toward her husband. "Peter, fill that stove and put another log on the fire in the fireplace," she said as she, as always, reached out her hand to John. They kissed, and Melanie said back over her shoulder, "Girls! Really, you sound like something from another planet."

"Why do I have to fill the stove?" groused Peter. "Make Michael do it. I've been doing it all day."

"You're such a dweeb," Michael said to his brother, but their quarrel was interrupted by their sister.

"Look, Mom, they're going to do another Ragged Rainbow video," Mia said excitedly.

John needed his wife's attention. He was taking things out of the bags and asked her, "Want to be my sous chef?"

"What're we making?" she asked.

He wiggled his eyebrows at her. "Love," he said.

"You guys make me sick," said Peter, plunking himself down on a kitchen stool.

Catherine was putting things away in the refrigerator, pretending not to hear, and John and Melanie ignored him.

Mia shouted, "Oh, Peter, shut up. Come watch Ragged Rainbow with us."

Michael sat down on the couch with the girls.

"Not me," Peter grumbled. "He wrecked our car, and I couldn't go to the gym. I need to practice. There's a competition coming up next month. If anybody cares."

At fifteen, Peter Giamo had not reached his adult height, nor even his eventual shape. Now, he was rather stocky. He looked more like his father than anyone else, but his eyes were truly green. He was a martial arts aficionado, and he was good at what he did, winning most of the competitions he entered. Peter had his first-degree black belt test coming up in two weeks, and his anxiety was making life difficult for the rest of the family.

Purposefully, John turned his attention to his younger son. "Is your black belt test before this competition?"

"Yes."

"Where's the competition?"

"I told you. Nobody ever remembers what I say."

Mia was on her feet now. "Peter, shut up. You're just whining, whining, whining. Mom always listens to you. You always get whatever you want."

They were really bickering now.

Melanie raised her voice. "Okay, that's enough. We're going to make dinner now. Mia, get back on that couch and stay quiet. Emmie, keep your BFF quiet. Peter, you—" But Peter was gone, stalking through the house to his room upstairs.

"Really, Melanie," said Catherine to her daughter. "You've got to do something about that boy. He's downright rude. What's his problem? You've spoiled him rotten."

"I know, Gram," Mia said from the couch where Emmie was fussing, covering her with the light wool throw.

"It's true," Michael injected.

"Everybody, get off my back," Melanie said good-naturedly. "He's just upset about his black belt test. He's always like this when the pressure's on."

"He doesn't need to inflict it upon the rest of the family. He's got to learn some control," the grandmother said firmly.

"Oh, Mother, he'll be fine. Are you staying for supper? John's going to make something yummy. You can give Dad a call."

"No, thank you. Your father and I aren't too fond of Italian food. No offense, John."

"None taken," said John, rattling around for the proper baking dish under the counter. Years ago, it would not have been so, but then Melanie had said she would marry him and the dynamic had changed. Nothing the Dearbornes could say from that day forward could raise his ire again. He had what he wanted.

Catherine pulled on her coat. "I'll go along home, then. I just wanted to make sure you were both okay."

She crossed the room and bent over Mia on the couch. No matter what their opinion of their daughter's choice for a husband, or the staid, antiquated Yankee standards they expected Melanie to adhere to, both Dearborne grandparents adored their three grandchildren. It was as though the loving emotions they had fought so hard to suppress while raising their own child had finally bubbled to the surface and spilled over, to be lavished on their grandchildren.

Catherine cupped Mia's chin in her long, patrician hand and kissed her on the cheek. "Do as your mother says, Mia," she said. "Try to rest as much as possible. Grampa will probably stop up tomorrow. You're not going to school, are you?"

"I was planning on it," said Mia, "if they have school. It's still snowing."

"Oh," her grandmother said, "I think school is out of the question for you, snow or no snow, for at least a couple of days." Then the older lady bundled her scarf around her neck and head and turned to leave. "Good night, everyone."

"Good night," chorused John, Mia, Emmie, and Michael.

Peter sauntered back into the room. "Night, Gram," he said pleasantly.

"Drive carefully going down that hill," Melanie called out as the door closed.

Instinctively, those in the kitchen waited, looking through the windows until they saw the lights of the heavy Dearborne pickup truck shining through the snowstorm as it stalwartly made its way down the hill.

"Your mother doesn't like my cooking," teased John.

Melanie made a face.

"What are you cooking for dinner, Dad?" Mia asked.

"Baked penne with sausage and Parmigiano Reggiano, your mother's fresh bread, and Caesar salad. Something warm for this cold night."

"And I'm making an apple pie," Melanie chimed in.

"Oh, wow!" Emmie clasped her hands under her chin. "I'm glad I'm staying tonight."

"Hey." Peter was still peering out the window. "Grammie's back."

The lights of a vehicle pierced the flying snow as it crawled up the road toward the house.

"Oh, no," said Melanie, going over and standing by her son in front of the window. "Maybe a tree is down across the road or something."

Michael joined them. "That's not Gram's truck. That's a smaller vehicle."

It was impossible to see through the storm.

"Well, someone's coming here," said Melanie. "It can't be through traffic. Not on a night like tonight. We're the last place for two miles, and the houses at the other end are easier to get to from the main route."

"They've got to be coming here," Michael said.

John snorted. He didn't want to face more drama.

Sure enough, as they all stood there watching the lights, the vehicle turned into the driveway.

"I guess we'll find out soon enough," said Melanie, going to the door. She went out into the mudroom to open the front door.

Everyone waited, curious and just a little apprehensive.

John heard the door open and a voice say, "Hello, Mrs. Giamo. I was wondering whether I could come in for a minute."

"Oh, my, what are you doing out on a night like this?" Melanie asked with surprise in her voice. "Of course, of course, come in, please."

Gabriel followed her into the warm living room, and Melanie closed the door behind them. Several things happened at once: the dogs started barking, the girls on the couch made a strange sound, and the knife that John had been using clattered to the floor.

Melanie said, "Please, Mr. Strand, let me take your coat."

"Thanks, but please, call me Gabe," said their guest over the ensuing mayhem. He handed her his coat and stood, looking around. "This is a great room."

The dogs swarmed him, barking, but he wasn't disturbed. He held out his hand, and they both sniffed, then started to wiggle and jump, begging for attention.

"Go lie down, you idiots," John said harshly to the dogs as he crossed the room.

The visitor extended his right hand. John shook it.

"What brings you all the way out here in this storm? Is there more trouble?" Melanie asked.

Strand looked away from John and smiled at Melanie. "I just had to make amends," the musician said. In his left hand, he held two longish paper-wrapped packages. He handed one to Melanie. "I'm really very sorry for crashing into you this morning."

She took the package and looked down through the top. "Ooohh, flowers," she said. "Thank you so much. They're beautiful."

Mia and Emmie were standing, struck dumb, beside the couch. The Ragged Rainbow front man handed the other package to Mia. John noted with some shock that his daughter had somehow managed to shed her neck brace and her arm sling. They were nowhere in sight. He could see his daughter's hand shake as she took the flowers. Emmie's face was flushed.

"Thank you," said Mia, almost in a whisper. "Thank you so much."

"Did everything check out okay with you at the hospital?" Strand asked.

Emmie nodded vigorously. She said rapidly, "Oh, yes! She's really, really good. They gave her a prescription for Vicodin, but she won't take it. She's not in that much pain. She—"

"I'm fine," said Mia, cutting her friend off. "Thank you for asking. Thank you for coming. Really. Oh, this is my friend, Emmie Cohen."

"Nice to meet you, Emmie." Strand extended his hand again.

Only her mother's good training and guidance throughout the years gave Emmie the presence of mind to shake his hand, John thought.

Melanie stepped in smoothly. "She's had some whiplash, that's all. Please, Mr. Strand—"

"Gabriel. I think Mr. Strand is my father," the young man said, laughing.

"Well, then, Gabriel," said Melanie, "please join us for dinner. My husband's cooking."

In the heat of the kitchen, Melanie had unzipped her turtleneck sweater. John saw the lace trim of her camisole and the gentle swell of her breasts. He also saw the musician's eyes flicker over Melanie's chest, but Melanie didn't seem to notice.

"Is that a good thing or a bad thing?" Gabriel asked, a friendly smile playing on his lips.

He snorted to redirect their guest's attention from his wife's chest. "That's a very good thing. Baked penne with Parmigiano Reggiano and sausage. Homemade bread and apple pie."

"I'll stay," Strand said, smiling at Melanie. "Can I do anything?"

"Actually, yes, you can," John answered quickly, handing him a bottle of Chianti. "You can open this—" he took three wine glasses down from the cabinet "—and pour us all a glass of wine."

Chapter Eight

Over the years, Melanie had slowly come to realize the effect she had on men and, in turn, the toll it took on her husband. In the early days of their love, she had been unaware that he might be jealous or insecure. He came home every weekend from college, and when she started college the next year, he had traveled to see her. She had expected it; she enjoyed it. Young and naïve, she hadn't been aware of his fear—fear that she would meet somebody else and leave him. It was Becky that first brought it up to her bluntly. "John's crazy about you. You've got to stop flirting in front of him."

"I don't flirt," Melanie had insisted.

"You just have to look at a guy, and they're mush," Becky had exclaimed. "You're too pretty and, and, too *something*, to smile at guys. It's just your manner, I guess, but guys take it as an invitation."

Sometimes, through the years, there was gossip to contend with, but John had seemed to settle his demons. She knew he trusted her, and he'd seemed to have come to the conclusion that there were things about his wife he would just have to accept. For her part, she made a conscious effort to let him know how much she truly loved him.

Suddenly, the realization washed over her, even as she listened to Gabriel Strand while he answered John. That was what had been missing lately: that conscious renewal of their love every day. When had it weakened? What had dulled the delicious sharpness of the leap of her stomach each evening he returned home? When had he ceased to slide his hand up under her clothes, under her bra, to cup her breast? And worse, why hadn't she noticed it before this? She felt the young musician's eyes on her chest. It felt good to be noticed. She turned toward him and met his eyes.

"I can handle that," the mesmerized man replied. "Corkscrew?"

Peter rummaged in one of the kitchen drawers and handed the smiling singer a corkscrew.

"And your name is?" asked Strand.

"I'm Peter." Then, in a burst of civility, he added, "And this is my brother Michael."

The three shook hands around.

Strand uncorked the bottle and poured the wine, handing a glass first to Melanie and then to John. The girls had not moved. They stood rooted beside the couch, their cheeks pink.

Melanie said, "Girls, come put these flowers in a couple of vases."

At her words, the two seemed to find their sensibilities. They took the flowers and went about the task.

"Let me propose a toast," said the guest. "A toast to the fact that everyone's in one piece, in spite of my California driving."

The glasses clinked, and everyone laughed.

"What are you driving now?" John asked, stirring the sizzling sausage in the pan with onions and garlic. The spicy aroma filled the room. "That's not your Mercedes."

"No, it isn't," said Strand, grimacing. "The Mercedes wasn't mine, either. It was a rental. Anyway, Bruce—Bruce Blake; he's one of the promoters—had this local girl cornered in the bar at the inn. She's a hostess there, I guess. She was coming on to him, and it looked like a hook-up to me, so I told her I wanted to see you, and she let me borrow her car. I think they wanted to get rid of me."

"Must be nice to be a rock star," John muttered, only loud enough for Melanie's ears. He added the crushed tomatoes and the cheese with another grumble. "Have a perfect stranger lend you their car. It'd be hard enough for *me* to commandeer one." He finished the preparations, his little rant seemingly over, and said more vocally, "This is ready to go into the oven."

Melanie stepped up and opened the oven door. The hot air blasted her face, and John slid the green enameled pan in next to her apple pie.

"Twenty-five minutes," he announced. He turned his back to the room, washing up some utensils in the sink.

"Here, chew on these while you wait." Melanie reached a mitted hand back into the oven and brought out a cookie sheet full of stuffed mushrooms. "There's crabmeat in these," she said to Strand, "in case you have allergies."

"Thanks. I don't. They look very good. Let me help." He took the spatula she had been holding, his fingers brushing hers ever so lightly.

"Oh," she said softly. "Oh, thank you. You can put them on this plate." She turned abruptly away, saying into the room, "Girls, set plates and silverware out on the kitchen table. We can help ourselves buffet-style and sit in the dining room."

The girls were slowly losing their shyness. Mia said, "Where do you live, really?"

"I live in Beverly Hills now. I just bought my first house," he said. "It's a nice one. I like it. It's not too big, but it has a great pool and a pretty garden. My mother likes to garden."

"Oh, your mother lives with you?" asked Emmie.

"And my sister. I grew up in a small town just outside San Diego. My father was in the Navy. I was an only child until I was twelve years old. Then, my sister was born! She's fifteen now. After I had enough money and I bought the house, I brought them there to live with me."

"Are your parents divorced, then?" asked Mia.

"My father died when my sister was five."

"Oh, I'm, ah, I'm sorry," Mia stammered.

"Food's served," interrupted John, elbowing through and setting the hot casserole dish on the trivet.

Melanie followed with the salad bowl, and John sliced the bread.

"Now everybody grab a plate and dish up. We'll go into the dining room to eat." Melanie handed a plate to each girl. "Michael, you sit at one end, Dad will sit at the other. Girls on that side. Gabriel, you sit between Peter and me."

As they helped themselves to their meal, a low sigh seemed to pass through the room. Gabriel looked up from the salad bowl, alert.

"Don't worry," Melanie said. "We don't have ghosts in this house. At least, we haven't seen them. That's the wind you're hearing. It's an old house."

John added, "The storm is about to blow itself out."

"I bet we got two feet," said Peter gleefully. "I'm going skiing to-morrow."

"If there's no school," Melanie said.

"Now is when we'll get a power outage," predicted John. "Some tree will go down under the weight of the snow or something."

The family and their guests took their places around the table. The dining room was long and narrow, papered in black and white toile. The long windows were draped in sheer curtains that reached to the wide spruce floorboards, shiny with the footsteps of the comings and goings of the generations of the past one hundred and fifty years. There were old family portraits on the walls, of those people and the horses they'd owned. A fireplace crackled at the far end of the room, and Melanie's cobalt glass collection glowed in its light. She loved to eat in the dining room. She felt oddly alive, as though a bothersome care had been lifted from her, as though there was promise yet to the night ahead.

Melanie noticed Gabriel, sitting quietly, looking around at the room. Ignoring her husband's sharp glance, she asked, "Is everything all right? You look a little sad."

"I like it here," Strand said. "You don't know, but I never get a chance to be normal. Not for years now. You're all so nice. It makes me miss my mother and sister. Does that sound cheesy?"

"Not at all," said Melanie. "How about a girlfriend? Do you have one?"

"Mom!" Mia gasped, scandalized.

The musician laughed out loud, his dark eyes sparkling and his hair waving irresistibly around his face. "That's okay. Everybody asks. I don't have a serious girlfriend right now. Being on the road all the time, it's really hard to sustain a relationship. Sometimes I take some time off, when we get breaks in the concert series, but I just go back to California. Then I lock myself in my room and write songs. I gotta keep this momentum going for a little while longer. I need to take care of the family I have before I add to it, I guess." He looked at Melanie, then quickly down at his plate.

Melanie said, "I think that's admirable. And from what I read, when you do decide to have a relationship, there'll be no lack of volunteers."

Strand gave an ironic laugh. "Ha! I've got to be careful of that, too."

It was then that the lights went out. All the little sounds that reverberate in the background of an active household ceased. The refrigerator quit humming. The furnace ground to a halt. The water circulating in the pipes gurgled to a stop. Everyone sat stock still around the table for a minute. The only sound was the crackling of the fires in the wood stove and the fireplaces.

"There it is," John grumbled. "Well, break out the candles, and we'll finish dinner."

Melanie was already up, moving more candles to the dining room table. John followed right behind her, lighting them. In the kitchen, they lit two kerosene lamps. Soon, both rooms were bathed in a warm yellow light.

"This is amazing," said the musician, smiling. "This is really cool."

John snorted as he returned to the table. "As long as it doesn't last too long. You get to miss your shower after a while, and it really gets old when you have to start hauling water from the pond for the animals."

"Dad, we really need a generator," Peter said.

Melanie ruminated over Peter's remark. The elusive generator came up every time there was a power outage. John always promised to install one before the next winter, and somehow, it never got done. She brought the apple pie in from the kitchen and cut pieces for everyone. At the end of the meal, she said, "I put aside some water in the dishpan in the sink. We can scrape our dishes, and I'll wash them. Everyone can help dry and put them away. Try not to open the refrigerator door."

Clean-up was done in half an hour.

"Now what?" Mia pouted, forgetting the important guest she had to impress. "This is just great."

"I'm sure your iPod is fully charged," her father said dryly.

"Read a book," said Melanie, "or we can have scintillating conversation! Actually talk to each other."

"I've got *The Thirteenth Warrior* downloaded," Peter said.

"Well, there you have it," said John, putting the last pan away. "No end of opportunity."

Gabriel spoke up. "I saw a piano in the other room. I can play. That I can do. Can I play and sing for you?" Above all, Strand was a performer.

"Oh, wow!" whooped Emmie, sounding just like her mother. "Wow!"

"I'm sure it needs tuning," said Melanie apologetically, "but we would love to hear you sing."

The family filed into the little-used sitting room off the dining room, carrying the kerosene lamps and several candles. It was a sedate room, more formal than the front room, where people usually congregated. In this room, Melanie had hung some of the old family paintings and photographs. The piano was in this room, as well as two tall bookcases full of books. The walls were painted a calm butter color, and contrary to the rest of the house, where the curtains were either absent or sheer, the drapes in this room were heavy embroidered crewel work, pulled shut against the storm and the cold of winter.

Melanie set one of the kerosene lamps on the piano and turned up the wick to illuminate the keys. Then she sat down beside the girls on the comfortable old sofa. Peter and his father sat in the big wing chairs. Michael leaned gracefully in the doorway. Strand settled himself on the piano bench and lightly touched the keys. Melanie noticed a change in the young man's demeanor. It was easy to see that here was the forum where he was comfortable.

"I play for my mother and sister sometimes like this," he said. "Just me and the piano. After my father died, sometimes it was the only way to get my mother to stop crying." No one said anything, and he said in a happier tone, "I try to do as much for them as I can. Hey, you know what I did? I bought my sister a horse! She's always loved horses." He had begun to fiddle with the keys. Little melodies escaped here and there as he talked.

"Really!" Melanie exclaimed. "We have horses. Does your sister show?"

"She does that dressage thing, mostly, I think," said Gabriel. "Her horse's name is Above the Clouds. She's won a lot of ribbons."

"I do endurance riding," said Mia.

"Do you win?"

"Actually, yes, I do pretty well," Mia answered.

Melanie was glad to see her daughter regaining some of herself back. The celebrity was beginning to burn off the man like early morning fog burns off a meadow.

"What's his name?" Gabriel asked.

"Greensleeves," answered the girl.

And now the bits of melody seemed to weave themselves together under his fingers. Real music came from the piano. Gabriel Strand was playing "Greensleeves." He began to sing the ancient song. His voice was beautiful, possessed of the clear sweetness of a classic tenor. It was one of the loveliest renditions Melanie had ever heard, and she was truly surprised. When he finished, they were silent, mesmerized.

Emmie finally said, "That was so beautiful!"

Everyone burst into applause.

"Can you do 'No Place to Park'?" asked Emmie.

The musician smiled widely. "I can," he said. It was their current hit, a rock ballad. "It's one of my own favorites that I've written. It'll be a little different without the bass or percussion, sort of Gabriel Strand unplugged."

He sang the song. It showcased his voice, and they were all charmed. He sang another and then another. She felt she could have sat there until the morning, but Melanie noticed her daughter's pained expression. She stood and crossed the room to stand beside Strand. Putting a hand lightly on his shoulder, she said to everyone, "It's almost eleven o'clock. With the power still off, the house is going to cool down. The best place for everyone is bed—especially you, Miss Mia."

Gabriel stood up. Melanie was aware of the muscles beneath the cloth, and just for an instant, her fingers twitched, fighting the urge to caress. "I'll be heading back to the inn, then," he said. "I really enjoyed myself tonight. Thank you so much."

"You must stay here tonight," Melanie said vehemently. "It's too dangerous to drive back to town. Power will be out all over. Probably at the inn, too." She turned to her husband. "John, call dispatch. Find out the conditions. Really, Gabriel, I insist. John, please."

It was the tone of her own voice that alarmed her. She caught her husband's eyes as a drowning person might catch a towline to save themselves.

"No, really, I couldn't impose." The musician shook his head.

John said, "Don't be ridiculous. If you drive off the road, it'll mean people have to risk their necks trying to save yours. You're here for the night."

"John's right," said Melanie. "Follow me. We've got a very comfortable extra bedroom with its own bath. It's probably more comfortable than the mattress Bill Noyes would have you sleeping on." She placed her hand lightly on his forearm and led him out through the dining room to a large room at the foot of the stairs across from the foyer. "Peter," she called back over her shoulder, "throw down one of your T-shirts and a pair of your sweat pants for Gabriel. A clean pair, please." She stood at the bottom of the stairs and caught a black T-shirt with "The Cure" written across the chest and polar-bear printed flannel pajama bottoms. She smiled as she handed them to Strand. "Well, not high fashion, but comfortable. The bedrooms will get a little chilly tonight with no heat, but there's a thick duvet on the bed and another quilt folded on the chair in the corner. You should be fine. Oh, and there's a flashlight on the bedside table. Just for times like this."

"Thank you, really," he said. "I always loved The Cure. You make me feel like one of the family."

"We like company here in Vermont. Sometimes the cabin fever gets maddening. Having you stay is like having my kids' friends over."

He looked at her then. "I'm closer to your age than theirs," he said significantly.

The color rose in her cheeks. *This is ridiculous,* she thought to herself. "Good night, Gabriel," she said. "I'm going up now to make sure the kids are all set. Mia doesn't know how sore she's going to be in the morning. John's and my bedroom is on the other side of the house above the kitchen. If you need anything in the middle of the night, don't hesitate to yell up the stairs."

"Thanks," he said. "I'm going to give my mom a call. It's not so late yet in California. I want to tell her about the baked penne and the apple pie. It's the best meal I've ever had on the road. Good night." He smiled at her and retreated into the room, closing the door.

Melanie climbed the stairs with a flashlight to check on her children.

She went into Peter's room first. He was already in bed, bundled under his flannel-covered duvet.

"Seems like a regular person, doesn't he, Mom?" he said.

"Well, sort of, I guess. I feel kind of sorry for him, away from his family like that."

"Yeah, he said he missed his sister. I can't picture it myself. I guess his sister isn't like my sister."

"Peter! What a thing to say!" But she smiled as she kissed him good night. "You love your sister; you know you do."

Peter pulled the covers over his head and curled up into a ball underneath. His mother patted the lump that was him and went down the hall to Mia's bedroom. The door was closed, so she knocked lightly.

"Mom?"

"Yes, may I come in?"

"Of course."

Melanie went into the room and shut the door behind her. The girls were in their pajamas, sitting up together in Mia's double bed.

Emmie said, "I don't think I'm going to be able to sleep just knowing who's sleeping downstairs."

"Well, it appears he's just a man, like every other man," said Melanie. "He has a job, and he does it. He does seem lonely, though. I feel bad about that. Poor guy."

"He's cuter, though, than any other man," Mia whispered.

"And he doesn't have a girlfriend," Emmie replied just as quietly.

"He's pretty cute," acknowledged Melanie.

Mia looked uncomfortable. "Mom, I don't feel very well. My neck hurts."

"Mia, you ditched your collar and sling," Melanie admonished. "You're going to feel the effects. Grammie was right, too. No school for you tomorrow morning, no matter what the weather. Here, take this Tylenol. Emmie, you come and get me in the night if Mia's having a lot of pain, okay?"

Emmie nodded vigorously. "Yes, I will."

"The electricity will probably come back on before too long," said Melanie. "Snuggle down together, and you'll be warm enough."

The girls scrunched down into the bed, and Melanie fluffed the big duvet over them. She kissed them both. "Try to forget who's sleeping downstairs. Remember, he's just another person, and it's to our credit we were able to make him feel less lonely for at least a night."

"This was better than going to the concert, Mom," said Mia. "Think of it. We had him right here in our house, and he played our piano and sang just for us."

"I'll never, ever forget this," said Emmie dreamily.

"Nighty-night," said Melanie, and she closed the door behind her.

She stopped last to see her oldest child. He was sitting up in bed, playing some kind of game on his laptop. Melanie looked at him. He would always be her first baby. Oldest son was not an easy slot to occupy. She kissed him on the top of his head. "It was a foolish thing to do, but I'm glad you're home," she said. "Sleep well."

Michael smiled up at her. "Night, Mom."

When Melanie returned to the kitchen, John was stoking the stove with firewood. He turned down the dampers, saying, "The stove should keep the house at least tolerable until morning. Hopefully, the power will be back on."

"I think it'll be fine," said Melanie, shutting off her flashlight. If it wasn't, she thought, they could close off the nether regions of the home. The living room and kitchen would stay cozy and warm. She glanced out the window. The snow still swirled, but the wind had come up again, and that usually signaled the beginning of the end of a storm. She looked at the clock on the mantel. It was late, and all she could think about was getting into bed with her husband, holding him close, and ending this odd, emotional, and slightly hysterical day of snow, car accidents, and wandering minstrels.

"John, I thought you'd be in bed."

"I was waiting for you."

He always waited for her, she knew. "Let's go to bed, then," she said.

They each bent over a kerosene lamp, blowing across the chimneys to extinguish the flames. John took the flashlight from her, and they climbed the stairs together to their bedroom overhead, the dogs following close behind.

John shed his clothes quickly and climbed, naked as he always slept, into the big bed. There was no running water without the pump, so they would forgo their showers. By the light of the flashlight, he watched his wife undress. He watched her as she stepped out of her jeans and then pulled the turtleneck sweater off over her head. She unhooked her bra and tossed it carelessly onto the pile on the floor.

Finally, she took off her underwear and stood naked for a brief second before throwing her long black nightgown over her head. She was beautiful, he thought to himself. Even after three children, her body was as small and fit as it ever had been. He couldn't remember a time since he had met her that he hadn't desired her. He lay back against his pillow while she went into the bathroom to brush her teeth with the bottled water she had set out earlier. She re-emerged and came toward the bed, a faint sweet scent about her. John lifted the covers, and she darted in under them. He pulled the blankets close around them both, reached for her, and drew her into the curve of his body.

"It seems so long since this morning, doesn't it?" she whispered, wriggling even closer to him.

"It was a long, strange day." Her husband sighed.

"Is it still snowing?"

"Yes, but I think it's letting up. It'll probably be clear by morning," he answered.

"I hope so. We've got plenty of snow. Do you think the bedrooms will stay warm enough?"

"Of course."

"I don't want the kids or Gabriel to get cold," she said.

"They'll be fine."

"Are you warm enough, John? Should I get another comforter?"

"I'm hot," he whispered into the back of her neck.

"Hey! How come every time there's a guest in the house, you get amorous?"

"Marking my territory."

"Is that what I am? Territory?" She giggled and turned in the bed to face him.

It had been a while since they'd made love. They had both been so busy, it was as though they'd forgotten. He reached up under her nightgown and cupped her soft, round buttock in his hand.

The heat of passion rushed over him as though it was the first time he touched her. How could he have neglected her for so long? He slipped his hand between her silky thighs, and she moaned softly, opening her legs to let him in. He entered her with his fingers first, probing, tickling, teasing. She writhed against him.

"Don't torture me," she whispered into his neck.

He laughed softly and covered her mouth with his own.

"More torture to come," he whispered back. He slid down in the bed until he could bury his face in the hot folds between her legs. Gently, he spread her open, pausing just long enough to agitate her.

"Please," she groaned.

Lightly, he licked at the center of her desire. Her breath quickened as he took the spot, hard with the yearning for fulfillment, between his lips, and sucked softly. She gave a little squeal and heaved her hips to meet his caress. He licked and teased, bringing her just to the edge of her ecstasy, before he withdrew his fingers and straightened up, kneeling between her spread legs. He came into her in one motion and began his thrusts. He could feel the heat from her transfer to himself, washing over his body and burning in his core. Harder he pushed into her, and harder still, until a kind of half-yelp escaped her. He felt her body jerk and twist. He held her tight against him, burying himself to the hilt inside her. He felt her orgasm as it clenched down in a small fury of passion. She shuddered as the waves of release swept over her, and he could hold on no longer. He gave into his own desire, spinning in a swirl of pure physical elation.

"I love you," he whispered.

In answer, she nuzzled into his neck, resting her head in the curve of his shoulder. He felt her relax over the next few minutes as her breathing slowed. Soon, she was asleep.

Sleep did not come so easily for John. He lay awake, continuing to cradle his wife even after his arm fell asleep. He thought about Melanie. They had been a pair since she was fifteen and had persevered in the face of disapproval from their parents, gossip from the community, and a poorly thought-out elopement. He wondered why he sometimes feared she would leave him. She had never once been anything but a faithful, loving, and strong life partner. She made him feel young, as though twenty-five years had not passed, as though he had not gained twenty pounds, as though his face hadn't grown swarthy and care-worn.

She had the same effect on him as she had on every other man, and he wondered what it was that caused such reaction. He stroked her silky skin. Was it because when she smiled at a man, he immediately was under the impression that he was the only man in the room whom she cared anything about? Was it because of her smile itself, open and inviting? Was it her small stature, round and firm and fit even after three children, that made a man feel more virile somehow? There was a passion to her that fanned his own desires into flame. It was a mystery to him, and it scared him sometimes. What if she were to find somebody else? What if somebody found her and swept her off her feet? Somebody with more passion than he had? What if this stranger in his own house tonight, this rock star, was that somebody?

John sighed as he gently extricated his arm from under her. There was no point in worrying about unfounded fears. He closed his eyes and drifted into sleep. He woke with a start, feeling strangely apprehensive. He opened his eyes and looked out the windows. It was as he had thought: the sky had cleared. Moonlight reflected off the newly fallen snow, spilling its silver watercolor wash into the bedroom. The electricity was still off. The face of the digital clock next to the bed was dark, but the old clock in the bookcase was wound by a key. He squinted to make out the position of the hands. Three o'clock. He was unsettled and wished it were closer to four in the morning, closer to First Cock Crow.

John's grandmother had told him about First Cock Crow. He thought he was probably one of the only people left who knew, or cared, what that meant. First Cock Crow occurred at approximately four o'clock every morning. You could find references to it in Shakespeare, Chaucer, and Jethro Tull—not the rock band—if you cared to, Grandmother had explained. John could see her sitting on the edge of his bed, soothing him after he had wakened from a frightening nightmare. "Listen," she had said. "It is First Cock Crow, the time when the rooster first crows. It is still dark, but he wakes, stretches, and calls to the sun and the light. It is a call to new beginnings and a warning to all who mean harm. With the cock's first crow, all the demons, worries, anxieties, and fears of the night are exposed for what they are: cruel and cowardly. They are like all bullies; they scare easily. The rooster crows, and they run away. At four in the morning, the sound of my roosters is the most comforting sound in the world." It usually lasted about fifteen minutes, and then the roosters would be silent again. He could turn over and sleep peacefully. Second Cock Crow came between six thirty and seven. It was a different sound, like reveille, an invigorating call to action. Time to get up and get going. In vain, he listened for Melanie's roosters to banish his anxiety, but he knew it was too early. They were still asleep.

"Are you all right?" He had not moved, but like all people who have slept together for years, she knew he was awake.

"I'm fine," he whispered, kissing her hair. "Go back to sleep."

"You were right," she said. "It's cleared. Look at the moonlight."

"Hmm. It's bright."

"The power's not come on yet."

It was then that his cell phone, on the bedside table, rang. His stomach leaped a little as he reached for it. Instinctively, he was on guard. "John Giamo," he said. It was the state police dispatcher.

"Emergency call from The Inn On The Green, Chief," said the state police dispatcher.

"Any details?"

"Yes. Bill Noyes at The Inn On The Green reported the shooting of a Gabriel Strand, a celebrity musician staying there."

John stopped breathing for a moment, trying to rise above his confusion and sort out what he knew.

The dispatcher said, "State Trooper Bernard is going to the scene. He's not death certified."

"I am," said John. In Vermont, a death of suspicious nature had to be inspected by a person who was referred to as "death certified." There were only a handful of them in the state, but John was one of them. "I'll get down there now. Let Bernard know." He terminated the call and got out of bed, crossing the room to where he had laid his clothes over the chair the night before.

Melanie was sitting up in bed. "John?"

"Did Gabriel Strand leave this house? Did you hear anything?"

"Why, no. John, what is it?"

"Dispatch says Gabriel Strand is shot dead at the inn."

"Oh, John, no! No!" She scrambled out of bed, rushing down the stairs in her black nightgown.

John hurriedly stuffed his shirt into his pants, pulling them around his waist and buckling his belt. He heard her footsteps rushing across the kitchen into the far end of the house. He grabbed up his sweater and rushed after her.

By the time he caught up to her, Melanie had burst through the door of the guest room, which stood open, the beam of her flashlight the only illumination.

"Ugh! Oh! What the fuck!" He heard the voice of Gabriel Strand.

John entered the room as Strand sat upright in his bed.

Melanie said, "Gabriel, come into the kitchen with me. Something has happened."

He was suddenly conscious of, and uncomfortable with, his wife's dishabille. It wasn't as if the robe was transparent, but he knew the other man would be aware of his wife's nakedness underneath. He put the petty thought aside and stalked back to the kitchen while Strand crawled out of bed.

"What? What happened?" John could hear the musician's confusion as he followed Melanie into the room. "Is it my mother? What is it?"

For a man who moved slowly and deliberately, John was deadly efficient when it came to his job. He stood in the kitchen, in full uniform, pulling on his overcoat. "I just got a call from Dispatch. They told me you were shot dead in your room at the inn. Obviously, it's not you, but some guy's dead, and he's in your room. Can you get dressed, please, and come with me?"

"Oh, oh, okay," stammered Strand. "I don't understand. Who'd be in my room?"

"Hurry," said John.

Ten minutes later, John was hastening out the door, a cup of coffee in hand, followed by Strand, still looking upset and confused. Conditioned by years of practice, John opened the garage door, backed the Suburban out into the driveway, and started down the road, all one-handed, without spilling a drop of his coffee.

The police chief glanced over at his passenger. "Coffee?" He offered his cup.

Strand shook his head, staring blankly into the night. "Thanks anyway," he said, "but this is the time when I'm used to going to bed when I'm on the road. I usually don't have coffee until three in the afternoon."

"Any idea who might want to break into your room?"

"No." The musician shook his head slowly.

John looked at him out of the corner of his eye. Gabriel Strand wasn't very old and looked younger than his years. Now, he looked positively childlike. John felt sorry for him, hunched over against the cold, in a strange place surrounded by strange people, with a dead person in his room.

"You okay?"

"I guess so. What the fuck! Just seems surreal, doesn't it?"

"Yes," John agreed, "it does. I can't remember the last time there was a suspicious death in Clark's Corner. I've investigated murders in other places, but here, on my home turf, no, never."

"That must be grim," Gabriel said.

"Pretty grim. Some are worse than others."

"Look, I don't know what to do. What should I do? I can call my promoter. Maybe they tried to break into his room, too. It's just down the hall from mine."

"Go ahead."

Strand punched some numbers into the keypad of his cell phone, then waited. Finally, he said, "He didn't answer. He probably turned it off. Maybe he got somewhere with that girl he was getting drunk with."

"We'll find out soon enough," muttered John as he maneuvered the Suburban onto the town common.

The buildings around the small town green were all dark, their windows appearing opaque, like blind eyes. A tiny feeble light shined from inside the inn. John thought it was probably the emergency lights illuminating the exits. Joe Bernard was already there. The blue flashers of his cruiser refracted eerily off the unlit windows onto the snow. John could see him standing on the porch, flashlight in hand. He was glad to see Joe. The man was a responsible, no-nonsense officer and a clear thinker, despite his young age. *Crap*, thought John as he climbed out of the vehicle, *everybody's younger than me*. Joe was hurrying to meet him.

"The crime scene is sealed off, sir. All the guests are downstairs in front of the fireplace, except the girl who found the body. Most of them were down there anyway, trying to keep warm after the power went out," reported Bernard. In Vermont, jurisdiction for the investigation of a suspicious death lay with the police chief of the specific township. Bernard had followed procedure properly, waiting for the Clark's Corner chief to take over.

"What girl?" John asked.

"She's a waitress, Chief," answered the officer. "I understand she was with the deceased earlier in the evening."

"Thanks, Joe," John said.

The two men strode through the snow back to the inn. John had almost forgotten Gabriel until he turned to see the musician struggling along in their wake. As they climbed the steps to the inn's porch, John turned to Bernard and said, "This is Gabriel Strand. Strand, this is Officer Joe Bernard of the Vermont State Police."

Bernard shook Gabriel's hand slowly. "Then who's lying up there dead?"

"Don't know," John said.

He heard another vehicle approaching and turned to see that it was a town police cruiser. It pulled up beside Bernard's car, and Steve Bruno and Tim Cully got out. John waited on the porch for the men to catch up. Bruno looked professional and alert, despite the fact that he couldn't have had much sleep that day. Cully was beside himself, twitching with excitement. John reasoned that he'd have to keep Cully busy with the rudiments of the investigation just to keep him out of everyone's hair. As always, Cully spoke first. As always, it was irrelevant.

"You're alive," he said when he saw Gabriel.

The young man nodded.

"Yeah, but somebody's dead up there," John said. "Cully, you get on the radio and get the Waterbury team down here. We're going to need them." The state crime scene investigation unit was located in Waterbury, near the capitol. They had a mobile lab. "Then call the state coroner's office and tell the medical examiner we got a body that's coming her way. Suspicious death."

"Yes, sir," said Cully, and he ran back to the cruiser.

John heaved his sharp sigh and opened the front door of the inn. With his officers and Gabriel close behind him, he stepped into the lobby.

Chapter Nine

John had never liked the inn. Although it had always been the primary go-to place in the area for weddings, meetings, prom night dinners, and every other function public, private, or municipal, the one-hundred-fifty-year-old ramshackle structure had always struck him as creepy. Melanie claimed it was because the place had always been an inn, cobbled on to every decade or so to accommodate a constantly evolving clientele. First, it had been a stagecoach stop, a small pub with a few rooms upstairs and a stable in the back where tired travelers and horses alike could rest and eat. More rooms were added when the railroad came through, and still more when people began to take automobile vacations to the Green Mountains. Finally, the last and biggest addition was in response to the blossoming post-war ski industry. Melanie maintained that she was sensitive to buildings, and because the inn had always housed a temporary population, it had never had the chance to develop a solid and established air about it. This transient population kept the building in a state of insidious and permanent disruption, she explained.

Consciously, John did not share her existential interpretation, but the fairy tales and ghost stories his grandmother told him were still there and not as deeply buried in his subconscious as he would like them to be. The building was huge, dark, and drafty. It seemed to John to be hiding something, and just being inside the place made him jumpy. Maybe it was as Melanie said: the old inn carried the mark of every owner it'd had since it was built. Every part of the inn except the original tavern had been built rather hastily and never properly cared for. For reasons most likely rooted in finances, each innkeeper down the years had maintained this tradition of neglect. Throughout the decades, only the most visible wounds had been dressed. A coat of paint would be slapped across the front, but not on the back. The original slate shingles had been sold off years ago and subsequent leaks in the roof were patched on an as-needed basis until the whole roof was a mosaic of mismatched asphalt. The rattley old windows were caulked here and there around the edges rather than replaced. Except for the chimney block, the whole building was wooden. John shuddered to think about the dry rot that must be prevalent in the sills and load-bearing beams. Sprinkler system or no, he thought, one mislaid match and the whole place would burn like tissue paper, taking most of the middle of town with it. Either that or an above-average snow load would prove to be too much for the rafters over the dining room that John had suspected for years housed a bustling metropolis of carpenter ants. He imagined the entire ceiling over the dining room, the only part of the inn with no attic, crashing down and squishing all the out-of-state skiers as they sat eating their prime rib and shrimp scampi. Still, the inn enjoyed widespread popularity. It was convenient for locals and quaintly country for urban tourists, who, on approach, only saw the wide front porch and the garden off the breakfast room and never got around to the back of the building.

So it was with his usual trepidation that he stood here now, surveying the huge, chilly room that was the lobby. The twenty-five or so guests, driven from their rooms by the cold, were huddled in a clump on the far wall in front of the fireplace. They were mostly dressed in pajamas, wrapped in the quilts off their beds, robes, or their ski parkas. Three or four children were curled up under blankets on the big, overstuffed pink and green floral couches. An elderly man sat in a wing chair. As one, they eyed John and his entourage suspiciously, but nobody spoke. The fire was the only sound. It spit and hissed anemically, not throwing much heat. Randomly, John reckoned that innkeeper Bill Noyes, cheap as he was, had probably purchased green wood.

John looked up as Noyes approached him, crossing the room from the innkeeper's desk in the opposite corner. The floor creaked under his step.

"This isn't good, John," the small, skinny man whispered. He shook his head rapidly back and forth, and his hands clenched and unclenched. "This isn't good at all. You gotta get that body out of my inn."

"Did anyone see anything? Do they even know what happened?" asked John.

Noyes had been married to John's cousin Susan for twenty-two years now, and although he was basically a decent sort, John still found him annoying.

Bill Noyes continued to shake his head as he spoke. "No. Most everybody had already drifted down here because of the power outage. Oh, they know someone died, but they don't know it was murder. No one heard the gunshot. Except Tiffany."

"Tiffany?" John raised his eyebrows.

This time, it was Joe Bernard who spoke. "Tiffany Carroll, sir. She was, ah, with the deceased. She's sitting in the back room with Mrs. Noyes."

"Hmm," said John. "Is she the girlfriend?"

"She's a waitress, sir. She works here."

Gabriel broke from where he had been standing beside Steve Bruno. He strode across the room and ducked under the "Police Line" tape that stretched across the stairwell.

John called out sternly, "Strand! Stop where you are!"

Gabriel was taking the stairs two at a time. John moved after him, followed by Joe. Steve held his ground, not taking his eyes off the guests, who formed a tighter knot around the fireplace like a flock of startled sheep.

On the landing, John was able to reach out and catch Gabriel by the arm.

"I said stop," he said quietly.

The musician caught his breath in a dry sob. He looked directly at John. "I think it's Bruce Blake," he said.

"Bruce Blake?"

"The promoter."

John looked back over his shoulder. "Where's the body?" he asked Joe.

"On the floor of the bedroom, just inside the door. He was shot from behind as he was entering the room from the hall. At least, that's what it looks like to me."

"Okay, let's see." He tightened his grip on Gabriel's arm. "I'm sorry if this is one of your friends, but this is a crime scene under my jurisdiction and a violent crime besides, so you stay right behind me and do exactly as I tell you to do. And don't touch anything, not even something you don't think is important. You could ruin crucial evidence. Am I clear?"

"Yes."

"Joe." John motioned for the state trooper to take the lead.

They entered the dark hallway, flashlights blazing. The chief followed Joe until he could see an open door.

"In there, sir," said the trooper, pointing with his flashlight.

He stood aside, and John entered the room. Pale light from the moon revealed the body, lying face down on the floor: a male, fully dressed in jeans, cowboy boots, and a hooded sweatshirt with "Vermont" across the back. One arm was stretched out over the man's head. The other was curled under his body. The victim had been shot once in the back of the head. A pool of congealed blood spread out across the floor, shining blackly in the moonlight. John turned his flashlight on the doorjambs and the door itself. Both were splattered with blood. He approached the body. Joe Bernard walked in behind him, but Gabriel stood silently in the doorway, staring at the body.

John knelt down beside the dead man. Without looking up, he addressed the musician. "Is this your friend?"

Gabriel's voice shook as he answered, "That's Bruce Blake. He wasn't really my friend. I really didn't know him all that well. He's a promoter in this part of the country. He's out of New York."

"Do you know why he was in your room?"

"Well, I did leave the key with him. He wanted some of the business cards I had in my guitar case. He'd said he was going to make some calls. I told him to help himself. I thought he was just going with that girl. They were drinking pretty heavily."

John was silent. He looked back at Gabriel. Suddenly, a tiny gleam of reflected light caught his eye. A shiny object lay on the floor right at the toe of the musician's boot.

"Don't move a muscle, Strand," said John, and he heaved himself to his feet.

The singer's eyes widened a little, but he stood still.

John knelt down. Taking a pen from his pocket, he poked it into the object and lifted it into the glow from Joe's flashlight. "Twenty-two caliber casing," he said.

"Good job, Chief." Bernard focused the beam of his flashlight to illuminate the shell.

"For all the good it'll do," John said with a sigh.

"Might have some fingerprints on it," Bernard said, persisting with his support.

John stood up. "Let's leave things as they are here," he said, "until the Waterbury lab crew gets here. They can get samples. Joe, go check on Cully and see what he's been up to. See that he's contacted everyone. We've got to clean up here. I wish that power'd come back on."

"Are you going to talk to the girl, sir?" asked Bernard.

"Yeah. Poor thing." He started back down the hall, followed closely by the other two men.

"What should I do?" asked the musician.

"Go with Joe. Joe, leave him with Steve Bruno. They know each other." Then, more compassionately, the chief said, "Don't worry, Strand. You stick with Steve, and we'll go back to the station together. I'll have to question you after I talk to the girl."

"Question me? Somebody should just tell me what the fuck is going on." Strand was beginning to sound hysterical.

John let out a long breath. "A man was found shot to death in your hotel room. You knew him. More than that, you were doing business with him. He wouldn't even be here if it wasn't for you. You're a key figure in this whole mess."

"I'm not, though."

"You are. You could be a suspect. What if you shot him before you came to my house?"

"What? I didn't shoot him!"

"Just go with Joe. I'll be out after I talk to the girl."

From the landing, John watched the young man — pale and slouched over — follow the state trooper down the stairs. Then he continued down the stairs himself, but turned into a short hallway at the bottom that led to the office and the kitchen and knocked at the office door.

"Come in," said a woman's voice.

John entered the small room lit by a kerosene lamp on the desk. Susan Noyes sat behind the desk, a cup of coffee in her hand. Sitting in a straight chair in the corner was a young woman. Her thin brown hair was pulled back in a messy ponytail, and her mascara was badly smudged. She looked up at John with wide, frightened eyes, gripping a coffee mug so hard that he noticed her fingernails were white.

The innkeeper's wife said, "This is Tiffany Carroll, one of our waitresses. I'll leave you two alone now."

John waved his hand towards his cousin. "No, please, Susan, stay. I just have to ask a few questions." He pulled up another straight chair and sat down.

"Well, all right, if you like," said Susan. "Shall I get you a cup of coffee?"

"You've got hot coffee?"

"Gas stove."

"Yes, please. That'd be great. Sugar and milk, please."

She nodded and disappeared through a door at the back of the office.

John turned to the young woman. "I'm John Giamo, police chief here," he said. "Your name is Tiffany Carroll?"

The girl nodded.

"And you work here at the inn?"

Another nod.

"How long have you worked here?"

The girl answered in a whisper, "A little over a year, I guess."

"Full time?"

"Mm-hmm, nights."

"Where are you from, Tiffany?"

"Springfield," she said.

At this point, Susan Noyes came back into the room and handed John a steaming mug of coffee. He reached for it gratefully and sipped. It was hot and it burned, but it felt good as the heat traveled slowly down his gullet, warming him from the inside out. Suddenly, the lights popped on.

"Well!" exclaimed Susan, looking around as though she had never seen the room before.

John could hear murmurs from the people in the lobby, and then that murmur rose into a sort of cheer. He heard the furnace kick, and the old radiator under the window shuddered. The chief sighed. He took another sip of the coffee and looked at his watch. It was ten minutes past four in the morning. He was glad the power was back on. The warmth and light might make the girl feel more comfortable.

He said to her, "I could ask you a lot of questions, most of the answers I'd know already, but I want the truth here. A straight story. You're an essential part of this investigation. Do you understand that?"

"Yes, sir."

"Did Bruce Blake try to hurt you, Tiffany? Did you shoot Bruce Blake?"

John put the hard question out first and watched the girl closely as her bloodshot eyes grew wide and dark with fear. Her mouth opened, and she gave a short gasp, sucking air down her trachea. Then, she gasped again, and again. She was hyperventilating.

Susan was on her feet. "Put your head down between your knees, Tiffany. Right now," she said, and Tiffany obeyed.

John waited.

After a couple of minutes, she raised her head slowly.

"Are you all right now?" John asked.

Tiffany nodded, took a deep breath, and as far as she was able, tried to compose herself. "You can go ahead and ask me questions, sir," she said in her small voice. "I'm okay."

Susan sat down slowly in her chair, but continued to eye the girl warily.

"Why don't I just let you do the talking?" said John. "You tell me what happened this evening. Start with when Gabriel Strand and Bruce Blake came into the tavern."

The girl took another deep breath, but her voice was steady. She stared at the floor, as if she could recall things better by concentrating on the grain of the old wood. "Okay, okay," she said. "Well, I was the cocktail waitress. That means I was the waitress in the tavern, not working in the dining room. There's usually only one of us that works in there. I serve the drinks. Sometimes I make them, too, if Bill is busy doing something else. I also get the tavern food for anyone who wants it. There's a tavern menu, you see. Not like the dinner menu; simpler food, like hamburgers and stuff. And some Tex-Mex stuff, too. And calamari. Fried."

John picked at his cuff to hide his impatience, but he decided to let the girl ramble a little. It might settle her down.

"Well, I had heard that Gabriel Strand was in town," she continued. "We heard from some fans who were gossiping in the lobby. They'd been talking to that policeman of yours, Tim Cully, I think, and he had said that Gabriel Strand was staying at the inn. A lot of people came into the tavern at first, and they were asking me questions, but I hadn't seen anybody, so I just said, 'I don't know. I haven't seen him,' and it was true. Then, later in the afternoon, I think it might have been about six o'clock or so, in they come."

"Who?"

"Gabriel Strand. And…and Bruce Baker. I thought the rest of Ragged Rainbow would be in, too, but it was only them. They're the only ones here, I guess. That's what I heard. Anyway, I was excited, but I tried to be cool, you know, and not be such a fangirl. So I was just doing my job. My shift was supposed to be over at six thirty, when Annette would be coming in. I went over and said, 'Can I get you guys something?' And Bruce Baker, he says, 'Do you know who this is?' And I said, 'Yes, you're Gabriel Strand, but I don't know who you are,' meaning Bruce Baker. At the time, too, they were the only ones in the room. I brought them two beers—I mean, one each. Then Annette came in, and she said, 'I'm on now. Did you cash out?' I said no, I hadn't. She told me the weather was bad and to just go along, that she'd do it, so I said thanks.

"That's when Bruce Baker says to me, 'Hey, sit down here with us for a minute.' Well, to be perfectly honest, me and my boyfriend haven't been getting along at all, and I didn't want to go home right then because I never know what mood he's going to be in, you know? And then, how often do you get to sit down with Gabriel Strand? So, of course I said yes. Then Bruce Baker switched his drink to margaritas, and he orders me one, too. Gabriel was still nursing his beer, but me and Bruce kept drinking the margaritas. He just kept ordering them. Then, Gabriel said he had to go see somebody, and I said, 'You can't go anywhere tonight.' He said he had to go see the police chief's wife, so I thought it was important, and anyway, I was having a good time, so I said I'd give him a ride. But Bruce said, 'You're too drunk to drive,' so I said for Gabriel to just take my car. I gave him the keys and told him how to get to your house." Here, the girl stopped and fidgeted with her fingers.

John and Susan exchanged looks, but the girl remained calm.

"Then what?" Giamo finally prodded her.

The waitress rubbed her eyes. "Well, I was pretty drunk, and then I was getting mad at my boyfriend." She stopped talking.

John prompted, "Tiffany?"

"Oh, I'm sorry. I'm so tired."

"Just finish the story, then you can get some sleep."

"I'm afraid to go home."

John rubbed his face in quiet exasperation, but Susan said, "You can sleep here in the downstairs room, Tiffany."

The girl seemed relieved. She went on with her story. "Well, I was pretty drunk, like I said. Then Bruce started getting pretty friendly. Finally, he said would I like to see Gabriel Strand's room and maybe get a band T-shirt. There was a box in there, I guess. I said, sure I would. He took me by the hand and led me up to the room. It was right across the hall from Bruce's room. Then Bruce said, 'That's weird.' I asked what he was talking about, and he said the door was open. I said he musta forgot to close it tight. Sometimes the doors stick. Then, oh, wow. Then, it was bad, Mr. Giamo." Now big tears rolled down her face.

John cleared his throat and urged her sympathetically. "Go on, Tiffany," he said softly. "You have to tell just what you saw."

Tiffany gulped and wiped her eyes. "I didn't see much, I can tell you that. Bruce opened the door. The room was all dark, of course. He went in, and there was a kind of pop or something. Like just a pop. And then I heard a crash. I—I guess that was Bruce falling."

"Don't think about that, Tiffany," instructed the chief. "Just say what you saw."

"Okay, well, I heard a crash, and just as I was going to, oh, wow, I was going to walk right in there. Just as I was going to walk in there to see what had happened, I heard a voice. I think it said, 'Now you've got what you deserve, Strand.' Then someone ran out. I was just standing there. It was, like, pitch black. Whoever it was pushed me back into the wall. Hard. Then they ran down the hall." Tiffany sighed again. Her hands were shaking. "I—I went in to ask Bruce what happened. I saw him lying on the floor. I ran out. I didn't even know he'd been shot. I just thought there was a fight or something. I ran to get Bill."

John looked up at Susan. "That's right," she corroborated the girl's story. "She came to get Bill."

"Well," said John, "this has been very important to the investigation, Tiffany. Thank you. When you heard the person speak, are you sure they used Strand's name?"

"Oh, yes." Tiffany nodded emphatically.

"Could you identify the person?"

"Oh, I don't know. It was so dark. I didn't even see a face. I don't even know if it was a man or a woman. The voice was kind of a high-pitched whisper. I can't explain it. Everything happened so fast. I'm sorry. I can't be sure of anything. The emergency red exit lights were on, that's all. I know that."

"Do you know what the person was wearing?"

Tiffany shook her head. "Can I go, please? I don't feel very good."

"Go ahead. I'll probably have to speak to you again in the next couple of days."

He waited as the girl murmured a hasty "okay" and hurried from the room.

The chief pulled at his nose. "Sounds like someone meant to kill Strand."

Susan said, "Sounds like it was over a girl."

John looked absently out the window where the first light of morning revealed snow up to the window sills. "Or it *was* a girl," he mused.

Bill Noyes came into the room just then. He looked like a giant scrawny heron, bundled in a snow machine suit with his long pointy nose sticking out from under a knit ski hat. He said, "There's almost three feet of snow out there. This would be good for business if this thing hadn't happened last night. Is there any way to keep this quiet, John?"

The chief was beginning to feel tired. He shrugged. "You certainly don't have to tell everybody there was a murder. Apparently most of the people were downstairs in front of the fire anyway and the gunshot wasn't loud, but don't forget the Waterbury team is on the way. They'll have to do their investigation and get the body out."

"I'll make them use the fire escape," said Noyes. "That way, they won't disturb breakfast."

Susan stood. "Speaking of which, I've got to get into the kitchen. Bill, you'd better arrange for clean-up after Waterbury leaves. Call if you need anything more, John."

John smiled in acknowledgment. Bill was still pacing, wringing his hands. John gave thanks for Susan's level head. He heaved himself to his feet. "I've got to get back to the station," he said to Noyes. "I'm sure Joe and Steve are still there with Strand. I've got to put together some sort of plan and make sure Strand's out of danger. See you later, Bill."

"Yeah, okay, Chief."

Chapter Ten

John walked out of the office and stepped onto the front porch. The world was completely silent and white. Despite a body lying upstairs in a pool of blood and everything else that had happened over the last twenty-four hours, despite his being bone tired and not yet finished with the business at hand, John could not help but be lifted by the beauty that surrounded him. He slogged his way to the Suburban. Bits of drifting, floating ice crystals hit him in the face. The cold sting was fresh and pleasant. It was these times that he, not a religious man, was assured once again that higher powers did exist and the follies of men were just that.

Still, he lived in this particular plane and had responsibilities. One person had purposely caused the death of another, and folly or no folly, it was his duty to see justice done and to restore the order demanded by the society in which he lived. He gave his characteristic short, sharp sigh and started up the Suburban. The plows had been down the main streets not two hours before so the road was clear to the police station. He glanced at his watch. It was six fifteen. Cully's cruiser, Bernard's state car, and Becky's little SUV were all parked there. Then John noticed his son Michael's car was there, too.

Puzzled, he entered the building. When he opened the door to the police offices, Becky was standing there, steaming coffee cup extended. He took it gratefully.

The telephone on Becky's desk rang, and she answered it. When she hung up, she said, "Waterbury's there. Are you going back?"

John shook his head and sipped his coffee. "No. She'll call me later. I'll write the preliminary report, and then I'm going home for a hot shower. I'll be back around noon."

He turned around to go into his office. Steve Bruno, Joe Bernard, and Tim Cully stood in the doorway. Beyond them, inside his office, he could see Gabriel Strand sitting slouched in the hard wooden chair. And beside him, sitting in John's own chair and holding the musician's hand, was his wife. His surprise must have been obvious because he noticed the three uniformed men shift on their feet uncomfortably.

He cleared his throat and addressed the men. "We can't do anything more about this situation until Waterbury gets done. I have to review evidence and proceed with the investigation. I'll start that this afternoon. In the meantime, Cully, you run the roads. Everybody's still digging out, and there's no school, so people will still be trying to run into each other with vehicles. Joe, you go back and just make sure everything's copacetic at the inn. Stay with the Waterbury team until they get what they need. Then come back here to do your report. Steve, you stay here with Becky. You've had a long couple of days. Call Jason and tell him to come in to relieve you at noon. Then you go home. I don't want to see you for twenty-four hours."

The men nodded and grunted, confirming their understanding, and moved off in their own directions. John went into his office and closed the door behind him.

"John." Melanie let go of Gabriel's hand and stood up. "This is awful, John."

He tried not to sound exasperated as he answered her. "Melanie, what are you doing here? The roads are still bad. This is police business."

"It's my fault, Chief," Gabriel said. "I called Melanie. I didn't know what to do. I guess I wasn't thinking."

Of course he called Melanie, thought John, but he said, "Melanie, let's just go home. I'll follow you in the Suburban. Strand, you come with me."

Melanie nodded and led the way out of the office.

Once in the car, with the heater on and headed toward home, John glanced over at his companion. Strand had been silent the whole time, and now he stared straight ahead. His face was pale, and there were blue shadows under his eyes.

John said, "The girl, Tiffany Carroll, who was with Bruce Blake said the person who murdered Blake thought he was you."

Strand looked genuinely surprised. "Why do you say that?"

"Because according to the girl, the person said, 'Now you've got what you deserve, Strand.' Something like that."

Gabriel shook his head slowly back and forth, then buried his face in his hands.

"Is there anyone you know who would want you dead?"

"No."

"Are you sure?"

"It's probably some deranged fan."

"Hmm. Maybe. You didn't have a conflict over anyone with a girl?"

"I don't have a girlfriend right now."

"Don't tell me you don't have girls on the road. I'm not stupid. Even I know about groupies."

Gabriel gave a kind of mirthless laugh. "I will tell you that there are girls on the road, as you say, but I'll also tell you that we're a lot more careful than…than people used to be. We've got to be. At least smart people are. And my band is smart."

"Bruce Baker wasn't so smart."

"No, he wasn't."

"So you're telling me there is no one out there you know of who has a grudge against you or felt slighted. Maybe someone whose feelings were hurt somehow. Did you fire anybody lately?"

"No, no, we didn't. Look, there's these fan sites online. Some of the people post pretty weird stuff. A couple of them say weird stuff about me."

"Like what?"

"Oh, like who I should be going out with or who I'm secretly engaged to. When you're in entertainment, it always happens. Sometimes they threaten you when you go out with somebody. Sometimes they threaten you when you don't. It's always a risk. Ask anybody."

"I don't know anybody in entertainment except you. So you're sure?"

"That's right."

John had been a policeman for twenty-four years. He knew a lie when he heard it, but this was going to take some time. For some reason, Strand wasn't telling him the truth. Maybe it was an internal problem within the band itself. "Okay," he said. "For now, all I've got to do is keep you safe. The killer still thinks it was you who was killed and won't know better until the news gets it."

Strand looked up. "Then what?"

John could hear the fear in his voice. "Well, then it'll be obvious you're not dead, and there may be a second attempt on you. These types stick around until they see confirmation of their crime in the news. They always like to see their work showcased. It's important to them. Then they bolt. Unless they're local. I'm going to have a look at those fan sites."

The musician nodded. "I can show you."

"These fans, are they mostly male or female?" John asked.

"It's hard to say. Mostly, they go by fake names and code words, so it's hard to tell what they are."

They drove on in silence until they reached the house. Once inside, John shed his outer clothes and heaved a sigh of relief.

Melanie, who had arrived home just ahead of them, threw her coat across the back of the couch, saying, "I'll make breakfast."

Gabriel sat down at the end of the kitchen table and leaned forward on his elbows. John sat heavily, facing the windows, blankly watching the chickadees hammering the sunflower seeds open with their tiny beaks.

Melanie bent across the table to set Gabriel's cup in front of him. The hoodie she wore wasn't zipped all the way up, and her breasts swelled provocatively forward, giving the musician a clear view of her cleavage. John stifled a sarcastic eye roll and pretended not to notice Strand's gaze as he lifted his own coffee to his lips.

Why did she have that effect on people, on men? Did she do it purposely? His mind wandered as he watched the wild birds. Could any of the local gossip here and there throughout the years be true? He rubbed his eyes. No, people were just jealous of her. The only daughter of a prominent family, the owner of the local news rag, well-to-do. Beautiful. He tried to objectively critique his own wife. Was it her beauty? Melanie was certainly that, with her trim figure and ruffled hair, her made-up eyes and brilliant smile, but there must be lots of women like that out there. Weren't there? Finally, in his mind, he acquiesced. No, there was something about Melanie. Something riveting and mercurial. Something that made her irresistible and drew you in.

He shook his head to clear his thinking, choosing to confront this another time. He said this to himself every time these questions rose, every time he heard a whisper, every time he saw the way other men looked at her. Every time he saw her smile at another man.

John noticed the young man fidgeting. "Calm down, Strand. There's nothing to be done right now. No one knows you're here. You're safe. We can have a look at those fan sites, though. I want you to show me what you were talking about."

Mia and Emmie came into the room, dressed in their baggy sweats. They plopped sleepily down at the table. Mia was wearing her sling.

"No school? I thought Becky said they had things up and running," said John.

Mia shook her head. "Nope. When the power came back on, the heat didn't. The school is ice cold."

"At least that's what my mom says," interjected Emmie.

"Want some coffee, girls?" Melanie asked.

"Thanks, Mom." Mia shifted in her chair. "My shoulder hurts. Right up into my head."

"I'll get you some Tylenol, baby," said her mother. "You're going to be sore for quite a while, I'm afraid." Melanie set the pills in front of Mia. "Any sign of the boys?"

"Yeah, snoring."

"Well, let them sleep."

Suddenly, Gabriel started as though a gun had gone off. "You'll excuse me, please. I want to call my mother before she sees the news this morning. You don't know what might leak out, and I really don't want her thinking the wrong thing."

Melanie put her hand on his shoulder. "We understand, Gabriel. Go call your family."

As he stood up from the table, she reached out and wrapped her arms around him. Gabriel embraced her in return and held on an instant too long. The chief watched as the musician's fingers spread out across his wife's back. Mia and Emmie watched, too. Finally, Melanie drew back. Gabriel left the room without looking at anyone.

"Jeez, Mom," said Mia.

"What?" Melanie smoothed her sweatshirt and took a seat at the table.

"You're old enough to be his mother."

Melanie's eyes narrowed as she glanced at her daughter. "Not quite."

John said, "He'll never go home if you keep giving him that kind of treatment."

Melanie smiled coquettishly at her husband. Then her face sobered. "The boy needed comforting."

"I think you accomplished that," John groused into his coffee mug.

"Who could be trying to kill Gabriel Strand?"

"There are crazy fans out there, is what he tells me," answered John.

Mia had slopped some coffee onto the marble topped table. She absentmindedly drew the drop out in long wisps along the tabletop with her spoon. "Probably that stalker," she said, not looking up from her creative endeavor.

"What?" John asked sharply.

"Mia!" said Melanie. "Stop making that mess!"

"I'll get a paper towel," Emmie said.

John persisted. "Mouse, what did you just say? What stalker?"

Mia sipped her coffee. "Well, apparently there's some stalker that's been giving his mother trouble."

"How do you know that?" John was incredulous.

Emmie spoke up this time. "We read it, Chief. It was in one of the tabloids."

"Yeah," said Mia. "I've got it in my room. Some mental harassment thing."

"I'll get it for you, Chief," Emmie said, jumping up from the table.

John put down his coffee mug and buried his face in his hands. Melanie reached over and sympathetically ran her fingers through his hair.

"What's the matter, Dad?"

John looked up at Mia, shook his head slowly, and sighed. "I knew when I questioned Strand that he was keeping something from me. I've got four cops down at the station embroiled in this case, and my teenage daughter just comes up with a crucial fact. At the breakfast table, no less!"

"Don't forget her friend," Emmie added as she came back into the room. She reclaimed her seat beside Mia and put the glossy magazine down in front of him. John smiled at her as he took up the magazine.

"Thanks, Nancy Drew." John looked carefully at the magazine. There was a picture of Angelina Jolie on the cover. She was wearing large sunglasses and carrying one of her children. Bulleted teaser headlines were listed down the left-hand sidebar of the publication. *Angelina — Pregnant Again? Lady Gaga — Who Is She? Jay-Z Wants More Children — Now.* There was nothing on the outside about Ragged Rainbow or Gabriel Strand. John thumbed through the pages.

"I think it's toward the beginning, Dad," instructed Mia. "It's in a section of news highlights. I think it's called Entertainment Legalities or Legal Entertainment or something like that. It's just a blurb."

He found the headline in bold print: *Ragged Rainbow Front Man Confronts Mother's "Friend."* John read aloud, "Ragged Rainbow front man Gabriel Strand filed for an Order of Protection against Richard Seeley, a college placement counselor and former math teacher. According to sources, Strand maintains Seeley, who once dated the singer's mother, has appeared uninvited numerous times at the family's Beverly Hills home, troubling both his mother and younger sister. Seeley claims to be a friend of the family and has made a statement, saying Strand is 'controlling and overreacting.' Ragged Rainbow is on tour. Strand was unavailable for comment." He looked up at the girls. "Anytime either of you wants a job as a cop, see me first. I think I may have to fire Cully. Now, I'm going to collect Mr. Gabriel Strand and take him back to the station for more questioning."

Chapter Eleven

Melanie had been sitting silently, listening to her husband read. "Can't you just talk to him here, John?"

The young musician had impressed her more than she cared to admit. Last night, when she had thought for a moment that the worst could have happened, well, she didn't want to think about that now. She buried the thought as deeply as she could. She avoided John's eyes when he answered.

"I don't think so," John said as Peter slouched sleepily into the kitchen and over to the coffee pot. "Too chaotic."

"Are we gonna be stuck here all day again?" Peter grumbled.

Melanie watched her son pour his coffee. He was the only one in the family who drank it black, something she always found curious. She turned her attention back to her husband and the problem at hand. "I'm sure we can get more out of Gabriel here."

"We?" said her husband.

She knew she was pushing the envelope, but she persisted. "I'll help you. He trusts me, John."

"Everybody with a Y-chromosome trusts you, Melanie."

"Wow! Dad!" Mia said, arching her eyebrows at him over her coffee mug.

"Will you girls get out to the barn and take care of the horses?" Melanie said impatiently. Everything seemed to be grating on her nerves right now, making her uncharacteristically edgy.

"He should have a lawyer," John said.

"Well, you can tape it, if he agrees to speak without a lawyer."

"Yeah, Dad," Mia said sarcastically. "He seems to like Mom."

Melanie raised her voice. "Girls! Get out this minute."

"What's going on?" grunted Peter, putting down his coffee mug.

"Dad's found out somebody's trying to kill Gabriel Strand," his sister said.

"Who is it, Dad?" Peter asked.

"We don't know that yet." John shook his head in exasperation. "Now, Melanie, this place is a circus. Look around you! Pretty soon, Michael will come down and want steak and eggs or something and will offer yet another opinion. This is a home, not a courtroom."

"Yeah, you should keep your work at work, Dad," said Peter.

"Peter! Don't talk to your father like that!" she snapped.

Michael came into the room, rubbing his eyes. "What's going on?"

John threw up his hands. "That does it!" He stood so quickly that his chair tipped backward, scaring the dogs. "I'm the chief of police! Somebody give me the respect I deserve!"

"Mom," Michael said, "can I have breakfast?"

"Get your own, ya big baby," said Peter.

John bent over and righted the chair.

It was hopeless, Melanie thought. Maybe John was right. Still, she was loath to let Gabriel out of her sight. "Everyone, listen to me," she said. "This is a serious situation. There was a murder last night at the inn."

Michael looked at his brother for explanation.

"Somebody's trying to kill Gabriel Strand," Peter explained casually.

Michael's eyes widened, and he opened his mouth to respond, but John spoke first. "Since you all seem to be so interested in my work, I just thought of another place you might help me."

The four young people were all quiet at once, for the first time that morning.

Michael spoke first. "Help with what, Dad?"

"Do you know anything about fan sites or, I forgot what they call it, where people discuss celebrities online, I guess."

Melanie could tell he was struggling with the current lingo.

"You mean message boards?" asked Mia.

"Ooh, yeah," cooed Emmie. "I read those a lot. There's a lot of real crazies on those. Why do you want to know, Chief?"

"Yeah, why, Dad?"

"Strand said that they sometimes threaten him through the Internet or say untrue things. He says he gets threatening e-mails sometimes, too."

Peter snorted. "Those people are just shut-ins from East Bumfuck."

"Peter!" John barked.

"Sorry," he answered somewhat sarcastically. "East Overshoe."

Melanie ignored the whole thing, trying to draw everyone's attention back to the problem at hand. "I think the point your father is trying to make," she enunciated clearly. "The point he's making is that there might be a clue or a real threat from a real killer on one of those pages. Perhaps you girls could scan the message boards. You seem to know how to navigate them."

Mia stared at her, then she perked up. "Emmie and I can do that, Dad!"

"They can, Dad," said Peter. "It's all they do anyway."

Melanie knew John had had about enough from his youngest. "Peter," he said quietly, "are you going to help with this, or can you find something to do, like bring in wood, clean the barn, help your mother with the laundry? What's the matter with you?"

"I want to go to the gym!" Peter whined. "Only, Mr. Music in there wrecked our car, so I'm stuck here."

Melanie began to load the dishwasher. "Peter, you work out too much anyway. I don't like it. You'll damage your joints and stunt your growth or develop arthritis or something. Why don't you and Michael go skiing?"

Michael said, "I gotta get back to school pretty soon."

Mia had left the room during this testy discourse, but she returned now with her laptop and sat down next to her father. Emmie sat on his other side. Melanie watched as they leaned into him, as they had since they were small children. They were at such a precarious age, she thought. They still smelled like just-bathed babies to her, but she could feel another energy, too. It was the adult in them trying to get out and be noticed. One day, it would prevail. It goes so fast, she thought, caught in this little glimpse of the transition taking place before her eyes.

"So," Mia said. "Look at this, Dad. Here's one. This is a message board on the Celebrity Scope site. See?"

Melanie leaned over her husband's shoulder, and they peered at the screen.

Mia went on explaining, "See these icons? You can pick. You can click on Television, Movies, Talk, or Music. So, say I just saw a Ragged Rainbow concert, and I want to learn the latest news—"

"Or lies," injected Michael.

Mia gave him a withering glare but continued, "What I do is click on Music." She clicked. "And then, in the Search bar, I type 'Gabriel Strand.'" Mia typed the musician's name. "There," she said, triumphantly. "Then the whole message board pops up."

Melanie leaned closer. It was a page of comments by different contributors with bizarre code names. There was L.A.girl90210... Lollypopkid...Phizzboy.

Mia went on, "See, there's pages of comments. Sometimes, they kind of meld together into a sort of conversation. Sometimes, people just post opinions."

"Are all these pages discussions about Strand?" asked John.

"Pretty much," Emmie said.

"These are old," said Mia. "I'll go more current." She clicked and typed and clicked again. "Okay, these are from, like, last summer. Ooh, here's a good one. It says, 'Finally hooked up with Gabe. He is divine. The rest of you people will be seeing pictures of us together soon.'"

"Who's that from?"

"Hmm, let's see. It's from LydiaHisLove, and it's dated June twenty-third. That's just about when the tour began, I think, so there's a lot on here around that time. Oh, look, then, Phizzboy writes, 'Lydia, I don't believe you. Stick to the truth. You went to a concert. Stop fantasizing.' Then Lydia replies here, and says, 'Jealousy never pays off. More details later. I'll prove it.' Then, oh, there's tons more comments."

John put his arm around his daughter. "Can you e-mail me that website? The link? I think I'm going to have Cully go over the entire site."

"Are there more sites like that?" asked Melanie. She suddenly felt trapped in her printed newspaper. The world was whizzing by her on the Internet, faster than she could keep up.

"Oh, Dad, there's tons."

"Hey, Chief," Emmie said brightly, "you don't have to get Cully to do it. He'll just get lost. We can do it. Me and Mia. We'll check out his e-mail on the Ragged Rainbow website, too, if you can get us his password."

Mia was furiously typing. "Here. Here's the website for Ragged Rainbow. Let's get into his e-mail."

"Hey." John put his big hand over his daughter's. "You can't do that. Isn't that hacking?"

Emmie giggled. "You forgot who your dad is, Mia."

Mia shrugged. "The password is Above the Clouds."

"And how would you know that, Miss Hacker?" Emmie asked.

Mia commanded a superior attitude. "My password is Greensleeves. Above the Clouds is his sister's horse's name. It's always the horse's name—if there is a horse, that is. Always. Never fails." She turned to John. "Shall I give it a try, Dad?"

"I don't think you better." He was cautionary. "I'll ask for his password myself and tell him what we're doing."

"Then we can do the research for you, Chief?" Emmie said eagerly.

"Yes, you can get started as soon as possible with that other site."

Michael jabbed his sister in the upper arm. "I'm going to read your e-mail."

"You brat! You read my e-mail anyway. You've always known my password. Get out. Dad, make him leave me alone."

Melanie broke into the conversation. "You girls go upstairs and get to work on that. Michael, find Peter and do the chores around here before you even think about leaving. You came home for your own convenience, but you get to leave at mine. The world does not revolve around Michael Giamo." She turned to her husband. "Let's go talk to Gabriel."

Chapter Twelve

"Talk to me about what?"

The family, engrossed in the petty conversation of the last few minutes, had not seen Gabriel enter the room. Peter, Michael, Mia, and Emmie scattered to do their respective chores. They knew the point past which they dare not go.

Melanie stood behind her husband, still seated at the table. As the musician walked through the door, their eyes met. She felt a slow heat rising in her cheeks. He was maddeningly attractive to her. It had been simmering under the surface, but she repressed it no longer. He stood in the morning light as it filtered in through the east-facing windows of the kitchen. Despite the stress of the last twenty-four hours, the energy and promise of youth and strength emanated from him. His thick hair dipped over his forehead, and his eyes, though serious, still had a spark that made her heart leap guiltily when he looked at her. And that was the crux of the matter. Her heart.

Melanie knew then that she was in some kind of situation, some kind of juxtaposition. It had crept up on her, like a cat on an unwary bird. She was acutely aware, also, that it was not one-sided. There was chemistry, or something, between them. She sensed Gabriel felt it, too. It was dangerous, and she was complicit.

She looked away, focusing her attention on John. His big face was phlegmatic as he said, "You didn't tell me you took out a restraining order on a person who was bothering your family."

"I didn't think it was necessary. That was over a month ago. We haven't been bothered since."

Melanie glanced at John, but he betrayed no emotion as he said, "I have to question you. I think it's time you got yourself a lawyer."

Melanie stepped forward and took the young man's hand in hers before she was quite aware of what she was doing. "Gabriel," she said, choosing her words carefully, "we're afraid for your wellbeing. Will you come into the parlor and just talk to John and me? He'll have to tape it. Will you agree to that?"

There was a silence as they looked at each other. Finally, Gabriel said, "I don't need a lawyer."

Melanie smiled at him and led him into the back parlor, glancing over her shoulder at her husband.

"I'll get the tape recorder," John said glumly.

John went up to the bedroom and rummaged around in the drawer of his night table, where he kept a small tape recorder. He wished he could shake this awful, oppressive feeling he had about Gabriel and his wife. It must be that he was tired, he thought. After this present fiasco was over, he would take some time off. Put Becky and Steve Bruno in charge and spend some time with Melanie. He didn't want his foolish insecurities to turn into a self-fulfilling prophecy. When he went into the front parlor, he found Strand and Melanie sitting close together on the couch. Melanie held both of Gabriel's hands in hers. John said nothing as he sat down in the big wing chair across from them. Melanie let go of Gabriel's hands and, straightening up, moved a little way away from him.

"We'll forget about the fact that you didn't tell me this early on," John said. He snapped the "record" button on the tape recorder. "John Giamo recording testimony of Gabriel Strand. Melanie Giamo present." Then he set the recorder on the edge of the piano. "Why don't you just start at the beginning and tell me about the relationship you had with Richard Seeley?"

"He taught in the same school as my mother. She's known him a long time, really."

"How long?"

"Probably ten years, all told."

"What precipitated you getting a restraining order? Was it stalking?"

"It was more of an annoyance, actually."

"Tell me about it, please."

John thought he could see some kind of change in the young man's face. The heretofore forced nonchalance evaporated. Another emotion struggled to gain control even as it was repressed. Anger? Fear? Belligerence? John leaned back in the chair to watch as well as listen. "Go on," he prodded.

Strand wiped his hand over his face and stared at the floor. "Richard Seeley knew my mother from working with her at the school where they taught. She met him way before my father died. Then my father died, and we got through that. Tough, but okay. Fine. And then, a few years later, Seeley's wife died. Well, that was too bad. My mother really felt for him because she'd been through the same thing."

"When did his wife die?"

Strand blew through his nose as he tried to think back. "I guess, well, we were putting Ragged Rainbow together. I'd just graduated from Berkeley. About five years ago, I guess. Yeah, that was it, because one of the first things he was around for was my sister's tenth birthday. She's fifteen now."

"Go on."

"After that, they started to hang out together."

"You mean they dated?"

"Yeah."

"How did you feel about that?"

"Look, I never liked the guy. He was always derisive about the band. He'd make fun of it, you know, even when we started to get gigs. I always laughed it off because of my mother, but she knew I didn't think it was funny. I really tried, though, because I knew she was so lonely, and he seemed good to my sister. He never had any kids of his own. He helped her with her homework and stuff like that."

"How long did Seeley and your mother date?"

"For about a year. Then Seeley quit his teaching job and became some sort of college placement counselor. He wanted to move in. Or actually, what he really wanted to do was to have her sell her house and then they would buy a house together. She didn't want to do that. He badgered her about it until it gave me the creeps. Like he had some ulterior motive. She held out, though. She told me she liked him, but not that much. From then on, the relationship was on the rocks. It didn't last much longer. My mother suggested they take a break from each other, and he agreed. I didn't think much more about it. My mother was still teaching, but Seeley wasn't around at all. I was busy with the band. We were starting to open for big acts—stuff like that. Finally, we hit it big with 'Rusty Heart' and—" Strand raised his hands and smiled "—here we are."

"Hmm," said John patiently. "When did Seeley show up on the scene again?"

"Actually, about a year ago. 'Rusty Heart' had just gone platinum. I can tell you exactly when it was. I was home on a short hiatus. My agent and the manager were planning the tour. This tour. Anyway, like I said, I was home, at my mom's house, with her and my sister. We were just sitting around. My mother was making dinner, and my sister and I were hanging in the kitchen, talking." Strand turned his dark eyes on Melanie. "That was when I promised her a horse. She'd wanted a horse for so long, and I finally had enough money. She knew just which horse she wanted, too. Above the Clouds."

John coughed. "We were talking about Seeley."

"Sorry." Strand looked down at the floor. "We were all there, and the phone rang. My mother picked it up and said something like, 'Oh, Richard. How are you?' Something like that. When she got off the phone, she said she'd invited him to dinner. That didn't make my sister or me very happy, but she was so thrilled about the horse and I was so thrilled to be able to do it for her that we just let it go."

"So he came to dinner?"

"Yes. Yes, he did. And you know what? From the minute he walked into the house, he seemed changed."

"Changed? How so?"

"Belligerent. Like he had a chip on his shoulder. He'd always been kind of a jerk, but he hardly spoke to my sister, even when she told him about the horse. He was always pretty nice to her before, but now it was like he didn't have any time for her. He kept asking my mother all kinds of questions, like whether she going to move now that the band was doing so well. And he asked me, since I bought my sister a horse, was I going to buy my mother a car? Stuff like that. And the weirdest thing was that he brought her a present."

"A present? What was it?" asked Melanie.

"It was an expensive bracelet. One of those wide ones. A cuff, I guess you call it. It was more than I figured he should be spending. Random."

"Did your mother keep the bracelet?"

"No. She told him it wouldn't be right, that it would make her feel uncomfortable. Anyway, he stayed for dinner, but it was a weird evening.

"After that, he called my mother a couple of times, but she wouldn't go out with him. I think it kind of pissed him off. One time, I answered the phone, and when I told him she wasn't there, he said he wished he could make the money I did by not working. I kind of freaked out on him and told him I worked all the time, sometimes all night long. And I wrote the songs, too, and that's not easy. Then he said that he knew my mother was there, which she really wasn't, and to tell her to give him a call when she could break away from her kids."

"Were you aware of any personal problems he was having at the time?" asked John.

Strand shook his head. "No. Not a clue about his personal life. And since he'd quit his job at the high school, my mother didn't know much about what he was doing, either, except it was supposed to be some counselor job. So, everything was quiet for a couple of months. It was a great couple of months for us because album sales went through the roof. Then, in March, my business manager told me I could buy a house. I freaked, man, I tell you. I couldn't believe it. When he told me how much I could spend, I freaked again. All of us in the band were, like, unbelievable, man. My mom and sister and I had the best time buying a house. My mom wanted a place where she could garden. And my sister wanted a pool and a place closer to where she kept her horse. We found a really nice house in Beverly Hills, with the right zip code, too."

"And where was Seeley through all this?"

"Well, I don't know. That's the weird thing. He had stopped calling my mother after those initial attempts to get back with her. Then, on the exact day we moved into the new house, I swear, the first call we got on the phone—on the landline—was Seeley. I don't even know how he got the phone number."

"Did he ask for your mother?"

Strand held up his finger, to make the point. "Here's the thing," he said, "that made it creepy. The caller ID gave me an unfamiliar cell phone number, and I thought it might be one of my band guys calling from some other phone. So I answered it and said hello. Richard Seeley said, without any introduction or anything, 'I know where the new house is; it's real nice. Tell your mother I said it was real nice. She's lucky her kid could buy her a house.' Then he hung up. I thought that was strange, and I told my mother. She just shrugged and said it seemed to her that the last time we saw Seeley, he had changed somehow."

"Meaning…?"

"After that phone call, he started calling every day. He didn't say anything threatening, but he would just ramble on to whoever answered the phone—me, my sister, my mother. I thought he was drinking or taking some sort of drugs. We got the landline number changed, and we all got new cell phones. Everything was quiet for about a week. Then, I had a gig in Seattle. We flew up there that day, did the gig, and we were supposed to stay overnight for an appearance on a local morning show. Well, really early in the morning, I get this call from my sister. She sounded upset, and when I asked what was wrong, she said she had gotten up early, before my mother, about five o'clock, and looked out her window, and she saw Richard Seeley in the street. Just standing there, looking at the house."

"At that hour? Was she sure it was him?"

"That's what I asked her, but she said, yes, it was him. I was really spooked, so I let Mike, my bass player, take the rest of the guys on the show, and I blew home as fast as I could get there. My mother had already called Richard to tell him that his behavior was unacceptable and to please leave us alone. I was angry that she had talked to him at all."

"Did he say anything to her?"

"He said something like she needed a life of her own instead of living off her son. He said that just because I had made a lot of money, I wanted to control her and my sister. Then my mother asked if he was in some sort of trouble. He said he missed her and just wanted to get back together. Then he hung up. After that, the weird stuff wouldn't let up."

"What weird stuff?"

"He kept leaving flowers outside the gate. Sometimes, he would ring the bell on the gate, and when my mother answered the intercom, he would say he just wanted her to know he was thinking of her. He followed her in his car a couple of times too, like to the grocery store or when she dropped my sister off at school. He went to the stable where we board my sister's horse, saying that he just wanted to leave a note for my sister. The girls at the barn didn't think anything of it, so they let him leave the note."

"What did the note say?"

"It didn't make any sense. It was a rambling letter asking why my mother had retired and that my sister and my mother had better get out from under my control, that he would help them. It said something about how he was sick of being ignored. Everyone ignored him. Stuff like that. I can't remember all of it, but that's when I went to the police."

"Was there anything threatening in the letter?"

"Not directly, no, but it was still sinister."

Melanie finally spoke. "It sounds like some sort of displaced anger to me. Like he was blaming you for your mother not going out with him. Or something worse, like mental illness."

"I think he wanted in on the financial gains, too," Strand said bitterly. "He was probably sorry he was such an asshole to me. Or that he had pushed my mother to sell her house." The musician sighed. "Who knows? Anyway, we got a restraining order."

"Were there any repercussions from that?"

"He made some sort of statement. That's what you saw in the tabloid, but other than that, no, there didn't seem to be. We haven't seen or heard from him since."

John stretched his legs out in front of him and shut off the tape recorder. He stood and looked out the window at the snow. The clock in the hallway struck nine. The chief felt like he hadn't slept for a week. He said, "I'm going to take a shower and get back to the office. We've got to find out where this Richard Seeley person is right now, before he has time to cover his tracks."

"You think it was him who killed Bruce?" Strand asked.

"I don't know, but we have to act on every lead. You haven't helped matters, Strand. It certainly sounds like he had a grudge against you, and depending on the depth of his obsession, who knows? Whether you like it or not, you've brought a lot of trouble to my town, and I'm not happy about it." John turned to leave the room. He was beginning to let his personal feelings influence his professional behavior. Besides, the lure of hot water was calling him.

"What'll I do?" Strand asked after him.

John looked back from the doorway. "You stay right here," he said wryly. "Stay here with my wife." Then he paused. "Actually, I do have something you need to do. I'd like a transcript of your personal e-mail. I need to see these threats we were talking about. Mou — Mia's on her laptop now, going over some of these message boards or whatever you call them for me, trying to find suspicious comments. Go see her. She can print it out for you, too. We can trace people through e-mail and do it pretty fast. Will you do it?"

Strand shrugged. "Sure," he said. "You want my e-mail from the band web site or my personal e-mail?"

"I'd like them both. And maybe you could highlight the suspicious ones. Now, if you two will excuse me, I'm going to take a shower." He turned and left the room without looking at his wife.

John lifted his face into the shower and let the steam and hot water wash over him. He had gotten his second wind somehow, and the shower reinforced it. He felt his energy returning. It was best not to think about lost sleep.

Above the rush of the water over his ears, he heard the bathroom door open. "Hey!" he cried. "I'm in here!"

There wasn't a place in this house where a person could escape for even a few minutes! Kids would barge in anywhere; they had no boundaries. He felt himself agreeing with his mother-in-law: it was their mother's fault. Even here, in his own bathroom that he'd carved out of the closet in their bedroom with his own hands, for the express purpose of privacy from the children, he could get none — but it was Melanie.

"What do you want?" he grumbled, soaping himself all over.

"I want to know what you meant by that parting shot." She sounded huffy, and he was glad.

"What parting shot?"

"You know."

"I don't."

"'Stay here with my wife.' What's that all about?"

"Nothing," he said innocently. He rinsed himself leisurely and then turned off the shower. "Hand me my towel, will you?"

She opened the glass door and shoved the towel at him. He began to dry himself.

"John, really," she protested. "You've been so…distant…lately. What's wrong?"

He wrapped the towel around his middle and stepped out of the shower. "It just looked as though you were the best person to leave him with," he said, not looking at her. "He has to be watched, and you don't seem to be able to take your eyes off him."

"Very funny! Are you jealous?" She sounded incredulous.

"Me? Should I be?"

"John, I'm nearly old enough to be his mother."

"Hmm. I was younger than he is when we took off and got married. It looks to me like you are carrying on a blatant flirtation."

"Stop it. Stop it right now."

John glanced at her sideways as he reached for his toothbrush. "Are you protesting too much?"

He'd disarmed her with his remark, and he watched as she studied herself in the foggy mirror. "That's the most ridiculous thing you've said in a while!"

"That's how it appears to me," he replied. He brushed his teeth quickly and rinsed his mouth under the tap. "Do you have to hold his hand all the time?"

"I don't hold his hand all the time!"

"Often enough." He spit vehemently into the sink. "I walk into my office. There you are, holding his hand. I walk into the room just now, and there you are again, holding his hands—both of them!"

"I—I'm just trying to—to calm him down."

"That kid doesn't need calming down. He has nerves of steel. He's playing you, Mel."

"You're being ridiculous! And just what's been going on with you lately? I've hardly seen you. Last night was the first time we've made love in two weeks, maybe more. I forget. What if I thought you had a girlfriend?"

He sighed. "You know I don't have a girlfriend. You haven't been particularly available either. The kids take up most of your time; the paper takes up the rest."

"You're blaming the kids?"

"All I'm saying is a family is a unit. Every individual counts. We don't exist for the kids; the world doesn't revolve around them. The whole family counts. We count, too."

"Is that what this is about — the kids?"

He jammed his toothbrush back in the holder and met her eyes for the first time since the conversation began. "We're getting off topic. No, it's not about the kids. It's about you carrying on with this rock star. I'm getting pretty claustrophobic with him in the house, but I guess there's nothing to do about it now. Look, I don't even want to talk about it. I have a murder case. I don't like murder cases. I don't like strangers coming into town and wreaking havoc. I'm going in to the station." He turned abruptly, and she followed him.

"John! We've got to get a grip. I have never seen you like this. For somebody who is so confident in his job, you seem to be real insecure about our marriage right now. And for no good reason! John, look at me."

He looked up, trying to keep all his emotion under control. "I said I don't want to talk about this right now. I'm not going to talk about it, Melanie."

"We have to!"

"Not right now we don't. It will have to wait."

She made a frustrated noise and whirled, stalking out of the room.

Chapter Thirteen

In the kitchen, Melanie poured herself a cup of coffee and sat at the table, staring blankly at her laptop. She pushed the cursor around, checking e-mail but not reading it, and skimming the headlines that showed themselves on her Twitter page. She couldn't bring herself to check Facebook. Social media had transcended fun communication and become a professional responsibility. *The Town Crier* had a Twitter account, a Facebook page, and a Gmail address. She checked these periodically each day along with her personal accounts. Sometimes, it was just a chore.

"I'm going now," John said, striding across the room toward the door.

She got up quickly. "Do you want a cup of coffee?"

"No, Becky will have some when I get to the office, or I can stop at Jiffy Mart."

"John," she said. "John, I — " Then she stopped. "Please be careful. It's still crazy out there!" She was glad to see him manage a little smile. Taking her opportunity, she went to him and kissed him on the mouth. "Call me later?"

"I'll call you." Then he was out the door.

She sighed, and her forehead wrinkled with conflicting emotion. What John had said was true. She was not completely innocent. She was drawn to Gabriel. She found him physically magnetic. It was not something she had felt with any man she could think of, except John. It was hard for her to be around Gabriel and not be close to him. She found herself touching his arm, reaching for his hand. She stopped herself several times from brushing his soft brown curls back from his forehead with her fingers. She longed to feel that hair through her fingers.

"Something wrong?"

"Oh!" Melanie jumped a little. Gabriel stood in the kitchen door, smiling at her. "You startled me!"

"Sorry," he said as he pulled out a chair at the table and sat across from her. "You looked very perplexed just now."

"Ah," she said, her cheeks flushing, "I'm just going over the paper's e-mails."

"I'm glad you were there when I was giving your husband that interview. He's kind of a formidable guy."

Melanie laughed. "John? Oh, no! He's a big marshmallow!"

"You could have fooled me. I don't think he likes me."

"Don't be silly. He's just doing his job. When it comes to his job, John is a consummate professional."

Gabriel changed the subject. "What paper are you looking at?"

"I publish a little local newspaper," explained Melanie. "Announcements, school lunches, wedding pictures, classifieds. Things like that."

He stood and rounded the end of the table to stand behind her. He bent over her to look at the screen of her computer. His chin brushed the top of her head. She could feel the warmth of him enveloping her back. His hands gripped the back of the chair on either side of her shoulders. If she moved a fraction of an inch either way, they would touch. She shivered slightly.

"Hmm. Is this it? *The Town Crier*?"

She could feel his breath in her hair as he spoke. Odd that this virtual stranger being so close to her did not make her feel like he was encroaching on her personal space. Instead, she had to fight the urge to lean back into him, to brush his hand with her shoulder, to lift her face up and back until it met his…

"Yes," she said, forcing herself to speak clearly.

"Interesting."

She sat, frozen in the moment, aware only of the seductive warmth emanating from him until, slipping his arm across her shoulders, he returned to his chair.

"You're an interesting person," he said with a smile.

She laughed. "Not really! Just an average small town wife and mother."

"You wear it well."

Her skin prickled at his words. She made an attempt to be light-hearted. "Ha! I try to fight the good fight!"

"Are you worried the Internet will put your paper out of business?"

She laughed again. "Thankfully here in Clark's Corner, we are woefully behind the times. I'm thinking it'll survive at least until I retire it or get sick of it." She had to break the spell he had cast over her. She stood and brought her coffee cup to the sink.

"Where are you going?" asked Gabriel.

"Out to the barn," she answered. "The snow has stopped and the horses need to go out, at least long enough for me to clean up their stalls." The cold air would feel good, she reasoned to herself, and the physical work would keep her grounded.

"Can I come with you?"

Her heart skipped a little. There was a moment of acute confusion in her mind during which she allowed no thought to manifest itself completely. She looked at him, at his snapping dark eyes, and said, "I'd like that. Here, put on Michael's parka and boots. You don't have suitable clothes for trudging through two feet of new-fallen snow."

He obeyed, and Melanie smiled at him. "You're just about Michael's size. You need a hat and some gloves." She rummaged through a large basket under the coat rack and came up with a yellow knit hat with a huge black pom-pom and a pair of insulated leather gloves.

"I don't need a hat," he said as she handed it to him.

"Suit yourself," she said with a laugh, "but it's still cold out there, and there's a little wind that makes it even colder."

"I'm tough."

He grinned as their eyes met, and Melanie felt herself blush. He was cute and charming, with his mischievous eyes and unruly, thick wavy hair. He had not a care in the world, and he made her feel the same freedom. He made her feel as though she was twenty again, and every day started a new adventure. He smiled into her eyes, and Melanie was reminded of her college days, when she and her friends, a giggling clot of girls, would cruise the bars in the college town, excited at the possibilities they might encounter. What cute guys would they happen upon tonight? Melanie remembered several liaisons of her youth fondly. Yet something had always drawn her back here, back home, back to John. It was a connection she had never been able to define. Certainly it was love, and as the years went by, it became deeper, if that was possible. Love was a pale word. There was so much to it. Still, some days she wondered. What if she had elected to stay in the city? What if she had stayed in the arts community? Where would that have taken her? To fame? To celebrity? To a rock star? A woman was allowed to speculate, after all.

"Let's go," she said, and led the way out the back door.

The back steps were covered. When she stepped off them, she found herself standing in snow over her knees. There was fully two feet of snow on the ground.

Gabriel spoke up. "Let me go ahead. I'm taller. I'll break a path for you." He placed his hands on her shoulders and stepped in front of her.

Melanie followed meekly behind him. She found it easy to be with him. He didn't invade her space; his touch seemed natural to her.

When they reached the barn, she moved forward and slid the big door open far enough for them to step in. The horses nickered softly in greeting. Gabriel looked around.

"This is cozy," he said. "A real old barn!" He turned and smiled brightly.

Melanie felt her stomach leap. She looked away from him to quell the feeling.

"They don't like being in for so long," she explained, "but the weather was just so nasty! They can go out now for a while. The cold doesn't bother the animals as long as they can get out of the wind and they have plenty to eat."

"I thought they already had their breakfast." Gabriel approached one of the horses and stroked his soft nose.

Melanie walked down the aisle of the barn and opened a wide back door. "They can walk out into their pasture this way," she explained. "I'm going to put a bale of hay out there for them to snack on for a while. Mia can put them in a little early this afternoon." She crossed the aisle and picked up a bale of hay from several of them stacked against the wall.

Gabriel ran up immediately. "Here, let me get that for you." He reached out and took the strings, lifting the bale from her. "Where do you want it?"

"Oh, well, I…" stammered Melanie. "You don't have to do that. I can manage."

His smile was charming. "Please," he said, "give me a chance to be chivalrous. And I'm not a complete stranger to horses and barns. I've helped my sister on occasion."

Melanie could not subdue a laugh. "Okay, then, take it out and divide it into two or three piles in the snow out there. I'll let them out."

He smirked at her and plowed out through the deep snow. Melanie opened the stall doors, and the horses, tired of being cooped up, trotted out the open door. The new snow invigorated them, and they danced and tossed their heads playfully before they settled down to eat some of the hay. Gabriel walked back to stand beside Melanie in the open doorway.

"They feel good," she said. "They love a new snowfall."

"I feel good, too," remarked the musician. "At least, I feel better. Being with you makes me feel better. It's not a good feeling, knowing somebody wants you dead."

"John will get to the bottom of this," said Melanie. Guiltily, she realized as she spoke his name that it was the first time she had thought about him since he'd left the house.

"Melanie," Gabriel said.

She turned to look at him. "Yes?"

"Thank you."

"For what?"

"Being there for me. Not judging me. Being with me because you care for me."

Melanie said nothing, but a sudden flush burned her cheeks.

Gabriel raised his ungloved hand and cupped the back of her neck, under her thick scarf. She was suddenly powerless to move. She felt confused and struggled to collect her thoughts. She couldn't seem to move any part of her body.

He bent his head down closer to hers and spoke softly. "I want you to know how I feel about you. I've never met any woman like you. You've captured me. I can't stop thinking about what it would be like to...to..."

There was an almost imperceptible motion, and before she was quite sure what had happened, his lips were on hers. For a split second, all her senses flared, fueled to a blaze by the fascination with him that she had tried to keep hidden. She was acutely aware of the softness of his lips, of their gradual, increasing pressure on her own.

Before she'd processed the feeling, before she was ready, he drew back from her. "I'm sorry," he said, but she knew he wasn't.

"It's okay." She knew her reply was wrong, but she said the words anyway. She turned away from him and grabbed up a manure fork. Facing him again, she flashed a big smile, saying, "I'm going to shovel horse manure now. Want to help me?"

"I've done it before," he answered easily. "Like I said, I've helped my sister at her barn."

"Grab the wheelbarrow down there at the end of the aisle. There's another fork leaning against the wall over there." Melanie pointed her finger.

They cleaned for a while in silence, Melanie furiously shoveling the waste into the wheelbarrow until it began to spill over onto the floor.

"Hey!" Gabriel said. "I think it's full. Where do I empty it?"

"You can push it right out the back door to the pile. You can see it there, steaming under the snow."

Gabriel nodded and pushed the load down the aisle and outside. Melanie stood watching him struggle to get to the manure pile through the drifted snow. Her mind was spinning at dizzying speed. Thoughts, or partial thoughts, flitted through her consciousness. *Did one of the kids see me? What if John came home unannounced?* She hadn't meant for it to happen. She'd wanted it to happen. She'd made it happen.

Melanie's heart was beating out of her chest. She took a deep breath and went back to put clean bedding in the stalls. She filled the hay racks with hay.

"I did it," said Gabriel from the aisle. "I put the wheelbarrow back where I found it."

"Thank you for helping me," she said stiffly. She was angry at herself.

"Look," he said, stepping into stall where she was, "I don't want things to get weird between us. I just want you to know how I feel. I want you to know what I want."

"Things are already weird between us," she said bitterly. "You made them weird, just now!" Tears welled in her eyes. Why was she playing with fire? "No, no…" She dropped her eyes to the floor and shook her head. "No. That's not fair. I let it happen. It's not your fault."

"Then — " he lowered his voice and stepped closer " — then you wanted it, too?"

Still fighting herself, she looked up at him and said defiantly, "I must have, mustn't I? I kissed you back. I'm sorry. It was a stupid thing to do!"

"Don't say that!" There was desperation in his voice. "Please. I can't take that from you right now." He reached out and took her gloved hands in his bare ones. "I like it when you wear the gloves," he said. "That way I can't see your wedding ring."

Her breath caught in her throat. "I am married, though," she said, looking into the dark wells that were his eyes. There was light shining in them, up from the bottom. It made her want to fall into them. "I am married," she repeated.

"I don't care," he whispered, and he kissed her on her temple, where her pulse beat hotly.

"Why are you doing this? What do you expect?"

"Why are *you* doing this?" he shot back to her.

"Do you think I'm some kind of bored housewife?"

"You said that. I didn't even think it. What if you weren't married? What if?"

"There is no point even thinking about that because I am."

"I want to know. Would you be with me?"

Melanie felt as though her knees might buckle. This was getting too murky. She sat down on a bale of hay in the stall. He still held her hand. "Yes, I would be with you."

Gabriel sat down beside her. He put his arm around her and drew her in to him. They sat like that for a few minutes, neither of them uttering a word. Melanie listened to him breathing, felt the gentle rise and fall of his chest. Finally, she said softly, "Gabriel, I cannot do this. I can't even give it credence in my own mind. It's far too dangerous. There are way too many people who could be irreversibly hurt. I could not bear that."

He pressed his lips to her temple again and whispered into her hair. "I wish we could go away. No, I wish everybody else would just go away. You make me feel things I've never felt. You have captivated me. You make me forget somebody's trying to kill me!"

He unzipped her parka and slipped his hand up under her sweater, cool on her skin that flushed hot with desire, despite her brave speech. She felt his fingers spread out across her ribcage, just below her breast.

Laying her hand on his chest, she slowly pushed back from him. "No," she said as gently as she could. "No, I told you how it is. I love my husband, Gabriel. I love my children. Under different circumstances, it seems that I might love you, but the reality is all around us. Let's behave like adults and get through this."

She allowed herself to kiss him, on the mouth, while his hand was still on her naked skin. These emotions had crept up on her. She had not been prepared for—was not looking for—an attraction of this kind. For a moment, she allowed herself to feel the true desire for him that burned in her now, to be transported by the thrill of his touch and the thought of what lying next to him would feel like. For a single moment, however brief, she allowed herself to give in to her desire and give that moment the depth and breadth needed to sustain it for a lifetime. She shook the glove off her hand and ran her fingers through the soft curls at the back of his neck. She kissed him deeply and honestly, savoring the taste of him and the lust that the weight of his body awakened in her as it pressed into her own. For one moment, they were the only two people in this sphere of existence. For that one moment, she was as he was: young and unfettered like a bird. She reveled in the rush of her desire rising to meet his.

But it was only for a moment. Melanie drew back from him and gently brushed her fingers through his hair once again. He looked longingly, questioning, at her as she rose.

"What now?" he asked.

Melanie smiled. "Now everything is back to the way it should be, the way it has to be here and now. And we are fine."

"I'm not fine."

"You are. How wonderful that we had this…this interlude. How wonderful to join with another person on so deep a level, however brief, however incomplete. Gabriel, I am so flattered by your attentions, by your feelings for me. It has given me the confidence I needed. You've made me see that I still have a depth of being that I was ignoring. Under different circumstances, well, things would be different, but we have what we have, and it's real. Now we must weave it into the rest of our lives, one more fiber to strengthen us."

"You are a very pretty talker," he said as he stood, "in more ways than one, but I still wish for another reality."

Melanie smiled. "Let's go back in. It's getting colder."

They walked slowly back to house, side by side, occasionally brushing together. Melanie felt a sense of peace, as though her power had been returned. She was in control of the situation now. There was only one problem left to her, and that was how to draw her husband back to her. No more automatic sex. No more bickering. No more sacrificing themselves on the altar of mundane daily life. Suddenly, she wanted her husband desperately, wanted to be held in his strong, familiar arms, wanted to talk to him and hear his low, soothing voice.

They went into the house. Gabriel said, "I want to call my mother. I want her know I'm okay."

Melanie nodded, and he drifted off to the guest room, his phone to his ear. She poured herself a cup of syrupy, leftover coffee and sat down at the kitchen table. She stared out the window at the bird feeder, alive with chickadees and juncos. Her mind wandered back, retracing her life with Police Chief John Giamo.

From the start, her parents had been vehemently opposed to the relationship. And as the years went by and Melanie graduated college, her mother and father had tried everything to dissuade their daughter from her continuing relationship with "that Italian boy," as they called him. They cajoled...

"You should break it off with him before you hurt him," said her mother.

"I have no intention of hurting him," Melanie said, amused.

"I think he thinks this is more serious than it is," her father said with a cough. He was not comfortable talking with his daughter about boyfriends or, in fact, any other scenario between males and females.

"It is serious," said Melanie belligerently.

"No, Melanie, it's not. You won't feel the same five years from now," insisted her mother.

"Of course I will. I've felt this way about him since I was a teenager."

"When you were a teenager, it was different. Now you are a young adult. You'll be starting a job in the fall. In the city. A museum curator. You were very fortunate to land that job. Aren't you excited?"

"Of course I'm excited about the job, but why can't I have John, too?"

"Melanie, the boy went to Boston College. He graduated near the top of his class, if I'm to believe town gossip." Her mother sighed. "And he chose to come back here and live with his grandmother and be a police-man." She said the last word as though she was being forced to commit blasphemy. It was the same voice she used when she said "sex" or "actor" or other words that suggested topics she preferred to avoid.

"What's wrong with being a policeman?" Melanie said petulantly. "They're necessary, aren't they? His job's more important than mine, really. Who needs museum curators?"

This time, her father spoke up. "Your mother is saying that there were probably better choices for him to make. He made a choice and took the path of least resistance. He's just not up to your standards."

"Oh, you two are ridiculous." Now her ire was up. "John wants to be a policeman. He likes living here. He loves me."

"Melanie, even if you could iron out all the particulars, like you living in Boston and him living up here on a small town cop's salary, you come from opposite ends of the spectrum."

"How do you figure that?" she asked between tight lips.

"He's Italian." Her mother's face looked like she'd just tasted something bitter. "What can you possibly have in common? Ravioli?"

"It's a different culture," her father said hastily. "Do they know any-thing about what you studied, about your interests and goals?"

"I can't believe you! Have you people heard of the Renaissance? Galileo? The language sung in most operas?"

"He's Catholic," said her mother, grasping to put John in a bad light.

"You're going to want a husband who can provide you with the things you need to raise a family your way. How are you going to afford your horses?" her father asked.

"There are more reasons to marry than just…just youthful attraction to someone," her mother said emphatically, trying to be wise.

Melanie squealed angrily. "You can't even say the word, can you? You can't say the word 'love.' Mom, tell Dad you love him."

"We're not discussing your father and me at the moment."

"Are you two serious?" Melanie looked from one parent to the other. "Can you hear yourselves? Am I in some kind of time warp, like eighteen ninety-nine or something?"

When cajoling didn't work, they tried bribery...

"This farm will be yours when we go," said her father.

"Where are you going?" Melanie asked deliberately.

"Melanie! Don't talk to your father that way. This is a very valuable piece of land. You will be a wealthy woman in your own right."

"As long as Mia Giamo doesn't rescind the water rights." Melanie let out a cruel laugh.

"You are impossible and ungrateful!"

"Well," she said haughtily, "I don't know anything about the water rights agreement. What is it? At least you didn't have to worry about it as long as Grandpa was alive. I hear they were pretty good friends." Melanie meant it to needle them, and it did. Her father stood and left the room because he could remember things she couldn't.

Then they simply forbade...

"You are an adult now," her mother said. "We can't interfere with your actions any longer, but we don't have to have them going on under our noses. If you continue this relationship with that boy—"

"He's not a boy."

"With that young man, then. Listen to me, Melanie Dearborne. If you continue your relationship with John Giamo, you will have to do so under your own steam. You'll have to move out. Your father and I don't appreciate watching you settle for something just because it's familiar when we've raised you to go after so much more."

"I am moving out, Mother," Melanie said triumphantly. "I'm moving out. I'm moving to Boston, and I'm continuing my relationship with John."

"Then we can't help you any longer. We're your parents, and we'll stick by you up to a point, but we can't support you in such a futile direction. It would be irresponsible. He's not the man for you. Can't you just give it a break for a while? Give someone else a chance? Give yourself a chance, another option? There are so many interesting people out there."

"I'm perfectly able to take charge of my own life. I've given several other guys a chance, and they bored me to tears or irritated me to distraction. I think I'll stick with this one." She flounced out of the room.

Chapter Fourteen

By the time John got back to his office, it was ten thirty. Becky was at her desk, but no one else was around. "Where is everybody?" he asked.

"Joe Bernard went back to the barracks. Cully is on Fleming Hill trying to divert traffic around old man Clemens's car, which is augured into the bank. He's waiting for Larry Sample. Jason came and went right to the inn. He called in a little bit ago. The Waterbury team was just finishing up there, and they were trying to sneak the body down the back fire escape. Bill Noyes didn't want it going through the lobby and out the front door. Steve Bruno finally went home. I hope he's sleeping."

The door opened, and Jason Patterson came in. Jason was Woody Patterson's nephew, but unlike his verbose, pudgy little uncle, he was tall and quiet and sure of himself. Jason's mother was a Griswold, and as Becky frequently pointed out, it was fortunate for everyone that her three children took after her.

"Jason," John acknowledged.

"Hey, Chief," answered the young man, taking off his jacket and hanging it on the peg behind the door.

"Come in my office and grab a cup of coffee," John said, leading the way behind Becky's desk and into his own office.

Jason followed him. "I'm coffeed out, Chief," he said cheerfully.

John gestured to the chair in front of his desk, the one, he rue-fully remembered, Gabriel had been sitting in, holding hands with Melanie. "Take a seat and tell me what you know."

"I probably don't know much more than you do," Jason said as he sat down. "The Waterbury team took the body. They were able to get it out the fire escape and into the van without attracting too many curiosity seekers."

"Good. That'll make Bill Noyes happy." He lifted his security blanket—the perpetual cup of coffee—to his lips. "Anything else?"

Jason shook his head. "No, not much. They're going to do a complete autopsy in Waterbury, but Sarah said it appeared that the cause of death was the obvious: a bullet in the brain. Twenty-two caliber hand gun. Close range. Poor S.O.B. Talk about being in the wrong place at the wrong time. Do you think the guy who did it is still around? I wonder if he knows he got the wrong guy yet?"

Sometimes, Chief John Giamo felt as though he were surrounded by kids, at home and at work, but if his men were young, if they were relatively inexperienced, if they made his hair gray from time to time, John still loved each one, even Cully. To a man, they were young and healthy with bright eyes, white teeth, and wide smiles. They might be naive, but they were honest. And they did not say "perpetrator" or "perp." They said "the guy who did it." They were honest and took their job seriously. To a man, they tried to do their best.

"I don't know." John shuffled some papers on his desk. Then, looking up, he said, "We do have a lead on a suspect, though."

"Yeah? So soon?"

"It appears Gabriel Strand took out a restraining order on an ex-boyfriend of his mother's, and the guy didn't take it too well."

"It didn't say anything like that in the initial report I read."

"He failed to mention it to me."

"How'd you find out?"

"Mia."

"Mia, your daughter?"

"Mia, my daughter."

"Hmm."

"She read it in a tabloid magazine. You believe that?"

Jason shook his head again. "Well, what do we do?"

"We've got to find out where this guy is. If he's been in California with an airtight alibi for the past three days, then we have to revise our plan, but I'm thinking he *hasn't* been in California with an airtight alibi for the past three days. I think he's been here."

"What makes you think that, Chief?"

John leaned over his desk, his wry smile on his face. "I've always wanted to say this. Here goes." He paused for effect. "Just a hunch."

Jason laughed. "It makes sense."

"You can hit the trail on the computer and the telephone, then," John said. "Try to find this guy. Find out where he has been. If you get him on the phone, let me talk to him."

"Cully's out there by himself," Jason said slowly.

"Cully'll be fine. He's not stupid."

Jason arched his eyebrows.

"He's just overzealous." John smiled. "There won't be much going on today anyway. He's busy right now getting Burt Clemens out of a snow bank. If you're needed, he'll let us know. Right now, I need you here so we can untangle this before it gets out of control. This town isn't set up for murders. I've got Strand at my house now for safekeeping, and fish and guests, even rock star guests, stink after three days."

Jason smiled, looked at the floor, and left the room.

The rest of the morning passed quietly. Richard Seeley had no criminal record. The only mark against him was the restraining order, but John found the detective at LAPD to be more than cordial.

"There are a lot of people," he said to John, "who don't have a rap sheet, but they're still out there doing the crimes, day after day. Sounds like you might have the right instincts, Chief. I'll follow up for you. Shall I call you or your officer?"

"Call me," John said. "I've got my officer trying to find out whether he might have gotten a flight east in the last three days or so."

"Smart move. Have you talked with the mother?"

"That's next. Strand will be getting restless pretty soon. He's got a concert to do at the winter carnival here. I'd just like to pin something down because I can't stop him from getting on stage and making a target out of himself."

"Yeah." The detective snorted. "I hear you. Look, I'll dig around and get what I can for you. Good luck."

John found he was right about Strand getting restless. No sooner had he hung up the phone than Becky called in through his partially open door, "Gabriel Strand on your line, John."

"Hello," he said. He hadn't meant to bark into the phone quite so loudly.

"Hi," the musician said. "Look, I can't stay under house arrest like this. I've been on the phone with my manager. The band's due in Boston tomorrow morning on the red eye. Then, it'll take them two, two and a half hours to make the trip to Dartmouth. I've got to be there."

"Strand, you're not under house arrest. You're under police protection. I can't force it on you, but I strongly suggest that you stay where you are while we at least try to determine where this Seeley is. I'm calling the newspapers next, and we'll get it out on the television news that there's been a murder. We'll let it slip that you're still alive. That should flush out an action or a reaction of some sort."

"I've at least got to have a conference call with my band. Melanie said she could get me down to her office and I could do it there. Then, if nothing's done by tomorrow, I've gotta leave anyway."

"You'll be a sitting duck, Strand."

"I've got security."

There was nothing more John could do. He sighed, said goodbye, hung up the telephone, and sighed again. He wiped his hand across his face and looked up to see Becky standing in the doorway, looking concerned and sympathetic.

"You all right, John?"

"Yeah, I guess."

He knew, and knew that Becky knew, that Melanie was often a topic of discussion around town. Even though everyone liked her, and men blatantly loved her, her behavior sometimes pushed the parameters of respectable-wife-and-mother to the limit, stopping just short of woman-to-watch-out-for. Not that John could ever cite an instance where he thought his marriage was compromised. Rather, it was when something akin to the current situation came up, putting his wife in close proximity to another man, be it professional or social, that he sometimes thought, in the deep interior of his soul, what if this is the time? What if this is the man? What if this time, the gossip turns out to be true? Usually, he was successful in keeping these thoughts and fears relegated to his sub-conscious, but he and Melanie had been so distant from each other lately. Even their lovemaking the other night, though enjoyable, had something of the ordinary about it. Had he drifted away, or had she?

He shook his head. "Yeah, I'm all right. I'm tired, and this rock star thing is getting to me, but I'll survive."

Becky smiled. "A guy by the name of Brad Dunning is on the phone. He says he's from the Hanover newspaper."

John raised his head. "Great. We've got to get this story out there. I'll talk to him."

After Brad Dunning, the police chief talked to newspapers in the southern part of the state, as well as three television stations. In each case, he was careful to reiterate the fact that Gabriel was unscathed and staying in Clark's Corner until his band arrived. As he hung up the phone once again, he felt his stomach rumbling. Glancing at the clock, he was shocked to see that it was almost one in the afternoon. He thought he would walk across to Chandler's Grocery and get a sandwich. He was just about to open his mouth to tell Becky his intention when the outer door of the police office flung violently open and Cully, covered with half-melted snow, burst into the room in a blaze of profanity.

"Cully!" Becky reproved loudly. "Watch your mouth!"

"I can't help it!" The young man threw his hat on the floor and tore his jacket off. "I've been stuck up on that hill with old Burt Clemens, who shouldn't be driving anyway, trying to get his car out. Then Larry, instead of coming himself, sends his cousin Mike, who's a moron and can't even work the wrecker. We finally get the car out, and then what happens? Clemens runs me over!"

John, who had been listening to the tirade half-amused, now rose from his desk and stood in the doorway of his office behind Becky.

Her tone of voice changed. "Cully, calm down," she said. "Are you hurt?"

The young officer shook his head vehemently, his eyes flashing. "No, but I would have been if the snow hadn't been so deep. He drove the car right over my leg! He ground me into the snow bank." Cully was slowly calming. "Mike Sample thought I'd been killed. Then the old idiot drove away down the hill. Never even looked around. He didn't even know he ran me over." Cully plunked himself down in the chair facing Becky's desk and rubbed his leg.

John said, "Cully, maybe you'd better get it checked out."

"Nah, Chief, I'm fine. I'm just mad. Really mad."

Becky came out from behind her desk and gave him a maternal pat on the shoulder. Then she picked the hat and jacket off the floor and hung them on the coat hook above Cully's head.

As Becky turned to get back to her desk, John noticed something. "What's that on the floor?"

Cully looked behind him, and Becky stooped again to pick up a grimy white envelope. She looked at it, turning it over in her hands.

"Hey, John," she said, "it says 'Gabriel Strand' on it."

"Bring it here," said John, taking the envelope from her outstretched hand. "Cully, what's this?"

Cully looked up. "Oh, that's a letter or a note or something some fangirl gave me yesterday to give to Strand. I stuffed it in my pocket and forgot about it. I showed it to you, remember, when I came back from the inn in the afternoon?"

"Yeah, I seem to remember you waving something," Becky confirmed.

John was opening the envelope carefully. As he peeled back the flap, he could smell some sort of perfume, like he'd smelled in magazines the girls brought home. Inside was a folded piece of note paper with writing on it.

Jason joined the confusion. "Hey, Chief," he said. "I got something."

John nodded at him to speak.

"That guy, Richard Seeley, did take a plane east. Friday evening, he took a red eye. American Airlines to Boston. Arrived six-oh-five a.m. Rented a car from Enterprise at the airport. He told the clerk there that he was on a ski vacation."

John forgot his rumbling stomach. "Is that so?" he said, starting forward.

"Yes, sir. I asked the clerk if he had mentioned where he was going, but he didn't."

"Did he use a credit card to pay for the car?"

"Yes, sir, he did. I've notified the credit card company, and they're faxing us the records now."

"Good job, Jason."

"Thanks."

John took the folded piece of paper out of the dirty envelope. The note was handwritten in a large, rounded script. He read the note to himself.

Dear Gabriel, I can't believe this is the end for us. I know you have conflicting feelings for a number of reasons, but we can work it out. I'm here for you anytime. Just let me know. Just communicate with me, please. I can't stand it when you don't call me. It drives me crazy. It's not too much to ask. I will never be far from you. Count on it. Please don't ignore me. Never ignore me. I'm too important to you. Just look over your shoulder, and I'll be there. There is something important I have to tell you. Yours, heart and soul, Kayla

He read through it twice, then he said, "Cully."

Cully looked up and got to his feet. "Yes, Chief?"

"Do you remember who gave you this envelope?"

Cully tilted his head and rubbed his jaw in an effort to remember. "No, Chief, I don't. I know it was a girl, though."

"Can't remember what she looked like?"

"Hmm, not really. There were a lot of people milling around. I was just trying to calm things down."

"I understand that," John persisted. "Try to remember, though. Just go sit in the office and see if anything comes into your mind. You should rest that leg anyway."

"Okay, Chief."

The telephone on Becky's desk rang. She answered it, "Clark's Corner Police Department." There was a pause, and she said, "Yes, sir. I'll put him right on." She turned to John. "John, it's the detective from LAPD."

He nodded, went into his office, and shut the door behind him. "John Giamo," he said.

"Hey, Chief," said the voice on the other line. "I did discover something, and I think you may find it quite interesting."

"What is it?"

"This Richard Seeley took a flight out of LAX Friday. American Airlines. He rented a car in Boston."

"My officer just found that same information, but thanks anyway, Lieutenant."

"That's not all."

"Oh?"

"Richard Seeley was born in Vermont."

"Really!"

"In a town called Rutland. I Google-Earthed it. It's not far from you."

"Yeah, it's right next door. That's quite a discovery, Detective."

"There's another thing, too. I don't know if it's connected at all, but it's another factoid, so to speak, about this guy."

"Go ahead."

"Apparently, after he quit his teaching job, he got a job as a college placement counselor. He worked out of his home for a company. Now that company has brought charges of embezzlement against him."

"Is that so?"

"Yes. I guess the guy was counseling and only reporting a fraction of the business he was doing and only turning in a fraction of the money he was making. They fired him on the spot when they found out, and now they're making their case."

"Well, that's interesting. Thanks a lot, Detective."

"I hope it helps you out, Chief."

"I hope so, too."

"Hey, let me know, will you?"

"I'll keep you updated."

"Good luck, Chief."

"Thanks." He hung up the phone and went back into the anteroom. Becky, Cully, and Jason all looked up expectantly.

He cleared his throat. "Turns out Richard Seeley was born in Rutland."

"You're kidding!" Becky exclaimed.

"The LAPD detective discovered it."

Becky shook her head. "I don't know any Seeleys around here."

"Me, either," said Cully.

"How about you, Jason?" the chief asked. "You know any Seeleys anywhere? The name is ringing some sort of bell with me, but I can't place it."

"Not me, but I don't know everybody. And there's places in those hill towns where nobody's been."

"This is true," John agreed. "We better get on it, though. Isn't there a part-time constable up there, Becky?"

"I can find out," she said.

"Good, I'd like to talk to him or her."

The telephone rang again. Becky answered and said, "Just a minute, I'll put him on." Then she turned to John. "It's Marian Strand," she hissed in a stage whisper. "Gabriel Strand's mother."

The chief arched his eyebrows. He pointed at Cully and said, "Don't go anywhere just yet." Then he turned on his heel and disappeared back into his office. He picked up his phone. "Mrs. Strand," he said. "John Giamo, Chief of Police."

"I just got off the phone with my son, Mr. Giamo. I want to thank you personally for watching after him. Since I received the call from the police here, I've been very frightened. I wanted to fly right out there, but the police have asked me not to." John noted that her voice sounded level-headed and reasonable.

"We're working as fast as we can, Mrs. Strand," he said. "I have reason to believe that an acquaintance of yours, Richard Seeley, could be involved in the murder of a music promoter, Bruce Blake. Did you know Mr. Blake?"

"I didn't. Apparently he's a promoter for these shows and concerts on the east coast. Gabriel didn't know him before he went east this time. The poor man."

"What can you tell me about Richard Seeley, Mrs. Strand?"

"I've known Richard Seeley for many years. We used to teach in the same school system. After his wife died, I kind of reached out to him, you know, because I felt so bad, having been through it myself. We started to go out once in a while. We were both lonely, I guess."

"How long did you go out together?"

"Oh, probably, around a year, on and off. It was rather sporadic—not every weekend, even—but then he lost his job as a college placement adviser." Here, she paused.

"And?" John prodded gently.

"And I believe he changed after that. He began coming over to the house unannounced, which I usually didn't mind, but sometimes it was obviously inconvenient, and he didn't seem to care. His attitude toward the kids changed, too. He was quite sarcastic with them. Rude, even. He seemed especially critical of Gabriel the more successful Ragged Rainbow got. For instance, one weekend they were opening for Lady Gaga. They were over the moon. Jessie, my daughter, was so thrilled because Gabriel said she could be backstage with them. It was their first appearance of that caliber. Richard happened to drop by the night the promoters confirmed, and we were just blathering away to him about it. Jessie, especially. Richard asked who was Lady Gaga? And Jessie answered like any kid, 'You don't know who Lady Gaga is?' She was only fourteen at the time, Mr. Giamo. You know how kids are."

"I've got three teens myself. I know how kids are."

"Girls?"

"One girl. In the middle."

John listened patiently while Mrs. Strand told her story. He was encouraged by the fact that she related the same basic information he'd received from Gabriel, nothing new. That meant Strand had told him the truth as he remembered it. It was reassuring to John to be pursuing the investigation along what appeared to be the right road. "Go on, Mrs. Strand."

Marian Strand continued with the more recent events. "Then one day this past spring, I was grabbing my coffee to hurry out the door to school. Gabriel was home, and he came downstairs just as I was leaving. He told me to sit down; he had something to talk to me about. Well, I did, and he told me to quit my job. Then he told me about the financial news his manager had given the band members the night before. Good news, Mr. Giamo. One thing led to another after that. I sold my house. Gabriel bought Jessie her horse and the house we're in now, and we moved."

"And Seeley?"

"That's when his behavior became, well, disturbing. He called the house. He drove past it. He left notes under the front gate and at the stable where we board the horse. Gabriel started to get really nervous. Ever since his father died, he's taken the 'man of the house' thing seriously. I never pushed it on him; it's just the way he is. He was nervous about being away with the upcoming tour. He insisted on the restraining order."

"When was that?"

"It was a little over a month ago. I haven't seen or heard from Richard Seeley since."

"Did you see the blurb in that magazine mentioning the restraining order?"

"Yes, I did. Jessie showed it to me. Mr. Giamo, do you think it was Richard Seeley who killed that man?"

"I really can't be sure, but he is definitely someone we need to talk to. If you hear from him, Mrs. Strand, call LAPD immediately. By the way, did he ever mention any ties to Vermont?"

"No, he never did, but I will definitely contact LAPD if anything untoward happens. I'm worried about Gabriel. I know he told me that he's staying at your house and that he's safe, but I worry anyway."

"We'll do our best."

There were a couple of minutes more of small talk, a polite good-bye, and then John hung up the phone and went back into Becky's office.

"Find anything?" he said.

"Yes," she answered. "I spoke to Rose, the town clerk in Proctorsville. She says there's a Bud Seeley who lives way the heck out on Shropshire Brook Road. Not a familiar name to me."

"Hmm," the chief mused. "I still have that feeling I should know that name. At any rate, I better go out and talk to this guy. Did you get any other information on the man?"

"Just that he's in his late eighties, still lives alone. His wife died quite a few years ago; the town clerk wasn't sure exactly when without looking it up. The old man has apparently done odd jobs to make a living—raises poultry, rabbits, that sort of thing."

"Poultry!" the chief exclaimed. "I think my wife might know him. I'm going to call her. I'm remembering something, but my mind's like a sieve lately. It's taking me longer these days to sort things out."

"Just like the rest of us, John. You know when young parents think their kids are so smart just because they can recite the alphabet or sing the 'Do Re Mi' song? Well, the kid's not that smart. It's just that there's nothing else in there. No bills, no mortgage, no husbands, wives, children, jobs. Who couldn't sing the alphabet song?"

John laughed and went into his office to call his wife.

When she answered, John gave their customary greeting. "Hey," he said.

"Hey."

"Do you remember some guy up in the hills named Bud Seeley?"

"Of course!" Melanie exclaimed. "My uncle used to take my cousins and me up there to buy pet chickens and ducks and things. It drove my mother crazy. The guy raised poultry of all kinds. He had this pet turkey who followed him around. We were scared to death of that thing!"

"I knew it!" John said, pleased with wife. "I knew you'd remember! You used to tell me about that guy."

"He was a real character. You never met him? He lived way up in the hills on an old farm. Why the interest?"

"It appears he could have a connection to our case."

"Really?" He heard her pause, then say, "Oh, John! Not Bud Seeley and Richard Seeley! How bizarre. Tell me more."

"We think that's where Richard Seeley went when he came to Vermont last week. I'm going up there now to talk to him."

"He's still alive?"

"So they say. Want to come along?"

"What about Gabriel?"

"Leave him at the house," John said shortly. "If he bolts, he bolts, but something tells me he won't. Not with you there."

"Don't be silly."

"Come with me."

"You never ask me to go with you on police business."

"I'm asking you now. Besides, you know the guy."

She gave an odd little laugh. "What's the matter with you today?"

He ignored the remark. "I'll leave the office now to come get you," he said.

In ten minutes, John strode into the kitchen of his home. Melanie and Strand were bringing in wood for the stove through the woodshed door. Michael and Peter were sitting at the kitchen table eating pie out of the same dish. Mia was nowhere to be seen.

John watched as the musician smiled at Melanie, taking the wood, one log at a time, from her arms. His eyes were bright, and his skin glowed from the recent exertion in the cold. John had a sudden, stabbing memory of what it was like to be a young man.

"Daddy!" Mia came into the room and immediately hugged him. "What are you doing home?"

There were definite compensations for age, he thought, looking at his three children. Still, the price you had to pay along the way was pretty steep.

"I came to pick up Mom," he said, wrapping his arm around her. "I need her to help me for a while this afternoon. Where's Emmie?"

Mia shrugged as she walked to the kitchen table. "She had to go home. Debbie finally got brave enough to drive up here." She set her laptop down and picked up a small pile of papers. "I brought up a lot of posts from those message boards. Here, I printed them out." She handed the stack to her father.

"Thanks, Mouse." Then John addressed the musician. "Strand, who do you know named Kayla?"

Gabriel bent down and deposited the rest of the wood next to the stove, then straightened up. "Kayla? Ah, I met a girl named Kayla at an after-party when the tour just started."

John searched the young man's face, but this time, he could detect no deception.

"Did you date her?"

"No, no." The young man shook his head vehemently. "The only reason I remember her at all is because she attached herself to our drummer. She spent the night with him, I guess, and the next morning, she thought she was coming with us to Chicago. She didn't take it too well when he told her she wasn't invited. I got some e-mails from her, too, on the band site, not my personal e-mail."

"Really? Were there any threats?"

"Not what I'd call threats, just weird letters, like I was telling you about. She was mad when we left after that first concert. She came to me and said she really wanted to go with the band and asked if she could go with me. I told her I was sorry, but it was business and maybe Justin would call her. I was only trying to make her feel better."

"Did Justin call her?"

"I don't know."

"Could you identify her?"

"I don't think so. Why? Did you find something out?"

The chief shrugged. "Maybe. Here, take a look at this. A female fan pushed this on my officer, Tim Cully, the day of the blizzard."

Strand took the note from John and read it. "Yeah," he said, handing it back to John. "That's a lot like what she was writing on the band e-mail site. Same stuff. Crazy."

"The question is how crazy," John said. "Have you checked your personal e-mail?"

"There's nothing on that except spam and stuff from my mother and sister."

John held up the bunch of papers Mia had handed him. "Have you gone through these with Mia yet?"

"No," said the musician, "I haven't seen them."

Mia broke into the conversation. "Well, there's a lot of them, and there's a whole trail of ones from Kayla, whoever she is."

"I'd like her to go through the band e-mails, too, Strand," John said. "Do you mind giving us your password? You and Mia could go over them together now."

"Sure, we can do that. My password is AboveTheClouds," Gabriel answered.

Mia punched her father in the arm. He ignored her.

Instead, he addressed Strand again. "Is that okay with you, then? Will you stay here until Melanie and I get home? Something's come up, and it involves your case."

The musician's back was to him. He was shoving wood into the maw of the woodstove. A new skill, thought John. He saw Strand's shoulders heave with a sigh. "Sure," he said resignedly. "I'll stay." Gabriel turned back to John. "What came up?"

"We think we've made a connection that could help us track Seeley. I'll tell you about it when we've got it confirmed. You know I can't hold you here. It's up to you, but I think it'd be better for your health if you stayed. Go over the e-mails with Mia."

"I'll stay," Strand insisted. "Besides, I'm a good babysitter."

Instantly, Mia lashed out. "There's only one baby in this house, Mr. Ragged Rainbow! 'Ooh! Somebody's trying to kill me! Ooh!'" she said mockingly. "I think the whole thing is a hoax! Did you see the body, Dad? Sounds like a publicity thing to me!"

Her brothers laughed, but Strand was taken aback. "Hey!" he protested. "I'm sorry. It was just a joke. I was just trying to be funny. This whole thing is getting to me!"

John considered the banter. Mr. Gabriel Strand was apparently not acquainted with the ferocity of a provoked teenaged girl, celebrity or no celebrity. "I saw the body, Mouse," he said. "The guy was dead."

Melanie admonished, "Mia!"

"Sorry," Mia said sulkily. "I guess we've got cabin fever."

"I'll play you a song," their guest said, nonplussed. "Hey, I'll *write* you a song."

"Really? For me?"

"For you." He was an entertainer, after all.

"Okay," Mia said cheerily.

"We'll be back in a couple of hours." John put his hand on the small of Melanie's back and guided his wife out the door. "It seems the Mouse has caught the swing of the Great Pendulum of Emotions back the other way."

They climbed into the police vehicle.

Chapter Fifteen

"It's girls," Melanie said as she fastened her seat belt. "Their nastiness is unfathomable. A teenaged girl is a force to be reckoned with. A force of nature."

"I don't remember you being that way."

"That's because I was *the* girl. You only remember what I wanted you to remember. Things boys remember."

"Hmm." He found himself remembering the things boys remember.

They drove in silence for a while. Then Melanie said, "Do you really think there's a connection between old Bud Seeley and this Richard Seeley? I didn't even think Bud Seeley was still alive."

"According to Becky, records show Richard Seeley was born in Rutland. Bud Seeley is worth talking to. There's got to be a connection there. It's not that common a name in this area."

They turned off the main route that ran through the center of the tiny village and took a secondary road to the north. Up they went, and up still, climbing the old narrow dirt road. John hoped they didn't meet anybody on the way down. The snow banks on either side were higher than the car.

"Any of this seem familiar?" he asked.

Melanie sat quietly staring out the window of the vehicle. "Well, I guess, sort of. Only, I'm not sure it wasn't some other back road in some other hill town. Oh, wait. Wait! Yes! There's the old school house. I do remember that! It looks like somebody's restored it—maybe living there. I think you take a left here." She pointed up ahead. "Yes, right here."

"That's what the GPS says."

"I haven't been here since I was a kid. A little kid."

"I think this is the driveway."

"As I remember, it was a beautiful piece of land. The buildings were really run-down, but the land was beautiful, with high meadows and huge maple trees."

They proceeded slowly down the long driveway. One narrow path, barely able to accommodate the Suburban, had been plowed. On either side grew huge sugar maples that John guessed may have been survivors of the 1938 hurricane and were over a hundred years old. They breached a little knoll, and the farmstead came into view. John looked around. Bud's farm was a dilapidated homestead set away from any visible neighbors. This was probably a good thing. At one time, there had been a house, a barn, and solid outbuildings. Fences had separated the various farm animal species, and there had been a lawn and garden as well. That had been long ago. Now, only part of the barn stood, housing several ancient dairy cows. The rest of the building had collapsed, making good cover for myriad mice, rats, and rabbits. All the paint had long since been removed from the house by the winds of the two hundred winters it had seen. The fences had fallen into disrepair, and various poultry and mammals now roamed freely wherever and with whomever they chose.

John drove into the driveway. "It's muddy underneath this snow," he said. "I can feel the tires slipping around."

"I think it must always be muddy. I remember being up here in the winter, spring, all the seasons. The driveway was always muddy. Hey! Look out for the dogs."

What seemed to be hundreds of dogs came barking from all corners of the property. There was even a litter of fuzzy puppies bumbling through the snow behind one particularly scrawny bitch. The dogs kept up their cacophony as John brought the Suburban to a halt. He was afraid of running over the puppies.

"Think he's home?" John asked as he looked around.

"I'm sure he is," answered Melanie. "He'll probably come out soon. Just look at those adorable puppies!" Then, more to herself than to him, she said, "It's just the way I remember it so many years ago."

Dozens of cats watched from the top of the rows of stacked firewood in the woodshed. Chickens, geese, and guinea fowl wandered in and out of the rundown shed that stretched from the house to the barn. A large draft horse and two Jersey cows eating from a round bale of hay nearby remained oblivious.

Suddenly, the door of the house opened and Bud came out.

"He looks exactly the same," Melanie whispered.

Bud was a tiny man, bent over with either arthritis or scoliosis. He was dressed in dirty overalls and high black rubber boots. Unshaven and muddy and missing half his teeth, he looked a hundred years old. He waved at them from the doorway of the house, smiling, then kicked his way through the pack of assorted dogs.

"C'mon," he called to them as he approached the car. "C'mon out. These dogs won't touch ya." His voice was that of the old Yankee, high and nasal with an emphatic twang on the vowels.

John got out of the Suburban and extended his hand. "Police Chief John Giamo," he said. Melanie stepped up beside him from the other side of the car. The dogs pressed around them, wiggling and smiling. "And this is my wife, Melanie."

Bud shook their hands heartily with a grubby, arthritic paw. "Glad ya came. Glad ya came," he said.

Melanie stepped forward. "I used to come up here with my uncle to buy chickens," she said. "He bought me some bantams. A trio of black rose combs. I won first prize at the fair with them."

"Oh yeah? Who's yer uncle?" He eyed her sharply, like a bird.

"My uncle was John Asher," Melanie explained. "He died five years ago, now."

"Oh, yes, yes, yes," sputtered the little man. "John Asher. Nice, nice man. I remember when he died. Too bad. Too bad. So you liked them chickens, did ya?"

Melanie nodded emphatically. "Yes, I did."

"John Asher. He bought lots of poultry off'n me. Good customer. Bred some nice stuff himself." The little man leaned closer to her, eying her intently. "You still got chickens?"

"Yes, I do," she replied. "I have a small flock of laying hens."

"What kind ya got?"

"I've got Buff Orpingtons and Brahmas and Cochins," she answered.

"Yeah, the buffs set good. You raise any chicks?"

"Oh yes," she said. "I let one or two of them set once or twice a year."

"That's good," he said. "You come to buy chickens today, did ya?"

"No, not today," said Melanie. "My husband wanted to talk to you today."

Bud turned a suspicious eye on John. "What can I do for ya, Chief?"

"Well," John said, "I need to ask you some questions. First, I need to know, is Richard Seeley related to you?"

"I got a grandson Richard Seeley," said the old man carefully. "You want ta come inside?"

Somewhat reluctantly, they followed him into his home. As they stood in the front hall, he hobbled around them and shut the door.

"There!" he said. "In where it's nice and warm. Come on in the kitchen." He led the way down the hall to where the kitchen stretched across the back of the house. He pointed to an old enameled table piled high with papers and dirty dishes. "Have a seat," he said, swiping the detritus into a far corner of the table. "I'll pour some coffee."

John and Melanie pulled out chairs and sat. John looked around while the old man rummaged for cups and spoons. It was warm, that was for sure. A wood-fired cookstove heated the room, its back against a huge center chimney block on the inside wall. The chimney block was a beautiful thing, made of old, thin bricks laid in the Flemish Bond Pattern, unusual for interior work. John saw his wife examining the chimney block, too. She loved anything old, and their own house was filled with the eclectic conglomeration of antiques she had collected over the years. John's family of recently landed immigrants prized anything new and modern. "Antique" to them translated to "used," and "used" translated to "junk." They had little use for anything that someone else had possessed before them, even houses. John's father and all of his siblings had built the houses that they lived in. They were not in the least bit envious of John getting his grandmother's house. Their houses had dry, finished cellars, where they put pool tables or kids' playrooms. They did not see the charm of a cellar where a drainage hole had been left purposely in the stone foundation wall for the spring melt to seep through.

The old man crossed the room to the ancient wood cookstove that stood against the massive brickwork. John unzipped his jacket. He noticed Melanie's cheeks were flushed.

Bud set the cups of coffee before them with a steady hand. "I got sugar, but I run out of milk. The cow dried up, and I forget to get it at the store." He cackled and shoveled about four teaspoons of sugar into his own coffee and then pushed the sugar bowl toward Melanie. "Sorry," he said. "I forget my manners, too. Ladies are supposed to be first."

"Oh, that's all right, Mr. Seeley," she said, flashing him her warm smile.

John waited. Melanie passed him the sugar, and he helped himself. No one spoke as he stirred the dark liquid. John lifted the cup to his lips.

"You haven't told me what you come here for, Chief."

John swallowed and set the cup down. The little man was staring at him with beady eyes, very much like a chicken himself. "I need to know whether there is a connection between you and a person I'm looking for. Mr. Seeley, you say you have a grandson named Richard Seeley. Did or does he live in California? In his mid-forties?" John shared the driver's license photo Becky had pulled from California's DMV records.

The little man never missed a beat. His glanced quickly at the picture and then looked again at John, his voice clear. "Yep. That'd be him."

"Have you seen him lately? Has he been here?"

"Well, yeah, he has. I ain't seen him for twenty-five years, that's the truth. Then, just like that, he shows up and wants to stay with me. He said he was on a ski vacation. What's he done?"

John ignored the man's question. "Can you tell me about him?"

Bud continued to stare at John. They were like two men bargaining over the price of a cow. It was a contest of patience. Who would speak first? Nearly thirty seconds passed before Melanie broke the silence.

"Mr. Seeley, we realize that even though you haven't seen your grandson in twenty-five years, family is still family, and blood ties need to be respected, but, Mr. Seeley, this is a very important police matter. We wouldn't be here bothering you, but people's lives are in danger. My husband is very straightforward. We'll tell you what we know."

Melanie's bit of diplomacy seemed to cut through the barrier the old man had thrown up. It was precisely why John had brought her. That, and some other stuff he'd been thinking about lately. He dragged his mind back to the business at hand. "Mr. Seeley?"

The old man pushed himself back in his chair and then leaned forward, both arms crossed on the table top. "I'll tell you about Richard," he said. As he talked, his nasal twang became more pronounced. John guessed he didn't get many visitors and didn't get to talk to too many people. An audience of this importance was an opportunity, no matter the subject. "It's kind of a sad story. My wife and I had two kids. We had Al and Carol. Carol was the oldest. She was a good girl, went to school, got a job, got married. She's a secretary or something, I can't keep track, at the state house in Montpelier. Her husband's head maintenance man there. Al was different. Him and me, we never got along. I know it bothered his mother bad, but there it is. He was always with the wrong friends right from the start. I got a nice place here. Plenty of land to make a living, even these days, but Al was never interested in farming it. He liked booze, girls, and making a quick buck, like his friends. He was still in high school, but he quit and got a job at the quarry in Barre. Lived in a flop house sorta place. Really upset his mother. He was eighteen when he started hanging out with Susan. She was only sixteen, but he knocked her up. Well, her old man was some upset, I'll tell ye. He comes down here with the two of 'em and says, 'What're we gonna do?' He don't want 'em up there in Barre, ruining his precious reputation or some such nonsense. Well, my wife says they gotta get married and they can live here. You see, nobody knew her here. Al can live up in Barre and come home weekends till he finds something closer to home. So that's what we did. They got married. Susan stayed here, waiting for the baby, and Al was coming and going." Here the old man stopped and stared off into the space between John and Melanie. He ran his hand over the top of his balding head, took a breath, and continued. "Well, one night, a state cop comes to the door and says Al run off the road and was dead. They said he was drunk. I don't know about that, but he was dead all the same. It broke his mother. Right there." Another pause, then he spoke again. "The baby came. That was Richard. We had the girl — his mother — maybe three, four months after that."

"Why?" asked Melanie. "Did she die?"

The old man snorted with disgust. "Nope. She run off. Run off and left the baby. Three-, four-month-old child. Left it."

"Did she go home?" Again, Melanie asked the question. John was silent.

"Nope. She did not. She took off to California. She wrote to my wife once, after she'd been gone near a year. She said she'd send for Richard when she could."

"Did she?"

"She did not. She did come back, though. Eight years later."

"She came back eight years later?"

The old man nodded. "Yep. She showed up one day, no notice, nothing. 'Course, Richard, he didn't know her, but she came with a policeman, and she says she wants her kid. Then, she takes him, just like that. There was nothing we could do, even though we had him for eight years."

The Giamos were still. It was an awful story. John said, "And did he make any contact with you before he came to Vermont this time?"

"Oh yeah," said the old man. "We'd hear from him, a letter here and there, a card at Christmas. His mother had married again and had a couple of other kids. Once he got on his own, he did come back for a visit now and again. I thought he turned out all right, though. Went to college, got married, no kids though, then he was doing something else. Anyway, we always kept his room, just in case he wanted to come back."

John blinked. "Is that where he's staying now?"

"Yep."

"Can I see it? I don't have a warrant, but I'm not going to search it."

"Sure, I don't care. And it's my house."

They followed the old man past the chimney block and up a stairway littered with piles of old magazines and newspapers and bunches of clothing. At the top of the stairs was a hall with two doors opening off it on each side. The hall was as cluttered as the stairs, and miscellaneous extension cords ran the length of it. A bare bulb with a pull string hung in the middle of the ceiling.

John pointed to it. "Can I turn on the light?"

"Sure, go ahead. Richard's room's the last one on the right."

John pulled the string and, followed by Melanie, went down the hall. He opened the door to the bedroom. The room was neat and clean. A homemade braided rug was on the floor. White, gauzy curtains hung at the window. The wallpaper was old, probably hung in the forties, but it was in good condition. Crocheted doilies were on a bureau and the arms of an overstuffed chair. There was a small bookcase in the corner. A double bed with an iron headboard was made up with a beautiful patchwork quilt. A bedside table with a lamp and a book on it completed the furnishings. There was a suitcase in the corner, flopped open. John walked over to it and looked in, but he did not touch anything. Melanie waited in the doorway.

"This is his room. Always was. We always kept it ready for him, and after my wife died, I did the same. He's been here three nights now. Guess the skiing must be pretty good, what with the snow we just got."

John had a sudden thought. "Mr. Seeley," he said. "Do you own a gun?"

"Well, now, let's see," said the old man. "I got my deer rifle. I got a shotgun, and I got a twenty-two pistol."

Out of the corner of his eye, John saw Melanie's eyes grow wide and her mouth move as if to speak, but she knew her protocol and remained silent. John said kindly, "Can we go back downstairs? I'd like to talk to you about why we have to speak to your grandson. Also, can you lay your hands on that pistol? I'd like to see it."

The old man eyed him again with his beetle-like stare, but he nodded. "Go on down to the kitchen," he said. "The gun's in the table by my bed. I'll get it."

John led the way downstairs, and they sat at the table waiting for Bud.

"What about fingerprints?" Melanie whispered.

"If he suspects anything, he's going to wipe that gun clean before he hands it to me," John said, keeping his voice low.

"I may be old, but my hearing's still good," yipped the little man from behind them.

Melanie started, but John only arched his eyebrows.

Bud came around to take his seat at the table. "I've always been a law-abiding citizen, Chief, and I'm not stupid, neither. I figured out pretty quick when you asked about Richard that he was in some kind a trouble, though I didn't reckon it had to do with guns. I didn't wipe nothing 'cause there was nothing to wipe."

John looked up at him.

"The gun's gone, Chief."

John said, "You didn't misplace it?"

Bud snorted. "I ain't touched that gun in twenty-five years. Just keep it there in case anybody comes snooping around. I live here alone, ya know."

John felt his wife's hand on his knee. He cleared his throat and said, "Richard Seeley is suspected of the attempted murder of one man and accidental killing of another in the process. Although we haven't even seen him yet, circumstantial evidence points to him as a person of interest. The crime was committed with a twenty-two-caliber pistol, and I wanted to come out here and talk to you, to make sure we were on the right track. Now that we've found that Richard Seeley is staying with you and that your gun is missing, we have enough evidence to at least pick him up for questioning. That is, as long as we can find him."

"You don't know where he is?"

John shook his head.

Bud placed his gnarled hands on the table. "He was here last night, but I get up at four thirty every morning, and he was gone by the time I had my coffee."

Melanie leaned forward and, as was her habit, took the old man's hand. "Mr. Seeley," she said, "are you feeling all right?"

John expected the hand to be withdrawn, the question to be rebuffed with a snort, but instead, Bud sat there, letting Melanie hold his hand. It was that Y-chromosome thing again, he thought.

Bud said, "I can't say I like sitting here with you telling me my grandson murdered somebody."

"Oh, Mr. Seeley—" Melanie started.

"We're not telling you that at all, Mr. Seeley," John said over her. "We're saying we'd like to talk to him and that there is circumstantial evidence connecting him to the crime. We need to know because the man who was meant to be murdered may still be in danger." The police chief stood. "I've got to get back to my office, Mr. Seeley. I want you to know how much I appreciate your cooperation and understanding. It's got to be very difficult for you."

Melanie released the old man's hand, patted it, and stood beside John. Bud stayed seated, staring at the table top. Melanie and John exchanged worried looks, but the old man rallied. He stood up, straightening himself as much as his bent form allowed. He reached out and shook the chief's hand.

"Like I said, I'm a law-respecting person. I'll help you, and if it turns out Richard's done all this, well, then, I'll help him, too. Sounds like maybe he could use it."

"Thanks, Mr. Seeley," John said, going out the door, "and if Richard shows up here, just give us a call and don't tell him we've been here. We need to talk to him."

With that, the interview was over. John and Melanie slogged back through the muddy snow to their vehicle and climbed in.

"The poor old man," Melanie said softly.

"Yeah, he's a real Yankee, though, isn't he?"

"Yes, he is. Stoic as they come, and realistic. Sometimes it seems that people like that bear more than they have to just because of their own attitudes and constantly trying to live up to, well, pre-determined, archaic standards that no longer apply."

"Like your parents?"

"Ha! I guess so, yes, but they've softened up a lot, John."

"Not at first. I thought they were both going to kill me."

"What? When we ran off?"

"Yeah. I'm still sure they would have rather seen you a widow than married to me."

"They thought I was pregnant."

"I know."

"I think it might have been the best day of my life."

"When you got pregnant?"

"No, oh, that was, too, but I was talking about when we got married."

"Really? Why?"

"Well, it meant we were together forever. It did to me, anyway. Didn't it to you?"

John smiled at her. "Yeah, I suppose it did."

"You sound dubious. What was the best day of your life, then?"

"The night we slept together for the first time."

Melanie blushed and looked down at her hands. "Good answer," she said. "Why, though?"

"Because it meant we were together forever."

"Really?"

John had slowed the Suburban to a crawl. "Yes, really. After that, I knew I couldn't live without you."

"I don't like the way we've been lately."

"How have we been?"

"You know," she said. "We've been distant. The other night was the first time we'd had sex in about two weeks!"

"That must be a record for us."

"It's not funny."

John sighed and wiped his hand over his care-worn face. "What's going on with you and Gabriel Strand?"

Melanie stifled guilt that bubbled to the surface at his question. She answered as evenly as she could. "Are you still fixated on that?"

He glanced over at her as he drove. "Yes. I am. Tell me about it."

"I'm old enough to be his mother!"

"Melanie!" He pulled the Suburban as far to the side of the road as he could and stopped.

She gave him a long stare and then looked out the windshield.

"Mel, what's going on? I need to hear it from you. This case is getting more and more convoluted. Who am I harboring in my own home?"

"There is nothing going on between Gabriel Strand and me." She spoke so quietly, causing him to lean in slightly to hear her. "There could have been. Yes, I have to tell you. There could have been something going on. He…he spoke to me in the barn this morning."

"Spoke?"

"John, he kissed me."

"He kissed you," John repeated. "In the barn. This morning."

"Yes. I didn't even know it was coming. He's just a kid, John, and he's frightened. I guess…I guess I was the nearest thing to hold on to."

John blew angrily through his nose. "And how did you feel about that?"

"What do you mean?" It was impossible to hide the unnatural tone in her voice.

"I mean, how did you feel when he kissed you?"

"I was shocked, I think. I — I don't know. I just stood there." She hung her head and let her voice trail off.

"Well?" he prompted.

"Well, I set him straight. I told him it wasn't possible. I told him I couldn't reciprocate."

"Thanks for that," he said sarcastically.

"Don't be cruel."

"Cruel! You tell me you and this rock star are locked in an amorous embrace in our barn. Who's cruel, Mel? Who's cruel? Did you kiss him back? How do you feel about him?"

She unbuckled her seat belt and whirled in her seat to face him. "How do I feel? I felt pretty damn good! I felt like somebody valued me. I felt like it had been a long time since I'd had that kind of attention." Panic had its cold hands around her throat, and she raged on. "If I were younger…If I were younger and single, he'd be just my type. He's a good person, and I like him. But this made me very aware of something, John."

"Oh yeah? What's that?"

"It made me realize how much I love *you*! It made me realize there will never be another man for me. Not ever. I love you. I miss you, John! I miss you. I'm tired. The kids wring everything out of me some days. They're just weaning themselves, and it's hard. They demand. The paper demands. The animals demand. I'm always serving everybody. I'm so sorry. I neglect myself, and because you're part of me, you're neglected, too. That's how I feel. That's all I can say. Where have you been, John? Do you still love *me*? Do you still want to be with me and nobody else? How do *you* feel?"

He sat staring at her. Tears had begun to brim on her lower lashes. "If something came between us," he said softly, "if we were separated by anything, I wouldn't want to live. I love you so much, Melanie Dearborne. I have loved you all my life, since we were children. Don't you remember?"

"Oh, John! We were really in love, weren't we?"

They looked at each other. Bundled in their winter clothing, it was hard to move, but Melanie put out her hands to his face. They leaned toward one another over the console and kissed. It was a romantic kiss, there in the wilds of Vermont on the white ribbon of road, the new snow making it appear littered with diamonds in the afternoon sun.

"Yes," he said, "and we're still in love, but it's different now, isn't it?" His hand slid down her parka to where her breast was under the thick material. "Like now, all I want to do is go home with you, get naked, and stay in bed for two days. We can't, though, because, as we speak, our house is inhabited by a horny rock star and three kids. Maybe more, for all I know. And two dogs and a wood stove and noise. All I want is you and a bed."

Melanie's guilt was retreating, jabbing at her a little less. She was feeling reassured by his protestations of devotion to her. "Those are the rewards of love," she whispered.

"No," he said, "this is the reward of love." His hands went up under her parka, and he caressed her. "Do you think we've got time before the next snow plow comes through?"

She laughed and pushed his hands away. "No, I don't. And how would it look for the police chief to be caught in a compromising position in the middle of the work day? In the town vehicle, no less!"

He sighed and scowled. His hands returned to the steering wheel, but the vehicle remained stationary. "We're husband and wife. We can compromise each other anytime we want. Twenty-five years ago, we would have done it, right there. No excuse could have stopped us."

Melanie nodded. "It is different, yes. But, John, you're my best friend in the world, and I love you more than anything. The only reason we would have done it here twenty-five years ago is because we couldn't go home and do it because we weren't sleeping in the same bed yet."

"Do you still…" he said softly. "Do you still desire me? Even with a couple extra pounds?"

Her guilt rose up and slapped her across the face. "Of course! You're the sexiest man I know. To me, that's all that's important. When we're somewhere, with bunches of people all around, you're still the only one I want to leave with." She spoke the truth, and it comforted her. Her attraction to Gabriel was fading in the heat of her husband's desire for her.

Involuntarily, she moved toward him.

"Get in the back seat," he said with a slight growl in his voice.

Her stomach leaped, and she scrambled over the console like a teenager.

He shut the vehicle off, got out of the front seat, opened the back door, and got in beside her. A click of the keys locked them in.

She watched as he took off his jacket, wadded it into a ball, and placed it against the far door. She felt his hand on her chest as he pushed her backwards. She searched his eyes. They were glassy and hard and boring into her own. He unzipped her parka and pushed her sweater up around her neck. Reaching behind her, he unclasped her bra, exposing her breasts. He squeezed them hard with both hands and bent over her, kissing her. She opened her mouth and let his tongue in. He bit at her lips and pulled away. Dropping his head to her chest, he played with her taut nipples with his teeth and tongue until she moaned and writhed. He gave a wry smile as he unzipped her jeans and slid them down over her knees. He pulled off her heavy snow boots and one leg of her jeans. Grabbing her thighs in his big hands, he forced her legs open, pushing one over the edge of the seat and hoisting the other up over the seatback. His roughness surprised her, frightening and exciting her at the same time.

Bracing herself with one foot on the floor, she surrendered completely to him, lying on the seat in her panties, trembling. He pulled the crotch of her panties to one side, lowering his head. His tongue penetrated her, and she moaned again. He straightened up, on his knees on the seat, and recklessly pulled off the offending panties. She moved her leg back on the seat, but he pushed it off again, cupping her mons in his hand. He squeezed her hard and then shoved two fingers into her up to their hilt. She cried out, and then his other hand was over her mouth. Her eyes closed in rapt pleasure as his fingers moved in her, working her to a fever. Her face flushed, and she nearly lost her breath.

He removed his hand and held his finger up to his lips. "Not a sound," he whispered. "Open your legs."

She obeyed.

"Wider," he said.

She opened them as wide as the space permitted. He spread the folds of her vulva until her clitoris, hard and throbbing, was exposed to him. He flicked at it with his fingers, pulled at it, squeezed it. Melanie trembled uncontrollably and arched her back. She opened her mouth. Instantly, his hand was covering it again.

"No sound," he said again.

She shuddered, crazy for her orgasm. Suddenly, he pulled back. The car was beginning to cool off, and her skin prickled with the cold, adding to the intensity of her sensations. Desperately, she reached for him, but he laughed harshly and pushed her arms back.

"Don't move," he said.

He was dominating her, she realized. This was about him. And yet, she was being driven to distraction by it. He reached under her with both hands and spread her buttocks, running his little finger over her anus, poking at it, rimming it, pushing at it until he pushed in up to his first knuckle. Now she cried out as delicious, sharp waves of lust washed over her. He laughed, pushing in farther, moving in and out of her, flicking at her engorged clitoris at the same time.

John straightened up again, pulling back from her. He tore off his shirt and unzipped his pants. His holster dropped to the floor of the car. He was erect and hard. He knelt over her for a second, one hand on the shaft of his penis, one hand on her belly. Then he buried himself in her wetness and began his thrusts. It was all she needed. Her orgasm flooded her senses almost before he entered her, and the muscles of her vagina squeezed him into her until she felt him give himself over to his passion and explode within her. He collapsed on her, and they lay, breathing in unison and waiting for their heartbeats to slow.

Finally he stirred and, partially raising himself, kissed her on the mouth. "Nobody could get me going like that except you," he whispered.

She gave a little laugh. "That was, um, a little different. Amazing."

"I love you," he said.

"And I love you," she answered, satiated.

They dressed. Melanie climbed back over the console, taking her seat demurely. She watched John as he stood outside, strapping on his holster, straightening his jacket, and pulling on his leather gloves. A thrill went through her again, and she sighed.

John got in and started the car. "We got away with that one!"

"We did," Melanie laughed. "I feel like a guilty kid!"

"Speaking of guilty kids, we've got a house full of them. We'd better get back."

"Our kids aren't guilty."

"They must be, of something. And Strand is definitely guilty — of trying to seduce my wife."

"John. Please, let's not re-open that."

"Shh," his voice soothed her. "I'm okay now. But please don't go kissing every man in town just so we can have hot make-up sex on all the back roads!"

She laughed at that, relieved. Then, more soberly, she said, "What about this Seeley person, though? Gabriel may be a horny rock star, but I don't want him getting hurt."

"Neither do I," John said, giving his short, sharp sigh. "I'm just hoping we can get to the bottom of this case and keep him alive."

Melanie glanced at her watch. "It's getting late. I told him I'd take him down to my office, where he could have a conference call with the band and fax them some of the production numbers."

They had come to the end of the white road where the snow shone like ice crystals. They were back in the real world. John pulled out onto the main route back to town.

Chapter Sixteen

"I've got to get back and find Richard Seeley and the mysterious Kayla." They had reached the house and kissed quickly over the console.

As Melanie stepped out of the vehicle, Gabriel surprised them as he held the passenger side door open. "Can I talk to you a minute, Chief?"

Melanie said quickly, "I'll be in the house. See you later, John."

John motioned to Strand. "Get in."

Strand climbed in and shut the door. He was not wearing a coat.

John turned up the heat in the idling Suburban instinctively, as he would have done for any child. "What is it?" he asked.

Strand sat staring at the floor, his brow furrowed in a puzzled scowl. "I didn't tell you everything about this Kayla person."

"Well, what a surprise." John usually didn't resort to sarcasm, but this time, he couldn't help it.

Strand looked up, chagrined. "When you brought it up, I felt uncomfortable talking about it in front of…of all your kids."

"And Melanie," John finished his sentence for him.

This time, Strand met the chief's eyes. "And Melanie," he acknowledged in a clear voice. Their eyes remained locked, the cool, hazel gaze of the police chief subtlety attempting to quell the defiant fire that smoldered beneath the surface of the young man's deep brown stare.

At least we understand each other, thought John. The fire was there, but John had the upper hand, and Strand knew it. He was the police chief. He was providing protection. He, John Giamo, was the husband.

At last, Gabriel looked down. He said, "She is a special woman."

John answered him generously and without guile, "Yes, she is. I'm glad you recognize it." He rubbed his hand over his face, regrouping his thoughts. "This isn't about Melanie, Strand. This is about you and a murder and your personal safety." The young man was silent. "So tell me about Kayla."

Strand laced and unlaced his fingers and then said, "What I said before was true. She did somehow get into the party after our concert. We had just made it big. She made a play for Justin, but he's got a girlfriend and is strictly monogamous. I don't think she had a particular person in mind, as long as it was a member of the band. I'd had quite a bit to drink, so I just stepped in. I told myself I was helping my friend deflect unwanted attention, but I was thinking of myself, too."

John stifled another sarcastic thought.

Strand talked on. "We spent most of the party drinking together. I guess we talked. I can't remember what we said. Stupid stuff. You know, party stuff. Then she came back to the hotel with us. We all went back together, but we had separate rooms. She came to my room with me and stayed the night. In the morning, I had a real early plane, so we had to get up and get out of there. She walked down to the lobby with me and I said, like, goodbye and thank you or something stupid like that. Then she says, 'I'll see you in Chicago.' I said, trying to be nice, something like, 'Oh, I won't have time in Chicago. I really enjoyed last night, but I'm on the road now for six months.' Then she said, 'I'll find you,' and she laughed and walked away." Strand stopped, took a deep breath, and laced his fingers together again.

John prompted him, saying, "And? That's it?"

Strand shook his head. "No. When I got to my hotel in Chicago, there was a big bunch of red roses waiting for me. No name. I thought they might be from my mother, but they weren't. Then, after the show in Chicago, we had a party like we always do, in our suite at the hotel. Somehow, this girl Kayla got in. We found out later that one of the security guys let her in. Anyway, I was surprised, but I didn't think much of it. We were really pumped, you know, because of this incredible, unbelievable success we were having. I don't think anything could have bothered me at that point."

"What happened?"

"Nothing. That is, nothing as I saw it. She hung around me, and we talked and drank together, but I was kind of attached to this other girl I'd met earlier in the evening, before the show. She was our manager's sister. She was pretty, she reminded me of, like, well…" He was talking faster now. "Anyway, she was pretty. I liked her. Actually, I *like* her. She's back in LA, and I'll probably see her when I get home. We were sitting in a corner, just talking, and Kayla comes up. I said hi and introduced her to Natalie—that's the girl I was with. She looked weird, man, like wild or something. She said, 'Who's this?' I said, 'A friend of mine.' She said I wasn't allowed to have friends that pretty. Then she laughed, and I got freaked out. I took Natalie by the hand and tried to move to another part of the group, but Kayla followed right along, talking to Natalie, saying stuff like she knew me."

"Like what?"

"Like, she said, 'Well, he always acts like this when he's on the road. It's all I can do to keep him in line.' Like we were a couple or something."

"Hmm," said John. "Go on."

"She wouldn't leave us alone. Finally, she goes, to Natalie, 'You can go home now, bitch.' Whoa! I told her that was out of line. Then, she said I couldn't treat her like that, and she shoved Natalie up against the wall."

"Physical assault?"

"Yes."

"Go on."

"I didn't fool around. I called our security guys, and they got her out of there. I haven't seen her since, but she's definitely gone creepy. It turned out that there was a bunch of red roses waiting for me in every hotel room on the tour. Also, I started getting those e-mails on the Ragged Rainbow web site. They spooked me because there were quite a few references to personal things, but then I realized there was nothing there that couldn't be found somewhere online, like gossip sites and stuff like that."

"Did Natalie press charges? For assault?"

"No, she didn't. The security guys said they would call the police, but she said she didn't want any trouble, to just let it go."

"What did the e-mails say?"

"You can read them. Mia printed them all out. Mostly they said stuff like, 'I saw your mother today. She was coming out of Los Rios Drive.' You can Google the street where I live and see that it transects Los Rios Drive, so that doesn't mean anything. The stuff that creeps me out is when they say things like, 'You think I'm just a girlfriend, but I'm not. I'm something else.' Stuff like that. Then there was a new one today."

"What did it say?"

Strand cleared his throat. "It was kind of scary. It said, 'First I was hurt. I couldn't believe it of you. Then I realized you are totally self-centered. Now I'm angry. You'd better watch your back.'"

"The e-mail said that? 'You'd better watch your back'?"

"Yes."

"Hmm. I need to see those e-mails."

The musician straightened up a little and slapped both his hands down on his knees. "This is a nightmare. Now there seems to be two stalkers. Bruce Blake is dead. I'm the one that the killer wanted dead, so that doesn't make me feel warm and fuzzy. And I've got a show." He looked straight at John. "And I'm going to do that show, Chief. If I start letting things like this get to me, I'm finished. My band is counting on me."

John blew through his lips. "We'll try to narrow it down before Saturday night. I think I've got a good lead on Seeley. I don't know what to do about this Kayla person. I'm sure we can trace her through her e-mail, but she may not be where her e-mail suggests she is. What do the blogs say? Or the message boards, I guess they're called?"

"I never read those things."

"Go back in the house, Gabriel. Go with Melanie and get your business done. Have your conference call. Then stop back at the station. I'm going there now, and we'll see where we get with some concentrated effort."

He gripped the young man's shoulder for an instant. Strand nodded in acknowledgment and got out of the car. John hurried back to the station.

Melanie was alone in the kitchen when she heard the door open. She knew it was Gabriel before she turned around. They hadn't spoken of the incident at the barn, but she could feel it brewing just below the surface. She turned to face him and smiled.

"Would you like some coffee? I just made a fresh pot. Then we can go down to my office and get this conference call out of the way."

"Okay," he said and took a seat at the table.

Melanie set a mug of steaming coffee in front of him. She sat across from him with her own mug.

"Where did the kids go?" he asked.

"To other parts of the house. They're afraid to hang around here too long. They're afraid I might ask them to do something."

Gabriel gave a little laugh, and then he said, "Melanie, I'm sorry about what happened in the barn this morning. I was out of line. I'm just freaked out right now."

"You don't need to apologize, Gabriel," Melanie said softly. "I kissed you back. I guess I'm as guilty as you are."

"You're very beautiful," he whispered, a slight smile playing on his lips.

Melanie blushed in spite of her resolve. "Thank you, but I'm nearly old enough to be your mother."

"That doesn't bother me," he protested as he took another sip of his coffee. "I'm in love with you."

"Oh, Gabriel! Think about what you just said! You aren't in love with me! You don't even know me."

"I am. I am in love with you. I'd get to know you in time, but I'm in love with you right now. Do you understand how that works?"

Melanie sat back in her chair and raised her mug of hot coffee to her lips. "Sounds like a guy thing to me," she said. There was just the slightest hint of sarcasm in her voice.

"Please don't mock me," Gabriel said. There was no mistaking the passion in his deep brown eyes as they stared into her sky blue ones. "I need you to know that I'm in love with you." Melanie was silent, so he went on. "I don't know how it happened. I didn't plan on it, but I haven't been able to stop thinking about you since I met you at the accident. I travel all over the country. I meet hundreds of people. I have to scrape the girls off me. I hardly notice them. I hardly ever meet a person who impresses me one way or another. And then, here I am, in the sticks of a tiny state in New England in the middle of a blizzard, and you come out of nowhere and break my heart!"

"As I recall, you're the one who came out of nowhere."

Gabriel smiled a little at that. "You know what I mean. I had to see you again. That's why I came up that evening. I just had to know who you were. I couldn't let you just fade back into the snow. Then—then, all this happened, and now here we are." He paused and sighed, studying some invisible spot on the table top. Melanie waited, and then he looked up at her and said, "I take back my apology. I'm not sorry. I'm glad. I'm glad I kissed you. I want to kiss you again, right now. I'd give anything just to put the world on hold for a second—no, a week. A week with you and nobody else around. A week with you on a South Seas island. I'd give up all the fame in the world for that."

Melanie laughed. "Now you're being silly!"

Gabriel didn't smile. "I'm not being silly. I'm not a child, Melanie. I'm a man. A man with a job. A man who has learned what he wants. I know the feelings I have for you are real. I've had relationships before. I know what I thought love felt like, but now, here you are, and the feeling is something I've never felt before. Melanie, tell me you have some feelings for me. Please, tell me what to do about this."

Melanie blinked back tears that burned at the backs of her eyes for reasons she couldn't fathom. *I must be tired*, she thought to herself. *This kid is getting to me.* Even in the wake of that spectacular love fest with her husband, not an hour ago.

"It would be hypocritical of me to sit here and say I didn't care about you, that I wasn't attracted to you, too, but I'm a married woman. Married for a long time to a man I love very dearly. I tried to explain that to you in the barn. A physical attraction, even an emotional attraction, can happen between people at any time. It's not unusual. However, I, for one, won't act on it. I'm absolutely flattered that a b—a man like you, young, extremely attractive, with testosterone oozing from every pore, a celebrity with his pick of women no less—would feel this way about me. You have no idea how it's touched me, this attraction we have, but Gabriel, I do love my husband, and I know, I *know*, he loves me, too. We met when I was fifteen, and I dated other guys, even thought I was going to marry one of them, but I always came back to John. We belong together. Our connection trumps everything. Always has; always will."

The young musician rubbed his hands over his face. When he looked up, he said, "Will you tell him about what happened in the barn?"

"Not all of it," Melanie answered.

"Why not?"

"Why?" she asked coolly. "What purpose would that serve? Nothing happened that would change the way I feel about him."

"Well, thank you for that," Gabriel said, smiling suddenly. "I wouldn't want him to find out and then conveniently let somebody take me out!"

Melanie laughed out loud. "You're funny!" She got up from the table just as Mia came into the kitchen.

"Am I interrupting something?" she asked sulkily.

"No," Melanie replied. "Did you have any lunch, baby? How's your shoulder feeling?"

"It's okay, I guess." Mia sat down at the table. "I'm not that hungry right now. I want to go somewhere, but we're short a car!" She glanced nastily at Gabriel.

"Hey, I'm really sorry," he said. "My trip here really put a kink in your whole family's plans."

Mia smiled. "Oh, that's okay. I'll be able to tell my grandchildren about how I was snowed in with Gabriel Strand."

They both laughed.

"Yes, we are short a car, and Gabriel and I have to get down to my office for that conference call. Call your brother down here, Mia. We'll have to use his car."

The pale winter sun was slipping down toward the horizon. Afternoon had descended.

Chapter Seventeen

"Rick wants you to know it's going to be a while for Melanie's car," were the first words spoken to John as he walked in the door.

Becky was standing behind her desk. She was the best co-pilot, wing man, and first mate a captain could want. She was his "brother-in-arms," personally and professionally, and had been since high school. She was at once pragmatic, practical, and optimistic, and he envied her that. She had an uncanny knack for being able to see the prize without losing sight of the trail or the details along the way.

"Why are you looking at me like that, John?"

"Do you remember when you sneaked Melanie out of her house the night we got married?"

"Please! Don't remind me. I was scared. I carried the suitcase."

"Well, it ended up fine, didn't it?"

"You know what they say about fools and drunkards."

He laughed. "You might have a point there."

"What made you think of that?"

"Melanie and I took a ride into the hills to talk to Bud Seeley. We were talking."

"And is he related to this Richard Seeley?"

"He is. He's his grandfather. Richard Seeley's been staying there, saying he was on a ski vacation."

Jason Patterson and Steve Bruno came into the room from their back office. "Does he know where he is now?" Steve asked.

John shook his head. "No, he doesn't, but he showed me the room where Seeley's been staying. His suitcase was still there. And here's the kicker: Bud Seeley, the grandfather, owns an old twenty-two-caliber pistol."

"No shit!" Jason exclaimed, forgetting himself.

"That's right," John said. "What's more, the gun's missing. The old man claims it's been lying untouched in the drawer of his bedside table for years. It wasn't there today when I asked to see it."

Becky spoke up, saying, "So the old guy was cooperative, then?"

John sighed. "Very. Made me sad. It's a long story. I've got to write it up, but obviously this guy hasn't left the area. If he is the guilty party, by this time, he must know it wasn't Gabriel Strand he shot. He's not going to go far. They never do. He's going to have to have the last word. Where's Cully?"

"He went to your house," Steve said.

"My house! What the hell for?"

"Mia called him on his cell phone. I guess her brother wouldn't give her a ride to a friend's house or something. She asked Cully to give her a ride."

"That kid is out of control!" John was mad. This was Melanie's bailiwick, not his, but Melanie was running around with this rock star kid at the moment. He gritted his teeth. "Becky, get Cully back here right now. I need everybody on, and I need everybody here right now!" He whirled on his heel and into his office. "She thinks the whole frigging world revolves around her!" he muttered loudly, not caring who heard.

With his office door closed, John called his contact at the State Police, informing him of the situation. After that, he called the "neigh-bors" — police departments in nearby towns — to put them on alert as well. Then he grabbed a clipboard and returned to his staff. Jason and Steve were still standing there, waiting patiently. "I've been on the phone with Ostrowski down at the State Police Barracks. They've put extra cruisers on routes one-oh-three, ninety-one, and eighty-nine. Rutland police have Bud Seeley's place staked out in case he shows up there. Personally, I think he's riding around trying to figure out where the kid is. He's going to try again. That means he's right here under our noses."

In the background, Becky was on the phone. "Don't bother, Cully. Just get in here now. Somebody will get Mia to her friend's house. I don't care! This is life and death. The chief needs everybody. Bring her in with you, then. She can talk to her father."

John shot her a thoroughly exasperated look over his shoulder.

They all waited impatiently until they heard the outer door of the big town office building open. They heard the footsteps come down the hall, and the door to their small cluster of rooms opened.

Mia was the first one through the door, Cully on her heels. She was bundled against the cold in a black goose-down parka. She wore a turquoise neck warmer, but her head was bare, and her blond hair was windblown and unruly. Her face was like a little thundercloud, blushing pink. "Daddy!" she demanded, swiping the hair from across her eyes, "I…"

He was ready for her. John could count on one hand the times he had spoken harshly to his daughter, but he spoke harshly now, cutting her off in mid-sentence. "Mia, go in my office, close the door behind you, and sit down." Her mouth opened, but if she meant to protest, he didn't give her the chance. "Not a single word from you! Do as I say. Do it now."

Mia clamped her lips together and stalked through the small knot of policemen, disappearing into her father's office.

"And don't slam the door!"

The door closed quietly. John turned to Becky and his men.

"Now, everybody pull up something to sit on, and let's get some action going here."

There was a scraping and clunking as the three officers pulled up various chairs. Becky sat behind her desk, and John remained standing.

He cleared his throat and said, "We have to close this one fast. Strand is determined to do that show on Saturday night, and there's no way we can stop him. It's his choice. My guess is that his hired security is worthless. We can suggest to Hanover police that they provide more security, but my inkling is they won't be very thrilled with the idea. We've got the state cops watching the interstates, and I called the neighbors so they'll have their men on alert too. I don't think the man's gone far. He's been staying with his grandfather up in the hills, and I think he thinks no one can find him there. He's probably made it a base of operations until he gets the deed done. That is, presuming he's the guilty party."

"Who else would it be, Chief?" Cully spoke up. "It seems pretty cut and dried to me. At least it's all we got."

"That's just it, Cully. We've got another suspect."

The three young officers exchanged surprised looks.

Becky said, "What's up, Chief?"

John shook his head and ran his hand through his hair. "It's this electronic age. Just now, when I was up at the house, Strand tells me he's been getting threatening e-mails from some psychotic fan. And apparently the same person has been posting comments on these blogs or whatever they're called."

"Message boards?" Cully asked.

"Yeah, that's it," John confirmed.

"How'd you know that, Cully?" asked Jason.

"I keep up." Cully gave a self-important shrug.

"Well, good for you," Becky said sarcastically.

"At any rate," John said, bringing his troops back to order, "as far as we know, it's a girl named Kayla. Somebody Strand picked up after a concert who didn't take it too well when he dumped her. My guess is it's the same girl who slipped you the note. He claims she attacked a girl he was with at another party, so according to him, she's capable of violent behavior."

"Where do these people come from?" Becky snorted. "Why are there so many of them?"

"How do we track this one down?" Steve asked.

"Well..." John sighed. "That's a problem. We don't know any-thing about her, where she lives, or where she is. We can apparently track her via the e-mail, but of course that will only give us the registered account she e-mailed from. It's better than nothing. Becky, you better call State Police and see whether they have any venue for accomplishing this."

Steve spoke up again. "I think we can do that ourselves from here, Chief. It might be quicker. At least we could get the name on the account and then go from there. If the server won't give us the name, then we have to go through the courts for a subpoena. We might as well try first."

"Hmm," John mused. "How long is that going to take, though? I wanted you all on the road today tracking Seeley." Jason was usually the person John set on any computer-related task, but he was also a valuable man on the street. "We'll have to call FBI in Burlington."

"Hey," Jason said, seeing his chief staring at him. "Is Mike still home? He's a computer whiz. He can do that. I know he can. Whenever I have a technical question, I call Mike first. He can usually talk me through it."

John nodded in relief. "Good idea, Jason. I'll get him on it." Now he needed to hand out the assignments and send his troops into the field. "I want everyone on the streets. Jason, you start down by the diner and go out into that neighborhood. We've got the car, make and model, and license plate. Becky's going to print you all out a sheet with the information on it, so there's no mistakes. I guess he could have changed plates, so keep an eye on any vehicles of same make and model, regardless of their plates. Steve, you can take the north side of town and watch those areas around my house, just in case. Cully, you go east toward Springfield. Check the stores, restaurants, and gas stations. I'm going to stay in the middle of town, talk to people, see whether I can raise some kind of clue as to this guy's whereabouts."

"What about the fangirl?" Tim Cully asked.

Johns shook his head, frustrated by his limited skills in the area of computer technology. "I don't know what to do about that right now. I'll call Mike when we get done here, see whether or not he can track down the computer and how fast he can do it if it's possible. Can we identify a specific computer, Steve?"

"Yes, you can, as long as the provider will give out that specific information. Then, it's a fast job. Otherwise, it's a subpoena."

"Hmm." John rubbed his face. "Well, get going, guys. Stay in touch, either with me or Becky."

Becky stepped forward. "Here, don't forget your information sheets. This has everything on the case we've got so far and what to look for. I'll be here all day."

Steve spoke up as he took the paper from Becky. "Do you think the guy knows we're looking for him yet, Chief?"

John shrugged as he opened the door to his office. "I don't know. I hope not. It'll greatly improve our chances. See you later." They filed out, but as Cully put his hand on the doorknob, John said, "Cully, I want to talk to you a minute."

Becky stood up behind her desk. "I'm going down the hall to the clerk's office for a minute, John," she said, and she made a judicious exit.

He tried not to raise his voice as he addressed the young officer who stood, looking at the floor.

"Cully, are you crazy?" He leaned over Becky's desk on his clenched fists.

"Are you talking about giving Mia a ride?"

"Yes, I'm talking about giving Mia a ride. Since when is babysitting one of your concerns? You were on duty, Cully."

"Sorry, sir, but I—"

"I don't want to hear any excuses. I'm sure there's a million of them. And I'm going to hear plenty when I go in my office. Cully, you've got to pay attention. Learn about teenage girls. One of these days, you're going to turn around and have one of your own."

"Sorry, sir."

"Well, if anything like this happens again, just call me. Or call her mother. Now please, go do your job."

John turned and went into his office, shutting the door behind him. He did not speak to Mia at first. Instead, he slipped behind his desk and sat down. Mia stared at the floor with knitted brow. John almost smiled, but he was still truly irritated, so he kept his face stern while he thought about what to say. Finally, he sighed and said, "What's going on, Mouse?"

"I just needed a ride, Daddy, and Michael wouldn't give me one. He said to wait until Mom and Gabriel were ready to go to Mom's office and he'd give everybody a ride in."

"I'm surprised you wanted to leave with Gabriel Strand in the house."

The girl made a sound through her nose. "Oh, he's totally smitten with Mom. It's 'Melanie this' and 'Melanie that.' You should say something to him, Dad. She's your wife."

John said sharply, "Don't change the subject. You can't call a police officer in to give you a ride, Mia." It was amazing how children always knew the buttons to push.

"It's just Cully. He was probably just eating lunch." Her tone was defiant, but she didn't look up from the floor.

"I don't care if he was picking his nose by the side of the road. He was on duty, and when he's on duty, he's mine. Is that understood?"

"I guess."

"No 'I guess' about it, Mia. I had to ream Cully out, too, and I hate doing that. You're not the only person affected by something like this. Why couldn't you just wait for Mike?"

"I told Ethan I'd be at his house by two o'clock, and I was already late. I'll be lucky if he talks to me again."

"Ethan Adams?"

"Yes. He called at, like, ten o'clock, and now it's almost three."

John sat still. Ethan Adams was Mia's new boyfriend. He didn't particularly like him. The boy was too polite and too squeaky clean, like the boys who used to follow Melanie home from college. John said irritably, "He'll be lucky if you talk to him again. Why didn't Ethan come and get you?"

"His mother took the car."

Things happen for a reason, John reflected. Two teenagers stranded apart were infinitely preferable to two teenagers stranded together. He sighed. "Well, look, Mouse," he said, capitulating, "you can come with me. I'm out on the street myself this afternoon. I'll give you a ride to Ethan's and then swing back through town."

Mia's face lit up. "Thanks, Dad," she said. "Oh, there goes my phone." She reached into the pocket of her parka for the device. She glanced at it and said, "It's Ethan."

John stood up and went out to speak to Becky.

"You just wait, Becky," he said. "Your kids are still pretty young. What are they?"

"Twelve and fourteen."

"Ah. Well, it's going to start pretty soon."

"I don't have any girls, though."

"Well, I can loan you one," he said sarcastically.

The phone rang, and Becky picked it up. "Clark's Corner Police." She listened for a moment. "Just a minute, Mike. I'll put him on." She handed the phone to John. "It's your son."

"Mike?"

"We just dropped Mom and Gabe at Mom's office," said Mike. "It says on my cell phone that you called me."

"Becky called, I think. I need you to stop here and do some computer work for me."

"It's almost three, Dad. I was going to drop Peter off at your office and get back to school before dark."

Everything was always on their terms, thought John, exasperated. He spoke carefully into the phone, tempering his voice. "Since when have you been afraid to drive after dark? Mike, I need you for police business. You don't have any classes tonight."

"No, but—"

"You can get up early in the morning and get there in forty-five minutes," said John. "I need you to find me some information regarding this Gabriel Strand case."

"Dad!"

"Michael…" John decided to go for the bribe. Parenting books forbade the approach, but time and again, he had found it useful. "I'll pay you."

"Dad!"

"It's your civic duty. You're the one always pontificating about politics. Well, here's something for your resume."

"I'll be there," his son answered in a sulky voice. Then, as an afterthought—or a threat, John could not be sure which—he added, "I've got Peter with me."

"Bring him, then. I don't care."

"He doesn't want to come."

"Both of you get in here now." He slammed down the phone and turned to Becky, who was stuffing some papers into the engorged file cabinet. "What the hell is going on with these kids? Is everything about them? Can't they contribute anything out of altruism?"

Becky outright laughed. "Didn't you just ask me a while ago to remember that night you and Melanie eloped? I guess you were thinking a lot about how her parents, and yours, too, would feel. I guess you were thinking about where you would live and how you would manage to eat. You didn't even have a car. I had to drive."

John gave a little smile. "Touché," he said. "I can tell you this, though. I wasn't thinking about even one kid at the time, let alone three of them in my hair!"

"You got good kids, John. All kids are a pain in the neck from time to time."

"I suppose you're right."

They heard the huge outside door creaking open, followed by footsteps down the hall. They heard Irene, the town clerk, greeting the boys. Then the door of the police station opened. The brothers walked in, Michael first, Peter just behind and to the left of him.

It was their unconscious formation whenever they were together. It was the way they worked, in tandem. Michael in front, making the decisions where to go, whom to talk to when they got there. Peter was the enforcer, who despite and contrary to everything he might say, was there to back up his brother. Peter was scowling. Michael's face was impassive.

"Hi, boys," said Becky.

"Hi," they both answered.

"Dad," Peter started, "can somebody give me a ride home? Just let Mike give me a ride up the hill. You don't need me for anything."

John's patience was at an end. "Peter, just shut up for a minute. I'll get to you." He grabbed a bunch of papers from Becky's desk. "Mike, I need you to get online and track down this URL for me. These are the e-mails and message board postings threatening Gabriel Strand. See how far you can get. We may have to call in the FBI or get a subpoena, but do what you can right now. Can you see where they're being sent from?"

"I can at least get the server, Dad, and they can identify the location of the computer. Depending on the server, well, I don't know how much information they're willing to divulge."

"See how far you can get," repeated John.

"Where's Mia?" asked Peter. "She can use Mike's car and give me a ride."

John's office door slammed at that moment. "I'm right here," Mia said, coming into the room.

"I thought you went to Ethan's," said Michael.

"Well, I didn't," Mia said bitterly. "Some selfish pig wouldn't give me a ride, and now Ethan's called and said he's got to go to work this evening in his father's office. Thanks a lot, Michael!"

Michael made no answer. He took the papers from his father and retreated into the back office. They heard the chair clunk as he settled down at Jason Patterson's computer.

Peter whined, "Can Mia give me a ride home, Dad?"

John held up his hands. "Look, you people are almost adults. You're not babies anymore. I have to work. I'm at work now, and right now, I'm supposed to be tracking down two people who may have committed crimes in our town. Murder, no less. That's my job. You guys work it out amongst yourselves. I don't care where you go.

I don't care who you go with. You can stay here. You can walk home. I've got to go to work. And Becky's working, too, so don't bother her."

He turned abruptly, yanked open the door, stalked out into the hall, and slammed the door behind him. He wasn't six feet down the hall before he heard scampering footsteps behind him. He knew who it was before he turned around.

"Come on, then," he said, putting his arm around his daughter's shoulders. The two walked out together to the Suburban.

Chapter Eighteen

John drove up to Main Street and turned left at the intersection where Gabriel had skidded into Melanie's car. It seemed like ages ago. Mia was silent. "How does your shoulder feel, Mouse?"

The girl shrugged. "It's okay, I guess. It's still kind of sore. When I was lifting the buckets today for the horses, I could feel it."

"You should wear your neck brace."

"Yuck."

He turned into the Jiffy Mart at the south end of Main Street. "I'm going to run in here and talk to the girls. They might have seen something. Want anything?"

Mia shook her head. "No, thanks, Dad."

John smiled to himself. She may be nearly eighteen, but she was still his baby. He knew she just wanted to be close to him. The ups and downs of being a father were exhausting. Inside the shop, John poured himself a coffee, loaded it with milk and sugar, and went to the cash register to pay for it.

"Hey, Chief," greeted the girl behind the counter.

"How are you today, Carla?"

"Not so bad," she replied, taking his money. "How about yourself?"

John put a picture of Richard Seeley down on the counter. "Have you seen this guy around here?"

Carla studied the print-out of the photo. "No, I can't say I have, but you know, I don't remember people anymore. They come and they go. If I don't know them, I hardly notice them, and I forget as soon as they leave the store."

"Hmm, well, keep your eyes open for this guy and give me a call if you see him."

"I will," she said. "Is this to do with that murder at the inn?"

You couldn't keep anything quiet in a small town. "Yeah."

"Nobody knew the guy who got killed. What happened with that Gabriel Strand guy? The rock star?"

"He's under police protection."

"Weird. Oh, well. Have a good day, Chief."

"You, too, Carla." He walked toward the door, sipping his coffee.

"Too bad you weren't looking for a girl," Carla called out after him.

John stopped in mid-sip. "Why do you say that, Carla?"

"Well, yesterday, a girl comes in here and asks where she can buy ammo."

"Ammunition? For a firearm?"

"Yeah."

"What else?" John turned to give the cashier his full attention.

She was flattered and elaborated. "Well, this girl comes in, and she was dressed kind of funny. Like she was almost dressed up, I guess you'd say, with high-heeled black boots on and her hair all done."

"How old would you say she was?"

"Oh, probably in her twenties or maybe early thirties."

"What did you tell her?"

"I said we didn't sell ammo, but I thought my boyfriend bought his at the hardware store. Then she left."

"Carla, I think I can use this information. Thanks. Thanks a lot for mentioning it."

Carla blushed.

His next stop was the hardware store. He pulled in, leaving Mia in the car with instructions to answer the radio if Becky or one of the officers called in. A father couldn't grill his daughter for the details of her relationship with a boy, John felt, or even question her about her feelings like a mother could, but he could give her something useful to do.

Ed Sanborn, the owner of the store, was at the cash register when John walked in.

"Hi, John."

"Hello, Ed."

"What can I get you?"

"It's police business, Ed. Can I see you in the back?"

"Sure. Just a minute." The proprietor's voice rose as he called out, "Hey, Travis, get up here and man the cash register for a minute, will you?"

A muffled "yeah" came floating back from an undefinable corner of the store.

"Follow me." Sanborn led the way into the back office, held the door for John, and shut it again behind them. "What's going on?"

"We're looking for a person, a female. She could be dangerous. Did an unknown woman come in here yesterday or earlier today wanting some kind of ammunition?"

"Yeah, she made a purchase when we first opened. What's up, John?"

"I want to question her about the shooting at the inn," John said. "Can you verify the sale?"

"Of course. Certainly. I can get you the receipt in about two minutes. Want it now?"

"If you will, yes, please. Was it twenty-two caliber?"

"It was. I waited on her myself. She was kind of a nervous thing. Really skinny, too. Laughed too loud. She had a lot of earrings in her ears."

They were interrupted by a frantic rapping on the office door. "What is it?" Ed called out irritably.

The door opened, and Mia hurried into the room, thrusting her cell phone at her father. "It's Michael," she said. "It's important, Dad."

John took the cell phone. "What is it, Mike?"

His son's excited voice came over the phone. "Dad, I started with the most recent e-mails and blogs first. It didn't take me half an hour to zero in on this. The server is Vermont Telephone for the last three e-mails and the last message board posting. VTel was really cooperative because this is a Vermont thing and Becky verified who we were. Her cousin is the executive assistant."

"Well?"

"The computer is the one in the lobby of the inn."

John was silent.

Michael repeated, "Dad, it's at the inn. Are you there?"

"Yes, yes, I'm here."

"The account holder is Bill Noyes. Somebody at the inn sent these e-mails and posted this message."

"You're sure?"

"Of course."

"Did you track down any other servers?"

"No. I didn't think it was necessary."

"I guess it's not. Good job, Mike. I'll head over there right away." He handed the cell phone back to his daughter.

"Did Michael find her, Dad?"

"He's hot on the trail. Come on, Mouse, I've got to get to the inn and talk to Bill Noyes. Ed, do you think you can get that receipt for me?"

"Sure."

"I'll pick it up later."

"Good luck, John."

John strode out to his police vehicle so fast that Mia had to skip to keep up. She jumped agilely into the passenger side. "Do you think that person is at the inn?"

"That's what we're going to find out." John stuck the Suburban's nose out into the street and peered around the giant snow banks. "If we're lucky, she won't have gone too far and it'll be the same person Strand told me about." John drove down the street and parked in front of the inn. "You stay here and man the radio again, Mouse. I'll talk to Bill Noyes."

He ran up the front steps and through the double doors. Surprisingly, Susan and Bill Noyes were standing there.

"Thank God you're here!" Bill blurted out, but it was Susan's silence and the look on her face that struck John.

"What's the matter?" he asked cautiously.

"Aren't you answering the nine-one-one call?" Bill Noyes persisted.

"No. What's going on?"

Susan said, "We've got a girl who's locked herself in the room where the murder took place. She's threatening suicide."

"This is awful!" The innkeeper rubbed his hand across the back of his neck. "I called nine-one-one. Who's supposed to respond to that, John?"

"It goes through the fire department. Dispatch probably called Caleb. He should be here soon."

"Aw, John!" moaned Noyes. "He's probably three towns away up to his knees in leaky pipes!"

The words had just left his lips when Caleb Cochran came through the door. By trade a master plumber, he was also the volunteer fire chief and an unusually handsome man a few years younger than John. He nodded at the police chief.

"Caleb," acknowledged John.

He knew he could count on Caleb. The man never broke a sweat, no matter what the crisis. Yet, years back, when his young wife died, John had seen the light go out of Caleb's eyes, and it had haunted him and the rest of the town as well. Everybody loved Caleb. Then, last fall, Caleb had married again. A beautiful girl, Lauren Smith. A prodigal daughter, if you will, of Clark's Corner. The whole town watched with satisfaction as the empty man filled with love again. The spontaneous smile, gone for so many years, returned, and there was renewed vigor in his eyes.

Caleb replied, "Do you know what's going on?"

"I just got here. Actually, I'm investigating that murder. We've got another suspect, and I've reason to believe that my suspect and the girl who is threatening suicide are one and the same."

"Hmm," Caleb mused. "Interesting."

"Well, can someone do something?" Bill Noyes was exasperated.

Caleb had yet to address Noyes. He was still talking to John. "The first responder call went out. I got Tim Cully coming in with the ambulance crew."

John sighed. "Couldn't the state cops respond? I'm not thrilled at having one of my guys pulled today."

Caleb smiled a little. "Well, Cully responded. He's on his way." Finally, he turned to Bill Noyes. "What's going on, Bill?"

Noyes blew through his nostrils. "Susan was at the desk, around noon." Suddenly, he threw up his hands. "I'm a wreck," he said. "Susan, you were there. You tell them."

Susan picked up the conversation calmly. "I was at the desk, as Bill said. There was a young woman who had checked in early on the evening of the murder. She was sitting over at the computer desk, typing. I had seen her there the evening before, too. She was there for about twenty minutes, I'd say. Then she went out—outside. I watched her through the big window. She headed down the street toward the hardware store. I wasn't here when she came back."

"The next thing we know is this!" Bill interrupted his wife as he waved a paper in the air and shoved it at John. "It was stuck in my office door."

John took the paper and read aloud:

At the time you read this, I will be barricaded in the room my Gabriel died in. I will be preparing my own death. I can no longer live with my grief. I am sorry to inconvenience anybody, but I cannot leave the spot where his blood was shed. Please forward my love to his sister and dear, dear mother. I look forward to joining my darling in the next life. The hour approaches when I must go to him. Please do not interfere. Only carry out my last wishes and bury me next to him.

"She's a crackpot!" snorted Bill Noyes.

While John had been reading, Tim Cully had come in to the lobby, with Mia close behind. Cully echoed Noyes's sentiments. "She's a nut! She doesn't even know he's still alive."

John said, "Or does she, and this is the beginning of some elaborate defense charade?"

"Good thinking, Chief," said Cully. "How'd she get into that room?"

John looked at Noyes. "I've no idea! We've kept it locked up tight," the innkeeper insisted nervously.

"Probably up through the fire escape," offered his wife. "Or she may have gone up the main stairway when we were all busy elsewhere."

"Mia, this is getting serious. Go back and monitor the radio," John instructed. "This woman is armed, or at least we know she bought ammunition earlier today. Twenty-two caliber, as it turns out."

"No shit!"

"Cully, you're on duty," John barked.

"Sorry, sir." The young man lapsed into silence.

"Dad, she's not going to kill herself."

"Mia, please, monitor that radio. Get a call in to Becky and have her alert Steve and Jason. Spread them out. Cully and I will be here for a while. Tell her to call State Police and send up Joe Bernard."

"Daddy, she would never leave a note like that if she were really planning to kill herself. She's a crazed fan who should be locked up! She just wants attention." Mia tossed her hair with such defiance that it hit Cully across the face. Then she stalked out of the building.

Caleb remarked, "Your daughter's got a point, John. We're either dealing with the murderer—the person who killed that promoter—or she's a real nut. Either way, it could be dangerous. For herself or anybody."

"Then let's do something!" Bill Noyes exclaimed, his clenched fists waving in the air.

"Caleb, you come with me," said John, ignoring Bill's antics. "We'll go up there and try to talk her out. I think we can tell pretty quickly where she's coming from."

Caleb nodded his affirmation and followed the police chief up the stairs.

Susan said abruptly, "Wait!"

Both men turned from the bottom step.

"Here." Susan extended her hand to John. "The room is still locked from the outside. You'll need this key."

"Thanks, Susan," John said gratefully to his cousin, and they continued up the stairs.

On the landing, Caleb said, "What do we do if we run into somebody in the hallway? Noyes isn't going to like any negative publicity."

"That's not our concern, Caleb." John was tired of publicity and its effect, negative or positive, on anything or anybody.

The men made their way to the upstairs hall, which John was thankful to find empty. He walked quietly to the room where Bruce Blake had been killed. It was not marked, but it had been locked from the outside with a padlock. John figured she must have crawled up the fire escape and in through a window. It would have been pretty easy to guess which room it was, especially if she had been the person who pulled the trigger in the first place.

John and Caleb took their places on either side of the door. John reached out and tapped. There was no response. John rapped harder, with his knuckles. They waited. Still no response.

Caleb called out in a kind voice, "Is there anyone there? Is the person who left the note to the innkeeper there? We don't know your name. We want to help you."

Finally a response came. "I'm here, and you can't help me."

"I don't understand why you want to die," Caleb said gently. "You sound like a young person, full of life. Would you explain to me?"

John knew the goal was to do anything to keep her talking.

"I caused Gabriel's death."

John's heartbeat elevated, and he arched his eyebrows at Caleb.

"Do you think you shot Gabriel Strand?"

"No! No! I love Gabriel. I loved him so, so much. I just didn't get here in time."

"I still don't understand."

"I think he came here to find a place where we could be alone together. He didn't tell anybody he was coming here before the concert. I e-mailed him to tell him I had something very important to tell him. He knew I'd find him. I always do. I'm always there, at every concert. He knew he could depend on me, and there was this other girl, and I know he got a room here so she couldn't find us. Now he's dead. He's dead, and I will be soon."

"Gabriel isn't dead." There was silence. Caleb repeated, "Gabriel Strand is alive. Did you hear me?"

The woman's voice went flat. "You're lying to me."

This time, John spoke up. "We're not lying. I'm John Giamo, Chief of Police here. Gabriel Strand is under my protection. What is your name?"

"You're just lying to keep me from killing myself. I know he's dead. I watched when they sneaked the body out through the fire escape."

"That wasn't Strand. Really, I promise you he's alive. What's your name?"

"Kayla."

"Kayla, open the door, please."

"Will you promise to take me to Gabriel?"

John and Caleb exchanged looks. John said, "We would have to make sure everyone was safe."

The voice sounded hesitant. "Safe from what?"

John said quickly, "Kayla, come closer to the door. I can't hear you very well. I need you to be able to understand me when I explain things to you."

The two men in the hall could hear footsteps cross the room slowly. John continued, "Kayla, are you listening to me? Do you have a firearm, Kayla?"

"I do. Yes, I do. I've always carried it, in my purse. You can't be too careful. People are untrustworthy. They backstab you. People try to hurt you. People try to hurt Gabriel."

"Kayla, we won't let anyone hurt you or Gabriel, do you understand me?"

"He doesn't love me, does he? That's why he won't come to meet me. He doesn't believe me. It's because I'm too fat. I can't believe it. We've been through so much together. I'm on a diet now. He doesn't love me, does he?"

"I can't answer that, Kayla," John said gently.

She began to talk faster. "He was only wounded, wasn't he? He wasn't dead. He doesn't love me, does he? He would have called for me. Did he call for me?"

Caleb opened his mouth to answer, but the girl rambled on, becoming more and more agitated. "This is his blood, but he wasn't dead, was he? They were sneaking him out past my window that night, but he was still alive, wasn't he? They thought nobody knew who was in that room, but I knew. I always know where he is. We're connected. We are. Oh, oh, Gabriel. Why didn't you just come to me? Why did you let that girl come between us? She's not fat, is she? Why did you even talk to her? Now it's brought about my end as well as yours."

They heard a click, and then another. Both men knew it was the gun. She was preparing to fire.

"Kayla," said Caleb gently, "when I fell in love with my wife, things didn't go easily. We had plenty of problems getting together, but we're married now, and we're happy." He was attempting to ingratiate himself, to make her identify with him. It would buy them time.

"Sorry to do this to you," came the voice through the door. "I can't live without Gabriel, and I can't live being called a fool. A fat fool. My face will be all over the tabloids as the person who let Gabriel die."

"Don't worry about that now," John said. "Just open the door, Kayla, so we can talk together about when you can see Gabriel."

"Now you *are* lying to me," said the girl. "And I don't want to talk anymore." The voice had changed its tone, and it scared John.

Caleb whispered, "Is it possible to enter this room from any other way?"

John shook his head. "I don't know."

"I'm going down to talk to Bill Noyes," Caleb said.

John held Caleb's arm and gestured for him to stay. Then he tried to jump-start the conversation with Kayla. "Don't ruin your chances of a relationship with Gabriel," he said desperately.

"Is he with that other girl? Is that why he won't come here? Does he want to hear my news?"

John whispered, "You stay here, Caleb. You're better at this than I am. My job is downstairs, anyway. I'm going to see whether we can get up there from the outside."

Caleb nodded, and John walked quietly away down the hall. He heard Caleb as he kept the conversation going, saying truthfully, "Gabriel isn't with any other girl."

On the way back to the first floor, John struggled to organize the jumble in his mind. His instincts told him the girl probably didn't intend to commit suicide, that it was just her unfathomable need for attention that motivated her along the path she had taken into the situation she occupied now. Still, he could not be sure enough to force the issue or to risk taking the conversation, however inane, to the level of an argument. He also doubted, but could not be sure, that she had shot Bruce Blake, thinking it was either Gabriel Strand or the girl she suspected of coming between them. And did she really have news, or was it a ploy? John's money was still on Richard Seeley as the perpetrator, and he was anxious to be done with this crisis and find his suspect. With Cully on scene, he only had two men in the field. He couldn't be sure Joe Bernard had joined the hunt. He reached the bottom of the stairway. Bill and Susan Noyes stood with Tim Cully in the lobby. John was exasperated to see Mia there as well, standing beside Cully, but he said nothing to her as he joined the group.

Instead, he addressed the innkeeper. "Bill, is there a way into that room from the outside, or at least a way to see inside?"

"Only up the fire escape. That's undoubtedly how she got in. There's two windows in that room. It's one of the bigger rooms—a suite, actually. I'm sure she got in by the fire escape."

"Actually, John," Susan interjected, "you could stand in the pergola, and perhaps, if the sun isn't glaring in the windows, you could see inside with binoculars. The windows in that room are pretty big."

"That's a good idea," John said. He could depend on Susan to get to the practical heart of the matter. He turned to Cully. "You take the binoculars in my vehicle, take a two-way radio, and sneak into that pergola. Try to hide behind the lattice work or something, although I don't think she'll be looking out the window. I'm going back upstairs. I think we're done fooling around. We'll just surprise her and take our chances. Hurry up, Cully. You got two minutes to get out there."

"Surprise her? How?" Bill Noyes asked, wringing his hands together.

"I'm going to kick the door down."

"Kick the door down! John!"

"It's all right," John smiled wryly. "I've done it before." He was back up the stairs two at a time.

John joined Caleb, who was still talking.

"…and I'm sure he'd be really upset if something were to happen to you. Like I said before, we can get by anything as long as we have the facts. Now, can you open the door? I'd just like to talk to you face to face."

John held up the key and signaled to Caleb to keep talking.

"I've got a gun."

"You have no reason to use that on me, now, do you?"

Silently, John unlocked and removed the padlock.

"No, no I don't. I'm terribly sorry. I really am, but I must join Gabriel. I must see him. I've got to warn him."

"Please, open the door now, and we can talk about the details."

There was silence. John shifted his weight forward, but Caleb held up his hand and mouthed, "Wait."

John stepped back and fidgeted. Now they heard the deadbolt on the door click. John saw the doorknob turn, and the door opened slowly.

There were no lights on in the room. The suite was located between the two rear wings of the old hotel, so even though it was still light outside, the gloom of evening had settled in the room, making it difficult to see. John walked in, trying not to betray his uncertainty. He could make out a figure standing in the shadows at the back of the room. "Kayla?"

He heard a rustle, but he could not see the figure move. "Kayla? I'm John Giamo. Do you mind if I turn on a light?"

"Please don't," the figure said.

John swallowed and flexed his hands. "I'm glad we can talk like this," he said. "We can talk about things now. Can I sit down?"

"Please don't. I'm not sure I should have let you in. I'm not sure what I'm going to do."

"Well," John said, trying to sound friendly, "just pretend that everything is exactly the way you would want it. What would you do then? Would you let me sit down? Would you talk to me? Picture that in your mind. What would we talk about?" As John spoke, he tried to get his bearings in the room. His eyes were adjusting to the light, or lack thereof, and he could see the girl in the corner. He had taken the required training pertaining to talking to potential suicides, although he had never had to use it. He thought Caleb would probably do a better job, being closer to the girl's age, but he could hardly have sent Caleb in to face an armed person.

The figure in the shadows stood still. It was a girl with long brown hair, not much older than Mia. John peered more carefully through the gloom. She was skinny. Not a natural skinny like Gabriel Strand—or Michael, for that matter—but skinny to the point of unhealthiness. John could see that she was most likely anorexic. She seemed heavily made up. She wore leggings, a short skirt, and a skimpy T-shirt. Her skeletal arms hung at her sides. In her right hand, she had a small, .22 caliber hand gun. He could see her tremble, as if she might be cold. Except for that, she didn't move. John held his position. Caleb stood stock still in the hallway.

Finally, the girl stepped forward out of the corner. "I want to leave. I want to go home now." Her hand wavered, and she raised the gun, pointing it at her own head.

Suddenly, the window behind the girl exploded, and everything happened at once. Shattered glass sprayed everywhere. The girl shrieked and raised both arms. The gun went off, but the bullet buried itself harmlessly in the ceiling.

When his children were very small, John had always found it a challenge to dress them. Inside or outside, they never seemed to want to wear clothes. John would stand in front of them, holding the offending article of clothing—a T-shirt, a snowsuit, boots. They would look at him with wide eyes and then whirl and try to make their escape on tiny, bare fat feet. John became very adept at scooping them up with one arm and holding them against his body until they stopped struggling and accepted their fate.

He did this now, instinctively, as the girl recoiled from the flying glass. Normally a slow-moving man, John moved quick as lightning, ducking under the gun and scooping the girl up with his right arm. The gun discharged and then clattered to the floor. He held tight. He prepared for the inevitable struggle, but there was no fight left in her. She hung like a rag doll in his arms.

Caleb rushed into the room. "John!"

"I'm all right."

"Is she hit?"

"She's okay." John scooped up her legs with his other arm. "I think she might have fainted."

"Let's get her downstairs where we can check her out. What happened? Did she shoot?"

The two men were hurrying down the stairs, John bearing the burden of the girl. He shook his head. "Not intentionally. The gun went off, but the bullet went into the ceiling. I don't know how the window broke."

"That gave you your chance."

Cully came running up to them as they stepped into the lobby. They laid the girl on the couch. She was crying silently, tears streaking down her face, but she lay quietly.

"Get the stretcher, Cully," John said softly. "You'll have to take her to the hospital." He bent down close to the pitiful, emaciated figure on the couch. The father in him, never too far from the surface, rose. He smoothed the lank hair back from her forehead, which was beaded with cold sweat. "Shh," he soothed. "Shh. You'll be better. We'll see to it. Just rest, if you can. Let somebody else do the worrying."

The girl nodded and turned her face away from him.

Caleb lifted the girl gently onto the stretcher. Cully secured the ties around her and covered her with a blanket. They prepared to carry her out to the waiting ambulance.

"Cully," said John, "as your chief, I have to tell you it was too dangerous, shooting that window out, but no one was hurt, so as a man, I want to thank you. It opened the opportunity for me to grab her. That was good thinking. Thanks."

Cully looked at the floor and then directly at John. John had known this young man for years. He saw something he couldn't quite identify. It wasn't defiance. It wasn't pride. He didn't know what it was. It was something like surprise, maybe satisfaction. Cully said, "It wasn't me, Chief. My weapon has not been discharged. You can check. Ask Mia about it."

"Cully!" The exclamation came from Mia, who stood off to the side behind him. "You promised me! You promised!"

"I didn't promise you, Mia," the young officer said. "I have to do my job. I have to tell my chief." He was as professional as John had ever seen him.

The chief kept his cool. "It's okay, Cully. Go with Caleb and get this poor girl to the hospital. Find out what you can. I'll talk with Mia. Thanks for the backup."

Cully and Caleb both nodded. "Okay," Caleb said. "Let's get going." They hoisted the stretcher and carried it from the building.

John turned to his daughter. "I need an explanation of your involvement in this."

Mia looked at her father defiantly. "I followed Cully when he went out to the pergola to keep watch," she said. "I could make out the silhouette of the girl against the window. Then I could see your shadow when you came in. Cully was watching through the binoculars." She stopped.

"Go on," John commanded.

They were alone in the big lobby now. Bill Noyes had retired to his office, and Susan had gone upstairs to assess the damage to the room.

"I could see your shadow," Mia repeated. "And when you came into the room, the light changed, and I saw that she had a gun. I told

Cully to shoot out the window, to cause a diversion, you know. It would give you a chance to disarm her. I was afraid if we waited, she might really be crazy and shoot you. Cully said he couldn't do that. He said it was too dangerous and he didn't have reasonable cause. I didn't argue with him, Dad. I broke some of the lattice work on the base of the pergola and got a stone from underneath. Cully didn't see me. When I saw her start to move toward you, when I saw her raise the gun, I threw the stone with all my might. I broke the window."

They stood facing each other silently. Then John sighed. "I can't have vigilantes running wild and disrupting police business. And you're a minor, Mia, a child. You might have been hurt." He wiped his hand across his face.

"I am not a vigilante. I'll be eighteen in the spring. I'm a citizen. I wasn't taking the law into my own hands. I was helping my father."

John and Melanie Giamo had brought their children up hoping that each one of them, as different as they were from each other, would develop the same qualities of intellectual curiosity, the ability to think for themselves, to ask the right questions, and defend the defenseless. They hoped to instill in their children courage, kindness, and social responsibility.

And here was his daughter standing before him, tall and straight, clear-eyed and strong, her head slightly cocked, partly defiant, partly beseeching. He saw that she was all of those things, and beautiful besides. He bit his lip to keep back the tears. He walked toward her, his hands palms up. He wrapped his arms around her and hugged her. "It was a brave thing to do," he said into her hair. "That's quite an arm you have." He released her and took her hand. "Let's go now. I've got to get back to the station and find out what Cully's up to at the hospital. I've got to catch up with Jason and Steve. We're not out of the woods yet."

"So you don't think she's the one who killed Bruce Blake?"

"No, Mouse, I don't. I think it was this Richard Seeley. I want to find him."

"You can just take me back with you, Dad. Debbie will pick me up," Mia said as she climbed into the police vehicle.

He smiled at her and pulled out into the road.

Chapter Nineteen

At the police station, Becky sat at her desk, writing furiously on a pad of paper, the telephone tucked under her chin. "Okay, all right. Get back here as soon as you can." She hung up the phone. She punched a button and said, "Mrs. Lewis? Mrs. Lewis, are you still there? Yes, yes, I know, but I don't have a single officer I can deploy right now. Yes, they can be a nuisance. Well, why don't I just call the school, and they can inform their parents? Yes, yes I will. Nice talking to you, too. Goodbye." Becky hung up the phone again and looked up at John. "Boys are running through Mrs. Lewis's yard again."

"Any word from Cully?"

"Yes, I just got off the phone with him a minute ago. The girl is a real train wreck. Cully spoke with the physician's assistant there. He said she was seriously anorexic and dehydrated on top of that. They're trying to notify next-of-kin now. Evidently she threw some kind of fit or had a seizure or something after they brought her into the emergency room. They won't let anyone talk to her until tomorrow, so Cully's on his way back here."

"Good. Where're Mike and Peter? Mike's car's still outside."

"I'm in here on the computer, Dad," his older son called out.

John peered around the corner to see Michael sitting at Jason Patterson's computer.

He held up a bunch of papers. "I've been tracking down all those e-mails and blogs, the message boards, too," he said. "I've created quite a paper trail. It'll come in handy, I think."

"It's valuable evidence, Mike. Thanks."

"Peter's in helping Irene. Some new contractor or architect or somebody was in looking at the tax maps and messed everything up. He's helping her get those big books straightened out."

"Irene's getting too old to handle those anymore," John said.

"Don't tell her that," warned Becky.

Peter came into the office. "What an idiot!" he exclaimed. "That guy made a mess. He just made a mess. Poor old Irene. She couldn't even lift the book, and he had left them all over the floor. It was cool, though. I saw the tax map of Mom's office building. Irene said he wanted to know who owned that piece of property. Maybe he wants to offer her a million dollars for it or something."

"In your dreams." Mia snorted and leaned back against the wall. "He wanted to know who owned Mom's building? That's weird. Who'd want Mom's building?"

Becky said, "He sounded like a new developer in town. I think he was just looking randomly for properties he found interesting."

"Hey," said Peter. "Maybe he does like Mom's place. There's a lot more land with that than I thought."

"That's because you only go into her office, rob the candy jar, and leave," Michael said.

"That building is worth a lot more to this family than you kids realize," John said as he riffled through papers on the corner of Becky's desk.

The building at the center of their conversation was the large, brick Federal-style house built in 1847, at the south end of town where Melanie had her offices for *The Town Crier*. It was a beautiful house, facing east toward the river. Four large windows, two on either side of the great front door, graced the face of the house. A carriage wing extended from the rear north side, and a charming, white-columned covered porch embraced the south and west sides. There were four fireplaces in the house, as evidenced by the two large chimneys on each end of the roof peak. There had been a barn, too, long ago, but it had fallen in, leaving its skeleton of a stone foundation. John had reason to be sentimental about the place. Melanie's grandfather, Tom Dearborne, had acquired the run-down building just before World War II, and he'd spent more time and money than his wife would have liked improving it. It was rumored that this was where he'd carried on his life-long affair with Mia Maronetti Giamo, meeting her here for clandestine trysts. Melanie thought it was romantic. John maintained the whole affair thing was probably hearsay, but secretly, he could not forget finding his grandmother crying alone in her bedroom the day Tom died.

Be that as it may, when old Tom Dearborne died, he willed the building to Melanie. She was twelve years old at the time, and her father, also Tom Dearborne, was named trustee to maintain the building and its grounds for her until she came of age. Melanie's father grumbled, but he kept the taxes paid and the roof and foundation in good repair. Her grandfather had left some money for the building's upkeep, but he could not have anticipated the inflation of taxes and maintenance costs. By the time Melanie came into her inheritance at age twenty-one, the house was run-down once again. Her father paid the taxes on it for one more year, until Melanie graduated from college. Then he told her, "It's yours now and your responsibility. You have the upkeep and the taxes. You can sell it, or you can keep it as long as you can afford it."

Luckily she did keep it, because the next year, she eloped with John Giamo. John could smile about it now, thinking back. The memories made John smile triumphantly. The Dearbornes could never quite understand from whence their only child came. She was nothing like her mother in looks or demeanor. While Catherine Dearborne's style was old-fashioned, Melanie wasn't afraid to show some cleavage. Where Catherine only smiled genteelly at the funniest of situations, Melanie laughed out loud — and often.

"What are you smiling like that for, Dad?" asked Mia.

"Oh, I was just remembering when your mother and I moved into that house just after we were married."

"Because Grammie and Grandpa wouldn't let you live with them," Peter said. They had all heard the story many times before.

"A married couple should live on their own," John said in defense.

"Why didn't your Nona let you live with her?"

"She would have, but she thought it was important for us to make our own life. She loaned us the money to fix the place up so we could live there."

The phone rang on Becky's desk. After a quick greeting, she said, "Okay, he's right here." She handed the phone to John. "It's Cully."

John took the telephone, not bothering to go back into his office. "What are you finding out, Cully?"

"I think you better get down here, Chief."

"Yeah? What's going on?"

"She's still in the ER. She's with the PA. They put a drip on her. The PA told me she was severely anorexic and the stress she'd been through could be dangerous. Anyway, while I was waiting there with her for somebody to see her, she started babbling away to me. At first I thought she might be hallucinating or something."

"What was she saying?"

"That she had to see Gabriel Strand, that he was waiting for her. She said she had news to give him."

"News?"

"Yeah. Get this: She said she wanted to tell him that Richard Seeley was in town looking for him."

John felt an instant surge of adrenalin. "Are you sure?"

"Yes, I asked her to repeat it. She kind of laughed and said she didn't think he'd be too happy."

"Then what did she say?"

"Then the PA came in and said they were going to start a drip and I had to wait until they gave me permission to talk to her again. I think you should come down, Chief."

"I think I should, too. She's not in danger of running, is she?"

"Nope. Too weak. Besides, she's enjoying it, if you ask me. I think she likes the attention."

"I'll be there shortly. Don't let anyone else get near her until I see her first."

John hung up the phone. "Becky, get hold of Jason and Steve. There's a new twist to this thing. It appears that our potential suicide is acquainted with our number one suspect."

"Seeley?"

"That's what she told Cully."

"Do you think they're in on it together, Dad?" Mia asked.

"I can't say that from here, but I intend to find out."

Peter's impatience surfaced again. "Can somebody give me a ride home? I don't want to be here."

John ignored him and said to Michael, "You make sure you've got copies of all the e-mails and blogs and message boards you can. Track as much as you can." He turned to Becky. "I'm going to the hospital to see what information I can get out of her."

Becky nodded. "Got it. I'll fill Jason and Steve in. Do you think Seeley might know she's at the hospital? Or that any of this has transpired?"

John had been feeling somewhat haggard, but this new bit of information gave him a second wind. He shook his head. "Don't know." He pulled on his jacket, fishing his black gloves out of the pocket.

"John, let me call State Police and get Joe Bernard to help us out."

"You can try."

"Dad," Peter nagged, "give me a ride home on the way."

"Peter, it's the opposite direction. Can't you see I've got my hands full?"

Becky stepped in. "Look, let your father go. As soon as I've got Jason and Steve set, I'll turn the phone over to State Dispatch and take you and Mia home."

Mia said, "I was going to Emma's."

"Well, I'll take you there, too, then."

"Thanks, Becky," Peter said.

John yanked open the door. "We are going to have a major summit meeting of this family as soon as things quiet down." He hurried out the door, closing it hard behind him. Through the closed door, he could hear Becky chastising his children.

"Your father's upset! That was just this side of a slam, and he *never* slams. Now sit somewhere until I'm ready."

Chapter Twenty

John drove as quickly as he could toward the hospital. The roads still weren't clear, and black ice was apt to be prevalent. He glanced at the sky ahead of him. It was cloudy and spitting snow. There was a damp chill in the air, and the gloom of the approaching evening was settling down between the hills. Soon it would wash over the river valley. He couldn't seem to get the car warm enough.

Orville Palmer Memorial Hospital, colloquially referred to "Opie," was a small community hospital built on thirty acres of Vermont hillside just outside town. Most of the people from Clark's Corner had been born there. John was as familiar with its floorplan as he was his own home. He pulled up to the parking area reserved for the police and fire department just outside the emergency room door and saw Cully waiting for him.

"Any more news?" he asked as he walked inside.

"No, Chief. I haven't been back in there. I figured it would be better with two of us listening. We could corroborate our facts that way."

John stifled a grin as he looked at the young officer. *Is he finally developing some sort of law enforcement instincts? And where did he learn the word 'corroborate'?* "I agree," he said. "Let's see what we can find out now."

They walked side by side down the hall to the emergency room reception desk. The PA looked up from his papers. He didn't wait for John to speak, but motioned for the two officers to follow him. "This way." He led them down the hall, past the curtained-off exam areas where nurses hurried back and forth among several patients, to a small room. The PA paused before he opened the door. "She's in here," he said. "She was very agitated when she was brought in. We have her on a mild sedative, so she may seem spacey or even be sleeping. It will keep her calm, though, until the psych guy can see her tomorrow. She appears to be textbook anorexia, so we're addressing that as well in the IV drip. Try not to stay too long."

John nodded and opened the door. The girl lay in the bed, covered with a light white blanket. Her eyes were closed. Her hair was matted underneath her neck, and there was a sickly pallor to her skin. She wore a hospital johnnie. One bony arm, the one attached to the drip, lay at her side on the outside of the blanket. Her nails were long, professionally manicured, with French tips.

"Kayla," John said.

Her eyes remained closed, but she answered, "What do you want?"

"It's John Giamo. I spoke to you in the room at the inn. I carried you down the stairs. I'm here with my officer, Tim Cully."

The girl repeated drearily, "What do you want?"

"Are you feeling well enough to talk?" Suddenly, all he could think of was the fact that here he was again, within a matter of two days, at the emergency room with another young girl. True, he reflected, this one was very different from the sleek, rosy beauty who was his daughter, but this girl was not very much older than Mouse. And who was to say that, given proper love and care, this poor thing would have bloomed in a similar way? He shuddered slightly.

"I'm not feeling anything," replied the girl. "Just say what you want."

He felt Cully shift on his feet behind him.

Before he could ask a question, the girl spoke again. "Where is Gabriel? He's dead, isn't he?"

"He's not dead," John said flatly. "He's still under police protection."

"If he's not dead, he will be soon. That's what I came to warn him about. That's why I was tracking him down." The girl rolled her head away from them, her eyes still closed.

John and Cully exchanged glances. John motioned with his head to the other side of the bed. Cully stepped around the foot of the bed and pulled up a chair. John did the same on his side.

Leaning forward slightly, he said, "Kayla, Officer Cully said you had news for Gabriel Strand. That's why we're here."

The girl's eyes opened, and she tried to focus. "That's why I'm here, too," she said in a slow, anguished voice as she struggled against the effects of the sedative. "I knew there was going to be an attempt on his life, so I followed him here to warn him. I tried to blog about it, and I posted it on the message board. I even e-mailed him about it. I didn't know whether anyone believed me, so I had to come in person." She seemed to be running out of breath. She gasped at the end of every statement.

Cully said, "Take a rest, Kayla. No need to hurry."

John looked at him and immediately felt ashamed that he had not spoken first. They waited. The only sound was the girl's breathing.

Finally, John spoke again. "We tracked all your postings and e-mails. We thought you were doing the threatening. That's what they sounded like."

The girl's eyes were closed. She wouldn't look at them. "I tried to warn him through a sort of code I thought we had together. I thought we really had something going on between us. I really tried to keep a close eye on him. When he didn't reply, I couldn't be sure, so I came here."

"Why don't you tell us about Richard Seeley and anything else you know about Gabriel Strand?"

There was a long silence. John and Cully waited motionless in their chairs. The girl lay on her back in the bed, her eyes shut. She gave a little hiccup, and John saw a tear slide down the side of her face. He glanced at Cully as the girl tucked her arms underneath her and struggled into a half-sitting position.

She cleared her throat, her ability to focus growing stronger. "I'm going to make a statement, okay?" she asked, her voice still slow. Another shift caused her to wince. "My arm hurts."

"Would you like me to call a nurse?" John asked. Both the chief and his officer sat, pencils and pads ready.

"No, I guess not. Can I make my statement?"

"Please. Anything you can tell us will be helpful. One man is dead, and Gabriel's life is still on the line."

The girl nodded and wiped the tear off her cheek. John fumbled at the bedside table and handed her a tissue. She accepted it gratefully and with an almost flirtatious smile.

Her voice was quiet and steady, without the hysteria of the last few hours. "Last June, I met Gabriel Strand for the first time. I had always been a fan of his music. I'd even been to a lot of their smaller gigs, really, right from the beginning. When they opened for Lady Gaga, that was special. I could see it in his face. Anyway, when they got their first hit, their managers got them a tour, and they were on their way. I tried to get to every show. Little by little, I got to know the road crew, you know. They're a great bunch of guys. They let me watch from backstage and then, in June, I got invited to the party at the hotel after the show." She was smiling broadly now. "It was such a thrill. And they were all so very nice. At first, the drummer tried to pick me up, but Gabriel had seen me from the stage, and he wanted me for himself, so he just came right over and took me by the arm and led me away into a private little corner of the party. He's such a gentleman. He got me a drink and a plate of the food. He sat with me. He really wanted to get to know me. I felt the connection right away. That was such a wonderful night. He brought me to his hotel room." She smiled and plucked at the sheet. Then she looked up again, right at John. "Ever since then, I've been going to every concert and making myself easily available to him."

"How do you know Richard Seeley?"

"When I first met Gabriel, he lived with his mom and sister in a small town outside LA. I started driving around, and I found the house. I thought it was important to know where he lived."

Cully quirked an eyebrow at her. "Didn't you think it might be an invasion of privacy?"

Kayla regarded him, dumbfounded. "No, of course not. How else would I get there when he called me if I didn't know where he lived? I was just being prepared. Actually, I'm sure he was flattered when he found out I knew the house. Anyway, I noticed that there was another car there often, and I knew it wasn't Gabriel's or his mom's because I had their license plate numbers memorized. Then, once when I was driving by, I saw a guy get out of the car. He looked kind of old, so I thought it was probably a friend of Gabriel's mom. I took down the license plate number just to be sure."

"Sure of what?" asked John. The pitiful pathology harbored by this girl was depressing him more by the minute.

"Well, for a positive identification if I saw him with Gabriel or something. You know, just to be sure."

"Oh. All right. Go on."

"Anyway, I think it was at the concert in Phoenix last August that I saw this guy again. I had just left roses at Gabriel's hotel room. I try to do that at every concert. It makes him feel good. I was coming out of the hotel, and Gabriel's mom and this guy were going into the hotel. He was talking away to her; I thought maybe it was her boyfriend. Then, I saw him again, at another concert, in Denver in October. I saw him in the hotel again. He was standing in the lobby. Gabriel's mom wasn't with him. I thought it was kind of weird, so I went up to him and asked him if he was with the band, and he said he wasn't, then asked if I was. Well, I just laughed and said I was always with the band. Kind of a joke. Then I asked him why he wanted to know. He said he was a friend of Gabriel's and just wanted him to know he was there. I told him I'd be seeing Gabriel later and I would pass the message along. I asked his name. He said Richard Seeley."

John said, "How do you get to go all these places? Don't you have a job? Isn't it expensive for you?"

Kayla laughed harshly. "I got a trust fund when I was eighteen. I can do what I want. I still live with my parents, but not really because I'm with the band most of the time. Sometimes living in hotels with a band is better than living with your mother and father. My father's a television producer in Los Angeles, so they're busy all the time. They hardly know if I'm there or not."

John nodded and said, "So, to get back to Richard Seeley. Was that the extent of your conversation with him?"

"Yes. Then it was weird, because about a month later, I saw a blurb in one of the tabloids that said Gabriel had gotten a restraining order against this guy. I remember it gave me goose bumps."

John thought ruefully that everyone must have seen that blurb in the tabloid except him. "And did you see him after that?"

"Yes. New Year's Eve. The band had just played Atlantic City. When the show was over, I sneaked in backstage because I wanted to see Gabriel. I knew that girl wasn't with him this time. I left the flowers at the hotel like I always did, and they told me at the desk that the band was traveling alone. That means just themselves and their roadies. Well, I saw him."

"Richard Seeley?"

"Yes. Backstage. The band members had gone back to the hotel. I was headed there myself to the party. They always have a party."

"What did he do?"

"He came up behind me and said, 'Will you be seeing Gabriel?' I jumped, then I recognized him. I tried to act like I didn't know anything about the restraining order. I said, 'You're Gabriel's friend, aren't you?' And he said, 'Yes, I'm his mother's fiancé. I need to give him something. Will you take it to him for me?' I said I would, and he handed me an envelope. He thanked me, and then we had a short conversation about how the band was headed to New York and then to Dartmouth College for the winter carnival. I asked if he knew where the band was staying in Vermont. I was trying to get information to give to Gabriel. He said Dartmouth was really in New Hampshire and they were probably staying right there in the town. Then he said he had to get going and he left."

"What did you do next?"

"I went back to my hotel room. And—and I sat on the bed, just looking at the envelope. I didn't know what to do."

"What do you mean?"

The girl started to cry again. John handed her another tissue. "I didn't have an invitation to the party. I couldn't get in. They wouldn't let me in to see Gabriel, even when I told them who I was and that I had a letter for him."

John nodded sympathetically. "Go on."

"I opened the letter."

"The envelope Richard Seeley had given you to give to Strand?"

"Yes."

"You read it?"

"Yes."

Cully could not contain himself. "Well, what did it say?"

Kayla dabbed at her eyes with the tissue and motioned toward her purse. "It's in there. You can read it yourself. I'm too tired. I'm tired of everything."

Cully looked at John, and John nodded. "Get the letter out of the purse, Cully."

The young man opened the leather bag and carefully withdrew an envelope. He put the bag back on the floor and took the letter out, unfolding it.

"Read it," John said.

Cully glanced at the girl in the bed. She lay back against her pillow, her eyes closed. He cleared his throat and read: "This is a warning to make it more sporting. I have a plan. It's a plan to take you out of the equation once and for all. All you do is confuse the issues at hand and make everyone's life miserable. You are important no longer."

"That's it?"

"Yes, Chief."

John wiped his hand over his face and sighed. "Hmm."

Kayla sat up, her eyes wild. "Don't you see? He's going to kill Gabriel. That's what the note means. That's why it's so important for me to talk to Gabriel. I have to warn him. If you're telling me the truth and he's still alive, then I have to warn him."

John put his hand on the girl's arm in an attempt to quiet her. "That's what the police do, Kayla. We'll warn him. You rest. That's the best thing you can do for yourself. You've probably saved his life just by telling us this. I'm going to take that letter, and we're going to find this guy."

Kayla lay back down, a look of worry on her face. This time, her voice sounded weak as she spoke. "He's here. He's here waiting to strike. I saw him in New York. He was hanging around the Garden, where the band was, and he was talking to this guy, this Bruce Blake. I talked to him, too. He was kind of a bossy, self-important little guy. He bragged to me that he was going to have a private meeting with Gabriel here in Vermont. He said he was going to make Ragged Rainbow the biggest band ever, because after this meeting, he was going to be their manager. That's how I knew he was here. He even told me the hotel. I'm sure that's how Richard Seeley found out Gabriel was staying here. From backstage. From Bruce Blake. He was such a loudmouth."

John and Cully exchanged glances. John said, "We're going to go now and let you rest. The people here are nice. They'll get in touch with your mother and father."

"Oh, great. That's all I need." The girl sighed and closed her eyes again.

"Have a good rest," John said. He left the room quietly, Cully at his heels.

"This just gets weirder and weirder, doesn't it?" Cully said, quickening his pace to keep up with his chief.

"What's that?" mumbled John, thinking of six things at once.

"I mean, we've got two stalkers, and one of the stalkers ends up stalking the first stalker and tries to outstalk him."

John gave a little laugh. "If it didn't involve life and death and a real murder, that'd be funny."

"He's going to show up real soon, Chief."

"I know that, Cully."

Chapter Twenty-One

John and Cully walked out of the hospital into the cold gloom of early evening. It was still flurrying as they drove back to the police station.

John spoke to Becky as the two men took off their jackets and knocked the snow off their boots. "Anything new?"

"Well, it's been busy with a lot of little stuff. There was a fender-bender over on Church Street. That bad corner. Then, that young guy from Boston who's was living with his girlfriend in the old Martin house called to say she'd kicked him out. He said he needed to get his stuff, and he was afraid to go in because she had a gun. Jason went over to see what was going on. Irene called from Chandler's to say they'd discovered the old back entrance open. They thought it was the wind, but they wanted to file a report in case it was a break-in and something turned up missing. Steve's over there now. That's about it. Oh, and sorry, but I got busy with these things, so your kids are still here. They've been quiet, so I guess they're resigned."

"Don't go apologizing for not running them around. No sign of Richard Seeley?"

"Not a single one, Chief. The boys have been just about everywhere, and Joe Bernard is circling through the whole town as we speak."

Cully said, "Well, we've got some news. And some evidence." He waved the envelope in the air and set it down on her desk.

Becky looked questioningly at John.

"That's right," John said. "It appears the dominoes are falling in sequence. We had quite the talk with this Kayla person. Cully, get going and write this up, will you? Here are my notes. Be as accurate as you possibly can. Then hit the road. Find this guy."

Michael stepped out of the back office and handed a small stack of papers to his father. "Here's everything I could get, Dad. Some of it's really interesting, but I didn't read it all. I figured you'd want to look at everything."

"Thanks, Mike." John took the papers and went into his own office.

Mia was sitting at his desk, typing away on his computer. Peter was leaning back in the straight chair, his chin on his chest, pretending to doze. Mia looked up as he entered.

"We're still here, Dad," she said dully.

John looked at her and sighed, but said nothing. Instead, he stood by his desk, looking through the pile of e-mails Michael had given him. There was a tap at the door.

"Come on in," said John, not looking up.

Becky stuck her head in. "Sorry, Chief," she said. "Peter, would you help Irene in the clerk's office, please? That guy who was in there earlier dropped a map down behind the copy machine, and she can't reach it. I think you can move the machine enough for her to get her skinny little arm back there."

Peter sat upright. For all his affected grumpiness, he liked to help people, especially when it required muscle. "Sure, Becky. I'll go right now."

John looked up and smiled. "Thanks for that, Peter."

Peter nodded importantly and left the office. He returned five minutes later. "That was weird. The tax map he copied was the map of Mom's office."

Three things happened at once: Michael came through the open door and said, "I don't understand why this guy is so interested in Mom's building." Then, John's cell phone rang, and a sudden wave of fear washed over him so profoundly that his mouth went dry and his knees became so weak that he had to grasp the edge of his desk.

A tremor went through him, and he struggled to regain his composure. He heard Mia say, "Dad, answer your phone. Dad! Dad, are you all right?"

He fumbled in his breast pocket for his phone. He knew without looking who it was.

"Melanie?" he said. Somehow, probably because of that tremor, he had hit the speaker button.

"John? Is that you?" Melanie's voice was oddly shrill.

He caught his daughter's eye and saw her rise from the chair. The boys were looking at him, too. "Of course it's me. What's up?"

"John, Gabriel and I are down here at the office, and I just wanted to call and tell you I'd be a little late. Sorry, I know this is an important date for you, but we've just got to finish this up."

Before he could ask what "date" she was talking about, she went on. "John, can you hear me?"

Now, Michael and Peter had moved in to stand beside their sister, their eyes still on their father.

"Of course I can hear you, Melanie. What is it?"

"This is very important. You've got to go back to the house and take the rhubarb pie out of the oven. Please, John, hurry. The rhubarb pie. I—I've got to go now. I just wanted to tell you that." Melanie ended the call.

Mia's hands flew to her mouth.

"Dad," Peter said. "Dad!"

"Mom said 'rhubarb,'" Michael added quietly.

John rubbed the back of his neck roughly. Everything was becoming clear and very rapidly.

"Mom said 'rhubarb,'" Michael repeated.

"I know. I know." John leaned on the desk. "Let me figure this out for two seconds."

It had started so long ago, when he had first taken a job with law enforcement. At first, it was a code between the two of them, but as the kids came and grew older, the parents included them. They all knew that if at any time they were in danger and couldn't speak of it, if they were kidnapped, held hostage, or needed to spread a warning without giving themselves away, they were to convey their danger by saying the word "rhubarb." No one else knew about it, only the five of them. It was only to be used in matters of life and death. They had never used it before.

John said, "Get Irene, Peter."

The boy ran out of the office and down the hall.

Becky stood in the doorway. "What's up, John?"

"Mom's in trouble," Mia said, her voice catching.

"I just got a call from Melanie," explained John. "I think Seeley has them." He rubbed his hand over his face, struggling to think clearly. "Mike, did she say she was at the office?"

"Yeah. She said she was there and would be late."

Becky said, "I'm calling in Jason and Steve. Cully, get out here."

Mia's eyes were awash with unshed tears, but her voice was steady. "What are you going to do, Dad?"

"I've got to go down there. I've got to try to find out what's going on."

The town clerk came into the office behind Peter.

"Irene," John said, "is this the guy who went through the tax maps today?" He handed her the computer print-out image of Richard Seeley that LAPD has sent him.

"Why, yes, Chief," she said. "That's just who it was. What's going on?"

"I think he's got my wife and Gabriel Strand hostage, Irene."

"Oh, Chief. Oh, no! Becky, can I help?"

John said, "The best thing we can all do is go about our business until I find out what's really happening."

"Absolutely! I'll be in my office if I can do anything helpful." With that, Irene left the room.

John's mind raced as Cully, Becky, Mia, Peter, and Michael stood looking at him. He needed a plan that would keep his wife safe.

"I'm going to drive down there. Cully, you follow me, but take your own car and go into the elementary school parking lot. You can hide there until I can call you about what to do from there. Hopefully we won't spook the guy." Then he did something he'd done only a handful of times before in all his years as the chief of police: he pulled out a key from his pocket and unlocked the gun cabinet behind his desk. Four rifles stood there. He took one and handed it to Cully, whose face was now ashen. Then he took one himself. "Mike," he said as he checked the firing mechanisms, "take your brother and sister home."

"Dad—"

John looked up. "Mike, please. I am deadly serious. Do as I say. Do it now."

There was a glaring match between John and his children. "I'll call you," he said. "I promise I will."

The three of them stood together. They were fifteen, seventeen, and nineteen years old, closing in fast on adulthood, but as he looked at them standing there together, he could only see them as three, five, and seven. His children stood as a unit. Michael was in the front, Peter two steps behind him and to his left, and Mia, the most courageous of all of them, at Michael's right elbow with her fists clenched. John fought back the tears that were breaking at the backs of his eyes. "I will not let anything happen to your mother." *I will not let anything happen to the one person I cannot live without.* "Now go home." He barked the order, and they turned as one.

Tim Cully reached out and brushed Mia with his hand. For a second, their eyes met, and then the three siblings went into the hallway. Moments later, John heard the big outside door creak open and click shut.

Chapter Twenty-Two

"You all right, Cully?" John asked.

Cully nodded. "Yes, sir. Are you okay?"

"I can function."

Becky stood in the doorway. "Jason and Steve will be here in two minutes. Joe Bernard and more state backup are standing by for orders."

As she finished talking, Jason Patterson and Steve Bruno walked in the door. They said nothing as they took the rifles Tim Cully handed them. John looked at them standing before him, young and brave and unconditionally loyal.

He drew a deep breath and said, "We don't know what we're facing. Melanie called in our Mayday code, so I know something bad is going down in that office. I can't say it's a hostage situation because I haven't heard from any hostage takers. I don't know if anyone's been hurt. All we do know is that an hour ago, Richard Seeley was in here looking at the tax maps of Melanie's building. That makes me assume that he must be there, at the office, threatening her in some way."

"Is Gabriel Strand with her?" Jason asked.

"That's another thing I can only assume. He's supposed to be. Let's just hope he's still alive." John wiped his hand over his face. "Becky, you call Woody Patterson. Have him close off the main route through town and redirect it down Route 10. I don't want any diversions or distractions."

"Yes, sir." She was on the phone before he finished his instructions.

He turned again to his officers. "Jason, you go with Cully. You drive in through the elementary school parking lot. You can see the back and north side of Melanie's building from there, but any time the lights are on, it's hard to see out through the windows from the inside. Steve, you come with me."

"What are we going to do?"

"I'm not sure yet. I'm not sure how I'm going to find out exactly what's going on in there. I'll have to figure it out on the way. Let's go." He sighed, slung the rifle under his arm, and led the way out the door.

John drove slowly out of the police parking lot and down the road toward his wife's office. He drove slowly because he was afraid he might at any moment be overwhelmed with the enormity of the situation. He was afraid he might lose control. As it was, his mind was racing in several directions at once. He had to consciously avoid thinking about exactly what scenario was playing out at the brick house. Any speculation was only speculation. To assume anything only threatened to push his thoughts to panic and undermine the ultimate goal.

Then he thought of the brick house itself. He knew it intimately from when he and Melanie had lived there early in their marriage: four large rooms downstairs, a wide center hall and staircase, and a kitchen wing out the back. The second floor had another four large rooms. Originally, there had been a stairway leading to the widow's walk on the roof that looked up and down the whole river valley. They had made love on the widow's walk more than once. Renovations early in their marriage meant access to the roof was now only through a manhole in the ceiling of the bathroom.

These days, the downstairs of the house served as Melanie's offices for her community newspaper. The upstairs was rented to a small accounting firm, but they'd likely be gone for the day. He thought about neighbors who might be in danger. The Sawyer family was just down the street; their boys would certainly come outside if they saw any commotion. Their home, however, provided the perfect vantage point. John called Becky on the radio.

"Becky, you call Alice Sawyer and tell her to shut off all the lights in her house and tell her and whoever else is in there to stay at the back of the house until they hear otherwise from the police. If she asks, just tell her we have a potential problem at Melanie's office. No need to say anything further for now."

"Yes, sir."

As he made his approach through the darkening winter evening, he confirmed that the accountants' offices upstairs were all dark, the employees all having left already. The only room in the house that appeared lit was the front office on the south side of the building. Melanie's office. There were four windows in that office. Two faced the street, and two faced down the valley. Cully and Patterson would not be able to see anything from the schoolyard. He glanced in his rear-view mirror. Cully was driving close behind and, as directed, turned into the school parking lot. John pulled into the driveway of Alice Sawyer's house, down the street and across from Melanie's building.

He took the binoculars and peered at the brick house, trying to see through the windows.

"What do you see, Chief?" Steve asked.

John's heart was pounding in his chest, but he said quietly, "I can see people moving around, but I can't make out who they are. The drapes are in the way. I can't even tell how many."

"It's getting dark real fast. I can sneak up to the porch and try to look inside. At least we'd know who was in there."

Before John could answer, the radio crackled with Cully's voice. "Chief?"

"Yeah, Cully, go ahead."

"Chief, we've got a situation. Mike's car is here in the school parking lot."

"Mike? Mike who?"

There was a pause before Cully's reply. "Your son."

John couldn't put the pieces together. His mouth was dry. Somewhere, in his fog, he heard Steve Bruno's voice. "What's the matter, Chief?"

John shook his head and spoke into the radio. "Cully, where are my children?"

"I don't know, sir. Mike's car is parked here, by the fence. There's nobody around."

John's fist came down hard on the dashboard of the Suburban.

"Sir? Chief? You there?"

"Yes, yes, I'm here."

"What do you want us to do, Chief?"

John started to answer, when the front door of Melanie's building opened. "Stand by, Cully, we got something going on." He put the radio back in its cradle.

"Chief?" Steve asked, shifting in his seat.

John held up his hand. "Wait."

A man and woman ran out the door, and John recognized them as Lisa Wright and Roger Bickley, Melanie's two employees. They held hands as they ran off the porch, neither of them wearing a coat. John and Steve watched as the two paused for a moment. Lisa seemed to peer through the encroaching darkness. Then she turned to Roger, and the two of them ran the hundred yards up the road to where the chief's Suburban idled in Alice Sawyer's driveway.

John cracked his window. "Get in quickly," he said.

The two fairly dived into the back seat. John could hear Lisa's teeth chattering.

"Grab those blankets, Lisa," he said. "Wrap them around yourselves. You need to tell us what's going on."

Lisa reached into the back and took the two wool rescue blankets kept folded there. She and Roger threw them around their shoulders. All the while, she stammered through violent shivers. "I'm not cold, John. I'm not cold. He made us leave. We wouldn't leave Melanie, and he made us leave."

John fought down the panic. "Tell me exactly what's going on in there. Are you two okay? Roger? Can you tell me what's going on?"

The little man with glasses nodded vigorously, although he, too, was shaking. "I'm fine, John." He glanced at his watch. "It's four thirty. He's been in there for about an hour now."

John and Steve turned in their seats to face the backseat passengers.

Roger pulled the blanket more securely around his shoulders and leaned forward. "Earlier this afternoon, Mike and Peter dropped Melanie and that Gabriel Stern?" He looked at Lisa. "Is that his name?"

"Strand," she corrected, her teeth still chattering.

"Anyway, the boys dropped them off. Lisa and I were working on next week's issue, as usual. Melanie introduced us around, showed

Strand what we do, and then they went into her office to have a conference call with his band. I guess they're up in Hanover. They're doing some show at Dartmouth over the weekend. She shut the door, and I could hear her put the phone on speaker. I could hear that they were having a conversation, but I couldn't understand what was being said. They talked for quite a while before I heard the phone hang up, and then I could just hear Melanie and Strand talking to each other. So, Lisa and I were working away, and I know it was three thirty because I glanced up at the clock just as this guy came through the front door. Our door was open, like always. He saw us and came into the room."

"Just a minute," Steve Bruno interrupted and thrust out the faxed likeness of Richard Seeley. "Is this the guy?"

Roger examined the picture closely in the half-light. "Yes, that's him. That's the guy." He handed the paper back to Steve. "He came into the room and asked if this was where *The Town Crier* was published. I said yes, and he said he had some news for Melanie Giamo and asked if she was in. I said she was, but she was in a meeting. Then he said he knew who she was in the meeting with and they were waiting for him. He turned and started to cross the hall. Lisa said she would go in and tell Melanie he was here. There was something about the guy. You know, you can just tell when somebody's not right. I got up and started to follow Lisa. He whirled on us and said don't bother, it was his business. I spoke up then and told him to come sit down and I would get Melanie. Then he shouted at me, 'You sit down!' Then he barged through Melanie's office door and slammed it behind him. Well, Lisa and I both rushed into the office. Melanie was sitting at her desk, and Strand was on the couch. They looked kind of shocked. The strange guy was blustering about something, I don't know, and I yelled, 'What do you think you're doing?' That's when he pulled a gun out of his jacket pocket." Roger stopped and took a deep breath. "A gun," he repeated.

John felt a cold sweat break on his neck and down his chest, but he kept calm. "What then?"

Roger went on. He was beginning to forget his initial fear, and John could see that he was getting angry. "He waved the gun at all of us and told us to stand against the wall. None of us moved, but I got scared then, and I asked him what he wanted. Lisa spoke up and said there was money in the safe and she would get it for him. He got real angry then and said he didn't want money. He went over to Strand and put the gun right to his head. He said he wanted Strand. He said he'd already killed somebody else by mistake, and he was sorry about it. He said it was Strand's fault that it happened. Then Melanie spoke up and said her husband was chief of police here in town and could she call him. She told him that since it was a mistake and he didn't mean to shoot anybody, he could probably get a manslaughter plea or something, so he didn't have to make it worse than it was. All the time she was talking, she walked real slow over to Strand and stood kind of between him and this guy."

John's stomach flopped like a fish out of water as he thought of his wife in the line of fire. He swallowed hard. "Go on," he said.

Roger took another deep breath, but he seemed to have run out of steam. He glanced at Lisa.

She cleared her throat and picked up the story. "Well, I was petrified, I'll tell you. This guy yelled at her and said if the police showed up, he would shoot everyone and himself. Then Melanie said, really nice, please could she call her husband, because if she was late getting home, he'd come looking for her anyway. So the guy let her make a phone call. That's the call you got, John, about the pie or something. I thought I was going to throw up. Anyway, she got off the phone, and he told us all just to sit down and shut up. 'Don't say a word,' he said. So we just sat on the couch. He was real twitchy, pacing back and forth, and then he went off into this rant, saying that everything in his life that had gone wrong was Gabriel's fault. He said if Strand hadn't had the band, he and Marian would be married by now and living a normal life, but Gabriel had elected to break up the family. Is Marian the kid's girlfriend?"

Steve Bruno said, "She's Strand's mother."

"Oh. Oh, my." Lisa blinked a few times. "Well, then he kept going on and on about how Strand turned Marian against him and moved away, and then he couldn't concentrate on his work so he lost his job. He said the losses he incurred had driven him nearly insane, and he had done some stupid things because he'd gotten mixed up with this Marian. He said he had, how did he put it, not been allowed resolution. He claimed no one would listen to him or help him, and he was here to resolve things once and for all. He said a lot more, but none of it made any sense. John, he nearly drove us crazy, talking and yelling on and on like that, but we were afraid of what he would do when he stopped talking." Lisa fell silent and sat, shivering. John could see that she was emotionally worn out.

He said to Roger, "How did you get out of there?"

"He made us leave, John," the man answered. "He said Strand was the only one he had business with, and Melanie might come in handy. Those were his words. Then he told us to get out."

"She was unharmed?"

"Yes, they were both just sitting there."

Steve had been watching the windows intently and said, "Chief, I'm going to call State Police and have them send up Joe Bernard. He's a trained sniper. I keep seeing Seeley pass by the windows. He could probably get a shot at him."

John shook his head. "I don't want to take the chance of hitting Melanie or Strand. Seeley's between the window and them. A misdirected bullet could be the worst thing possible. Go ahead and call him, though. We can use the backup. I think I'm going in there. Maybe I can talk to him, offer him some sort of deal or something for turning himself in."

Tim Cully's urgent voice crackled over the radio. "Chief, your kids are running across the back lawn of *The Town Crier*."

"What did you say?"

"Peter's in the lead. I didn't get there in time to stop them. I was afraid to call to them. Seeley might have heard me."

John knew he had to act fast. "Cully, stay where you are. I'm coming over. I need to assess this for myself."

"Yes, sir. You don't have to tell me that." The radio crackled again and went silent.

"Oh, John," Lisa gasped from the backseat.

No one moved as John strapped on his Kevlar vest and zipped his jacket over it.

"Chief—" Steve began.

John held up a hand to stop him. "I'm going over to the school. I have to see what my children are up to. Once they're safe, I'll go into the building. I can't go in there armed. If he sees me carrying any kind of weapon, we don't know what he'll do. Steve, you're in charge. I'll get a signal to you somehow. Watch for it." He gave a sharp sigh. "We haven't had any communication from the gunman.

All we've had is the call from Melanie. I'm going to try to call her. We might find out something." He took the cell phone out of his breast pocket and pushed the call button, his hand visibly shaking. The phone rang and rang until her voice mail answered. Frustrated, John called again, only to get the same result. Anger swelled in him. "I just wish I had something to go on." He spoke more to himself than anyone, when his phone, still in his hand, vibrated to indicate an incoming call.

"Yes?"

"Daddy, it's me," Mia said. "Daddy, I know you must be furious, but please, just listen to me."

John nodded, forgetting she couldn't see him. In the back seat, Lisa began to cry softly.

"Daddy, Peter, Michael, and I are going to climb up to the widow's walk and get Mom. We just need her to go into the bathroom. Can you talk to her?"

John now had to talk to his daughter as his peer. There was no point in trying to argue, cajole, or get angry. Any discord might result in tragedy. He would just have to go along with it. "I tried her cell phone, but she didn't answer. I'm going to have to go in."

"Try to call her again, Dad. Tell her to go into the bathroom. Peter will lift her up through the manhole."

"Peter can't do that. He's not strong enough."

"Of course he is. He's been training his whole life for something like this. Michael will hold onto him, and we'll pull them back into the stairwell. We just need to distract that guy and get him to let Mom go to the bathroom."

John could hardly see. Her words "his whole life" rang in his head. He couldn't let this be his son's whole life. The three of them were plowing ahead, fueled by their teenage bravado. They had seen their father work. They had ridden with him on some of his minor duties. They knew about law enforcement, but none of them had ever been hurt. None of them had ever seen what a man with a gun could really do. They were secure in the expectation that their plan would work. They had been sneaking up and down from the widow's walk for years. It was just another covert caper. Their naïveté made them afraid for their mother, but not for themselves. They knew where they were and assumed they were safe.

His phone beeped, and he glanced at the screen. "Mouse. You stand by. Your mother is calling me." He pushed the talk button.

"Melanie?"

"John, I'm here."

"Are you okay?"

"Yes, yes, I'm fine. Please listen, John. Richard Seeley wants to talk to you."

"Melanie, get into the bathroom." He had not been sure she heard the order, but then he heard her say, "My husband's waiting to talk to you, but Mr. Seeley, may I go use the bathroom? We've been here for hours and—"

"No," the man barked.

"Please. There's—there's only a tiny window there. Look, if you leave this door open, you can watch the door to the bathroom. I'll only be a minute. Please. Just while you talk to my husband."

"Make it fast. I'm watching the door."

John heard the words garble as the phone changed hands.

"Is this Police Chief John Giamo? This is Richard Seeley."

Chapter Twenty-Three

Something was going down. Melanie heard her husband's order to go into the bathroom. She didn't know what might be happening, but she trusted him with her life. She would do whatever he told her to do. She glanced over to Gabriel. He sat motionless in a straight backed chair beside her desk. She knew she had to get to the bathroom, but she was frightened to leave the young musician by himself. She walked over to him and spoke softly as Richard Seeley raved at John over the phone. "Don't move," she said. "John is working this out. Don't be frightened. He'll get us out of this. I'm going into the bathroom. I'll be right back."

Richard Seeley's eyes were on her as she left the office and crossed the hall to the bathroom. He stood in the open door of the office, staring as she went inside, shutting the door behind her.

A dim fluorescent light shone above the pedestal sink. Melanie turned it off and pressed her face to the high, small window that looked out onto the back yard. She could see better without the back light. Was John planning to get her out, or was he trying to shield her when they stormed the place? She couldn't know. Her heart pounded. She just hoped it would end soon.

Suddenly, she saw three figures crossing the lawn under the window. She squinted in an effort to get a better look. With horror, she realized it was Michael, Mia, and Peter. If her heart had been pounding a minute ago, now it nearly stopped. Surely John would not have planned anything involving the children! It couldn't be! And then she realized with a mother's intuition that they had acted independently of their father. As soon as she heard the light thuds from above, she knew the three had sneaked up to the roof. Since the day Melanie had first forbade them to do so, the Giamo children had been climbing up to the widow's walk. From the outside, they could scramble up the ancient grapevine, over the roof of the kitchen ell, and along the peak to where the clapboard ell joined the main part of the brick house. From there, they would shimmy up a huge blue spruce, whose branches dipped over the roof, and leap to the roof of the main house and the widow's walk.

Melanie looked up through the window to see them huddling together, and though they spoke in low voices, she was able to catch most of their conversation.

Peter sounded enthusiastic. "Do you think Dad got the message to her?"

Mia said, "I don't know. I told him, so let's just hope she's in there!"

"No lights," said Peter.

With this remark, Melanie flicked the light on and then off again.

"She's there! She's there!" Mia whispered excitedly.

Melanie was able to make eye contact with Mia, who held her finger to her lips. Melanie nodded. She was catching on to their plan and wanted them to know she was complicit.

From inside the house, the sound of Richard Seeley's voice reverberated. He was still ranting to John, which was good; it would give her more time, and now that her children were involved, she wanted as much time as she could get. Above her head, Melanie heard the iron ring of the trap door on the roof rattle.

"Is it frozen?" Peter asked.

Michael answered, his voice muffled. "I put my knife in there. I think its okay. I didn't feel any ice."

Peter said, "Got a light?"

Michael must have produced that smallest of flashlights, hanging from his keychain. "Hold it in your mouth," he said to Peter. "Don't use it unless you have to."

"I'll just need it to see the latch on the ceiling door."

Michael said, "Hopefully Mom will still be there."

Tears welled up in Melanie's eyes. She knew what her children were about to do, and she'd never felt so helpless in her life. One peep out of her, and Seeley would be on to her, putting the children in grave danger. All she could do was wait. Her heart beat in her throat, a combination of fear and pride filling her for what her children were doing to save her.

"This is Chief Giamo," said John. "I'd like to talk to you, Mr. Seeley."

"Oh, no, Chief." Seeley laughed condescendingly. "It is I who wants to talk to you."

"Go ahead, then. Tell me what you want."

"I want a clear exit from here. I must tell you I did not intend to kill Bruce Blake. In fact, he tried to help me when we were in New York. Ironic, isn't it?"

John said nothing, and Seeley continued. "I have a place to go. I can drop out of sight altogether and never bother anyone again. Sound fair?"

John kept his voice steady and patient. "What do you want, Mr. Seeley?"

"Right from the start, the only person I've had an issue with is Gabriel Strand, but he seems to be immune to my plans to get even. So, you'll be relieved to know I've changed my mind. Now, I'm willing to let everyone go. Everyone can go back to their former lives. No more need for embarrassing restraining orders. All I want in return is safe passage out of here. I want to drive away from here and know that no one will follow me."

"Let them go, then," said John. "When I see them walk out the door, I'll make the necessary calls and see what I can do."

"I said I changed my mind, Chief." Seeley's demeanor had quickly changed to anger. "I'm not stupid. I'm taking them both with me until I'm sure I'm in the clear. I wouldn't want to put the burden of a broken promise on you."

John told Roger and Lisa to stay put. He got out of the Suburban and looked around. Cully and Jason's cruiser was behind John's vehicle, and Joe Bernard had pulled up as well, but stayed a few car-lengths back, shaded from the street light. John held his phone to his ear as he and Steve Bruno walked back to Cully's car. Joe approached silently, his high-powered rifle resting ominously in the crook of his arm. The five policemen stood together between the squad cars. John turned the phone to speaker.

"Got yourself quite a posse, there," Richard Seeley said.

"Seeley, let my wife and Strand walk out of there. We'll even give you an escort."

"Yeah, sure, and shoot me while I'm escaping. No thanks. You listen, and I'll tell you what to do, Giamo. First, I'm going to throw out my car keys to you so you can start my car. I'm going to take Strand and your wife here, and I'm going to drive out of town. When I'm sure no one is following me, and I reach a place I think is safe, I'll let them go. I promise. Now listen further; this is the important part. I've got nothing to lose in this venture. All I'm asking is to be left alone, but if I'm not left alone, it's nothing to me to mess things up real good. I mean it. Do you understand me?"

"I understand you," John assured him.

"So, you understand that if you mess up, the deal's off, and I'll make you incredibly sorry."

"I want to see my wife, to know she's unharmed," John said.

"No go."

"Then let me talk to her."

"She's not here right now. She went to the bathroom."

John's heart started to pound. "I'll come in there and wait for her, then."

"Chief, I might change my mind. I'm agitated. If you don't shut up, I'll change my plan."

"Let me talk to Strand, then. I need to make sure everyone is okay."

"Strand's fine right now. I'm not feeling good about things, Chief. I'm feeling rather desperate, like I'm being tricked. I won't go to prison, Chief. I'll make a clean break or no break at all, do you understand? And I've got the feeling that our little agreement is going to be sabotaged. I can't trust you, Chief. My patience is running out, and I'm sick of talking." The cell phone clicked off.

"Try to get him on the phone again, John," Joe said. "I'll get up close to the house and see if I can get a clean shot at him."

"My kids and wife are there. The kids are coming down through the roof to get Melanie. It's my whole family, Joe."

"Cully told me. Let's wait and see if he calls us back." The state cop's eyes never left the brick building as he reached into his pocket, pulled out a piece of gum, unwrapped it slowly, and nonchalantly began to chew.

"Mom."

Melanie heard the whisper and looked up at the ceiling of the bathroom.

Her youngest son was dangling, head first, out of the manhole in the ceiling. He reached out to her. "Mom, stand on the toilet and grab my arms. Don't make a sound. Michael and Mia are holding me. I'll pull you up. We can get out on the widow's walk."

All her strength left her. Her legs nearly buckled under her. "I can't have you risking your lives like this. This person is a madman. Peter, get out of here. Please. Please. If he finds me gone, he could lose it and kill us all."

Her words failed to compromise her son's confidence. He ignored her and said, "Mom. Pay attention! Stand on the toilet seat and reach up. I'll do the rest. Dad will get Gabriel out."

Unbidden, memories of the countless times she had reached for him, pulling him from danger — out of trees, up steep embankments, off busy roadways, out of the path of some horse or cow or angry sibling — ran through her mind. Now, he was reaching for her. She swallowed hard and stepped up onto the toilet seat, lifting her arms over her head and extending her fingers.

"Lower me some more," Peter called behind him, and he was cautiously lowered inch by inch. "I can reach," he whispered finally as his hands made contact with Melanie's arms. "Grab hold of the waist of my jeans, Michael, so I don't slip down."

Melanie clutched her son's forearms, and Peter gripped her under her biceps.

"Pull. I've got her," he said.

She could see Mia and Michael on either side of Peter, grasping him tight as they began to pull both of them up. Michael wrapped both arms around his brother's middle and braced himself against the wall. It creaked, but it held and gave Peter the leverage he needed to pull Melanie up into the stairwell. Once Melanie's body was safely through the manhole, Mia started back to the rooftop.

Michael said, "Climb over Peter. Follow Mia up the stairs. We're right behind you."

Melanie looked up. She could see her daughter had already made it to the widow's walk, her tiny frame silhouetted against the starry winter night. She clambered over her son and made her way up the stairs.

Chapter Twenty-Four

John was frustrated. "I'm going in there. Maybe I can at least cre-ate a diversion so you can get a shot at him, Joe." He started out across the street, when his cell phone rang. He stopped, and all the men took one step closer to him.

John looked at the number and recognized it as Seeley's. "Yeah?"

"I don't want anyone to do anything, Chief," the man said. "I'm getting angry. I don't believe you'll let me go. I don't deserve to have my life ruined like this."

"Look, Seeley, let me come in and talk. We can work this out. You don't need to panic."

"Panic? I'm not panicked. I'm angry!"

"I'll do my best for you, Seeley. Right now, you accidentally killed a man. That's not first degree. You've got bargaining power here."

"You bet I've got bargaining power; I've got Strand and your wife."

John began walking toward the house, the cell phone to his ear. He could see Seeley in the window, talking to him on the telephone. He could see the revolver in his hand as he wiggled the gun barrel up and down, side to side. John's skin prickled with some desperate emotion he did not give himself the luxury of identifying. He could not see far enough into the room to guess where his wife or Gabriel were. Once again, he could only assume.

Then he could make out the form of Seeley peering out one of the long front windows.

"I can see you coming across the street," he said to John. "I'm going to throw my car keys out to you. Go start my car."

"What's your plan, Seeley?"

"I'll let you know along the way. Just do what I say." The man's voice rose. "Just someone do as I say."

"Okay," said John. "Throw the keys out. I'll stop right here until I see you do it."

"That's better."

John tried to gauge the movements he saw inside. He still couldn't see anyone except Seeley. The door opened a fraction, and light from the front hall spilled out onto the porch. He heard the keys hit the sidewalk leading up to the building's entrance. He waited.

"You there, Chief?" Seeley said through the phone again.

"Yes."

"Do I have your word that you will do exactly as I tell you?"

John was silent. His fear was fading as his anger increased.

"Do I have your word? Answer me."

"I'll do as you say."

"Start my car and back it out into the street. Park it so the driver's side is facing the building and leave the door open. Then get out and leave it running. Do you understand me?"

"Yes." John took the keys. He opened the driver's side door to the rental car, a late model Oldsmobile. He got in, started it up, and backed into the street as instructed.

"Now get out. Leave the car running. Tell your posse across the street that I'm coming out with Strand and your wife. If anyone so much as twitches, I'll kill them. This isn't a bluff, Giamo."

"Understood," John said. He only wanted to lay eyes on Melanie.

Over the phone, he could hear voices and shuffling. Then he heard a sort of strangled roar and a crash, as though someone had stamped hard on the floor or put a fist into a wall.

"Damn it!" Seeley shouted.

"Seeley," John barked into the phone, "what's going on? Seeley, if my wife so much as breaks a nail, my men will mow you down so fast, you won't know what hit you. That's a fact."

"She's gone!" Seeley's voice shrieked into his ear. "Your wife got away, Chief, but she's done more damage than she realizes. Just stick to the plan and back away from my car."

John's mind raced, exhilarated that she'd been able to escape, but she and their children weren't out of danger yet. Making Richard Seeley angrier *wasn't* part of the plan. He tried to keep his voice calm as he said, "Let me talk to Strand."

"No way, Chief. You stand back. I'm coming out. I've still got Strand."

John clicked off the connection and rejoined his men across the street. "He's bringing Strand out," he told them. "Nobody move."

The group of officers, standing in the shelter of Cully's cruiser, lifted their arms in acknowledgment. All except Joe, John noticed. The officer had kept out of sight, and now, slowly, hidden by the night shadows, he'd leaned on the hood of his own cruiser and lifted his rifle to his shoulder. Luckily, Seeley's request for positioning his car on the street ensured Joe's line of sight was clear. The weather had calmed, but there were no clouds overhead to hold in what little warmth the pale winter sun might have imparted during the daylight. The night was becoming bitterly cold. The snow squeaked under his feet as John shifted his weight in anticipation.

The front door opened slowly. The first person John saw was Gabriel. He walked slowly out onto the porch, with Richard Seeley close behind him. Gabriel's right arm was twisted up in back of him. Seeley obviously had it in a death grip as he pushed the musician along ahead of him. He also had the gun pressed to Strand's head, just at the back of his ear. Melanie and the kids were likely hiding on the roof or in back of the house. Either way, they were smart enough to stay hidden. John figured his best option was to go along with everything Seeley demanded and hope that a chance to overcome the gunman would avail itself. Unstable as Seeley was, there would be no second try. John stood still beside the car as Seeley and Strand approached.

Finally, they were close enough for John to make out their faces in the darkness.

"Are you okay, Strand?" he asked.

"Shut up," said Seeley through his teeth, but Gabriel managed to nod his head. "Stay away from my car." The man pivoted so that Gabriel faced the chief as he walked to the passenger side and backed up to the open door of the idling car. "I'm going to leave you with two things, Chief: a corpse and a bullet in the brain."

The words had barely left Seeley's lips, and John did not hesitate a moment longer. Any further attempt at negotiation might prove fatal for someone. He leaped the ten or so feet that separated him from the gunman and his hostage. He grabbed Gabriel, holding him in his arms as he kicked out at Richard Seeley. He heard a strange explosion, like a gunshot and yet different, followed by a cry as he and the musician crashed to the ground.

In the next few seconds, many things went through John's head. He thought he might have been shot, or maybe it had been Strand. They both lay face down in the street, his arms still wrapped around the young man. John rolled over just in time to see the car, with Seeley behind the wheel, speed down the road. Steve Bruno and Joe Bernard took off in pursuit in Bernard's cruiser.

There was a warm feeling on his exposed hand. He sat up and, by the street light, saw a dark pattern on the pavement. Blood. He knew by then that it wasn't his blood. He gripped Gabriel and pulled him into a sitting position.

"Where are you hit?" he asked, his voice urgent.

"I — I'm not hit. I don't think so." The musician was gingerly looking at himself.

John stood. On the ground near where the car had been parked lay the .22 caliber revolver. The old gun had misfired and exploded. The blood was Seeley's. John grabbed Strand by the shoulders and pulled him to his feet.

"Where is my wife? Where is Melanie?"

"I don't know. She said she had to go to the bathroom before he got on the phone with you. When he smashed in the bathroom door, she wasn't there."

Melanie was safe; the kids had rescued her and knew enough to stay out of harm's way. The relief that John felt made him feel lightheaded.

"John! Are you all right?" Firefighter Caleb Cochran was now standing in front of him, searching his face with worried eyes.

John nodded.

"Take care of Strand, Caleb," he said. "Get him checked out."

Caleb nodded his acknowledgment. He stepped up and put a blanket over the shoulders of the shivering musician. John ran to his Suburban and climbed in. Patterson and Cully were already there. He flipped the lights on, and the bulky vehicle careened down the snowy road, south out of town. Its sturdy snow tires allowed them to catch up to the chase underway. Ahead of them, they could see the Oldsmobile going too fast for the conditions, slipping around on the slick pavement. Joe Bernard's cruiser, its lights flashing and siren blaring, was bearing down on it.

"He's trying to get to the interstate," said Cully from the back seat.

"He can't go that way," Jason said. "The bridge is out."

The bridge *was* out. John had forgotten. Already, he could see the yellow warning lights as they flashed in the darkness. The Oldsmobile was speeding right toward them. Just ahead, they saw Joe abruptly turn his cruiser into a side street.

"He's giving him room to turn down River Street," Jason said.

John slowed the Suburban to a stop in the middle of the street. The lights flashed their eerie blue light on the snowbanks.

"The fucking idiot is going right through the lights," muttered Cully.

Joe's cruiser poked its head out of the mouth of the side street. Helpless, they all watched the Oldsmobile ram through the barricade. The yellow warning lights sailed into the night sky and shattered as they hit the street. The wooden barricades splintered, and the fluorescent orange and white barrels bounced frenetically in every direction. The Oldsmobile disappeared into the darkness.

"Fucker's in the water," Cully yelled, vaulting from the vehicle and grabbing the emergency bag. He raced down the road on foot, the others right behind him.

John held the huge spotlight.

They made their way through the wreckage of the barricade as quickly as they could manage. Standing on the edge of the damaged bridge, John swung the spotlight down into the river. Fifteen feet down, they could make out the rear end of the car. It had gone nose first through the ice, and the current had wedged the vehicle up to the back doors under broken ice pieces. The black water swirled around the wreck, piling the ice higher and higher.

Cully was pulling on a harness. "Lower me down there," he said, tossing the end of a rope to Jason.

John stepped forward. "You can't do that, Cully. Not in that water with no protective gear. You know that. There's a guy at the fire station who's a diver. They're on the way."

Cully writhed and struggled with the harness.

"Cully, stop."

The younger man looked at John and finally ceased his efforts. He took a deep breath. "Ken Fellows," Cully said, still looking down into the water.

"What?" John asked.

"The diver's Ken Fellows."

"Hmm, okay," John said.

He put his hand on Cully's shoulder and turned him back toward the street. As they all turned, the ambulance came shrieking up the road and stopped at the junction of River Street and the damaged bridge. The diver, unrecognizable in his wetsuit, was already being lowered down the steep river bank by the time the group of police reached them. Caleb stepped up to John.

"Strand will be fine, John," he said. "He's dealing with a little bit of shock, but otherwise seems okay. I had him taken to the hospital to get checked out."

John and Caleb stood side by side as the men on the road lowered a basket-like stretcher down into the ravine. The diver, steadied by ropes held by more men on top of the embankment, pulled the stretcher toward himself with one arm. Now they could see by the sporadic illumination of the several hand-held spotlights that the diver clutched a man with his other arm. With a great effort, the diver heaved the body onto the stretcher and waved. Slowly, both the stretcher and the diver were pulled up out of the river.

John and Caleb walked over to the diver as he peeled back the head covering of the wetsuit. The three of them looked in the direction of the ambulance. Inside, first responders were working on the man furiously. The drivers were closing the doors. The lights began to flash, the wailing of the siren split the frigid air, and the ambulance pulled away, headed for the hospital.

"What've we got?" Caleb asked the diver.

"I think we got a corpse," he answered.

There was a clanking and grinding and the sound of a large laboring engine behind them. John turned around to see Larry Sample and his beast of a wrecker. The wrecker came to a tenuous stop and stood shuddering on the bank of the river. The door of the cab creaked open, and Larry jumped lightly to the ground. He was dressed in the same greasy hat and clothes he'd worn days ago when he hauled Melanie's Jeep away. He sauntered over to the men, the ever-present tobacco wadded in his cheek.

"What's going on?" he said to John.

"We were in pursuit of a suspect, and he screamed right through the barricade and into the river."

"I gotta get inside," said Ken. "Good to see you, Larry."

Larry nodded as the diver left the group. "Dead?"

"We think so. Ambulance took him away."

"Hmm. Think it was an accident or suicide?"

"I don't know, Larry," John said, shaking his head.

"Well, I'll get the winch cranking and drag her out." He spat reflectively over the bank and walked back to the truck.

"Chief?"

John looked up. "What is it, Cully?"

"Becky radioed in and said your whole family is stranded on the widow's walk."

John wiped his hand across his face, but he smiled. "Think you can get me a ladder, Caleb?"

Caleb smiled back. "Right away."

John turned to Steve Bruno. "I'm going back to get my wife. Wrap things up here."

The young officer nodded acknowledgment.

Chapter Twenty-Five

John walked up the dark road and got back into his Suburban.

Caleb climbed into the passenger side. "I'll ride up with you, John," he said. "We'll meet the guys up there."

John nodded and turned the vehicle around, heading back into town. They could see the small fire truck as they approached. Two men were carrying a long ladder over the deep snow to the south side of the big brick building. John parked the police vehicle and left the lights flashing, and he and Caleb climbed out. They ran to catch up to the two men carrying the ladder — Cully and Strand. He wanted to ask the musician what was he doing here when he was supposed to be getting checked out at the hospital, but he didn't care anymore. The four of them lifted the ladder into place.

"I'll go up," Cully said and was three rungs up before John could comment.

He watched as the young officer scaled the ladder and reached the top. Looking up, he saw the enormous sweep of the Milky Way. He could see the outlines of his family against the starry sky. The next thing he saw made his heart leap: Melanie was stepping over the railing and coming down the ladder.

"John," she called before she had reached the bottom.

"I'm right here." He held his arms up.

She turned on the ladder, two rungs from the bottom, and he caught her as she reached out to him. They held each other.

"The kids are okay?" he said in her ear.

"Yes, the kids are wonderful." Her tears were hot on his neck, but her body shivered.

"You're freezing," he said, pulling off his jacket. Her teeth were chattering. He wrapped the jacket around her and held her close.

"So, the guy went into the river?" Peter asked.

John looked up and saw his two boys approaching. Beyond them, he could see Cully and Mia standing close together. Some dim realization raised itself in his mind, and his forehead furrowed, but he squelched the feeling immediately. Whatever it was, it would have to wait for another day.

"Peter," he said and wrapped an arm around his youngest son. "Yes, he drove into the river. The diver thinks he's dead. I'm going to have to go to the hospital and confirm it, but I'm going to get you all home first. Where's Gabriel?"

"I don't know," Michael answered. "I kinda forgot about him. He was with Caleb. Do you know, Mom?"

"He was here, I thought, a minute ago."

"I had sent him to the hospital," remarked Caleb as he, Cully, and Mia joined the group. "I don't think he went. He was here helping with the ladder a minute ago."

"I'll have to talk to him at some point," John said. "Let's just get home. Michael, leave your car here. We'll get it tomorrow. Is everyone all right?"

"Yes, Daddy," Mia said. "Everybody's fine."

On the way out of town, up the hill to their home, John's family filled him in on the details of the rescue.

He shook his head and fought back tears of emotion. "You were all very brave, very brave," he said, "and it's hard for me to even think about any of you being in that kind of danger. Michael, you were driving. You didn't do what I told you to do. You could have been killed. That person was certifiably insane. He wanted to kill someone and it could have been you."

His three children were silent.

His wife said, "John, I — " and then was silent too.

John held up his hand. "It's all right. It's all right," he said. "I've had to develop a certain resiliency with this job. Mostly, for me, as long as you're all safe, it's okay. And I am proud of the way you executed your plan, foolhardy as it was."

"We got what we wanted," Peter said sullenly.

"Yes, you did, Peter. The police department couldn't have done a better job. We didn't know what was going on, and you three got your mother out of harm's way. That's what's important."

When he dropped them all off at the house, he hugged each of them. He held his wife for a long time, then finally kissed her and let her go. "Go take a hot bath. I'm not sure when I'll be home. I'll have to go to the hospital and then try to catch up with Gabriel. I suspect he'll be calling you. If you hear from him, let me know." He kissed her again and watched her until she was inside the house.

At the hospital, John learned from the attending physician in the ER that Richard Seeley was, indeed, dead. He had a wound on his right hand from the explosion of the old revolver, but that had not been life threatening. He had drowned, probably already unconscious from where his head had struck the windshield on impact. John sighed. It was terrible to think of people being so desperate, so unable to communicate their distress, so unable to help themselves. Worse, he was saddened to think that he would have to tell old Bud Seeley, all alone up there on the hill. He could give the nasty job to Steve or one of the state police, but it wouldn't be right. Because he was chief, and more importantly in a small town, because of the connection with Melanie, as remote as it might be, the job was his, as distasteful as it might be.

"Thank you," John said, shaking the doctor's hand on his way out.

"Don't mention it," said the doctor automatically. Then he added, "Things have been pretty busy, Chief. I hope they settle down for you now. Are you feeling okay yourself?"

"I hope they settle down, too," John said, smiling wryly, and he walked out the door into the frigid night. He started the Suburban and headed for the inn. It was ten o'clock, but for some odd reason, he didn't feel tired, even though he couldn't remember when he had really last slept. He took a back street and drove past the police station. There was a light still on. He stopped and went in to see who was still there or, as he had to do quite frequently, to shut off the lights the last person to leave had left on.

Steve Bruno and Jason Patterson were pulling on their coats as he opened the door.

"Hey, Chief," Jason said. "We thought you were still at the hospital. Becky just left. Me and Steve were locking up."

"Thanks, but you should both be home. State dispatcher will keep an eye on things. Did Cully go home?"

"He went with Caleb to help him with the fire engine. I guess he'll go home after that. Or sleep at the fire station."

"Who's on tomorrow?"

"I think I am," Jason said.

"Why don't you call in a couple of the auxiliary guys for the weekend. And you both stay home," said John. "I don't anticipate any uproar this weekend."

"We didn't anticipate the last three days, either," Steve said, cramming his hat on.

"You're right, there. I guess I should keep my mouth shut. Call the auxiliary anyway and go home. I'm going to the inn to speak to Strand, and then I've got to go up into the hills and tell old Bud Seeley his grandson is dead."

"That's rough," Jason said.

John nodded, said good night, and took his leave.

The door to the inn was open. There was a dim light at the front desk, but no one was around. John could hear noises from the kitchen, so he went in. The chef and the kitchen crew were cleaning up after the dinner crowd. Bill Noyes was going over receipts at a little desk in the corner.

"Hey, John," he addressed the chief. "What now?"

"I think everything's pretty much blown itself out," John said. "I need to talk to Strand."

"Not here," said Noyes.

"Really? Do you know where he went?" John would have put money on finding him at his own house, talking to Melanie.

"A limo came after him a while ago. Here, come with me. He left some stuff for you."

John followed the innkeeper out to the front desk. Noyes went around back and shuffled through a pile of papers. He surfaced with a large manila envelope. "This is for you. He told me to make sure you got it before tomorrow."

John took the envelope. "Anything else?"

"He told me to tell you he had to leave tonight. He couldn't be away from the band any longer, what with the concert coming up tomorrow night. He said to say thanks to you and Melanie. He's staying at the Hanover Inn if you need to talk to him."

"Hmm," John muttered. "Well, thanks, Bill. Good night."

"Good night, John," said the innkeeper cordially.

Chapter Twenty-Six

John headed out of town toward home. He tossed the envelope on the seat beside him. He would look at it from within the comfort of his own kitchen. As he approached his house and swung the Suburban into the driveway, he could see all the lights on. Debbie Cohen's car was there, as well as his in-laws' pickup. The third vehicle he recognized as Tim Cully's truck. He sighed, but he was grateful to have his family intact and healthy after the threat they faced.

"John." Surprisingly, it was his mother-in-law who approached him first. She put her arms around him in a light embrace and brushed her cool cheek against his. "I'm glad you're safe," she said, releasing him.

John was amused. Catherine Dearborne had touched him only once before in all the time they had known each other. Immediately following Michael's birth, as she gazed at her first grandchild, she had laid her hand on his arm and told him his son was beautiful. Well, he thought, every twenty years was better than not at all. "Thanks," he said.

Automatically, he put out his left arm, and just as he unconsciously expected, Melanie was there beside him, her arm around his waist. "Nobody's tired," she said in an effort to explain the houseful of family and friends.

He squeezed her as he said to Cully, who was standing on the other side of the room with Mia, Emmie, Peter, and Michael, "Cully, you should go home. You need to rest now."

"Just following up, Chief," the young man said, flashing a brilliant smile.

Tom Dearborne, taciturn as usual, said from his chair at the kitchen table, "Glad you're back safe, John."

"John. John!" Juxtaposed to his father-in-law, Debbie enthusiastically threw her arms around him. "I am so very, very glad to see you! Oh, we were all beside ourselves, what with a murder and a blizzard and a rock star!" Conversation was never hard for Debbie.

"It is pretty unbelievable," he conceded. "Everybody all fine here?"

"Everyone is fine," his wife said. "Come sit down at the table and have some tea. We've all got to unwind. Where is Gabriel?"

John took his chair and leaned on the table. "I thought he'd be at the inn, but when I went there, Bill told me a limo had picked him up and taken him up to Hanover. Personally, I was irked. I thought he'd come here. I still have to ask him some questions in order to put this whole fiasco to bed."

"He had to get to his band," Melanie said. Debbie set a steaming cup of tea in front of both of them. "That's what we were talking about when Seeley burst in on us. He said they always did a new song at every concert, and this concert's song wasn't finished yet."

"Ah, the poor guy's got problems, then," John said sarcastically, making Tom's lips curve almost into a smile.

John sipped his tea. Debbie hovered around the back of his chair, ready to help her friends should they wish the slightest thing. It was her nature.

John said to Melanie, "I have to go tell Bud Seeley about his grandson. Will you go with me?"

"Oh, my, how awful," Debbie said with a sigh.

"Of course I'll go," said Melanie. "We should go tonight, shouldn't we?"

"I'm afraid so."

"I'm ready when you are," she said.

"Let's see what the famous Gabriel Strand has left for us, first." He put the manila envelope on the table and opened it. Inside was a letter and a pile of badges on lanyards.

"What is it, Dad?" Mia asked, sidling up close to her father. "What does it say? Read it."

"Shhh," John said. Then he began to read. "Dear Chief Giamo. It sounds weak, but thank you for saving my life. Please understand that I didn't try to avoid you after this evening's incident. I just had to get back to my band. It's been a week since I've seen them, and we have a song to complete before tomorrow night's concert. I would like to invite you and your officers, as well as your whole family and any friends you might want to bring along to the concert. I'm enclosing backstage passes—" Here, John was interrupted by shrieks and screams of delight. Mia and Emmie were hugging each other and jumping up and down. He raised his voice and continued. "Backstage passes for everyone. Just tell them who you are. I hope I can get to see you after the show. Again, thanks for everything you did for me. I know you saved my life. It's hard for me to think about, but as they say, the show must go on. Tell Melanie I thank her for everything, too. Gratefully, Gabe."

"This is totally, totally awesome!" Mia said. "Backstage with Ragged Rainbow!"

"Hmm," said her father. "I guess we'll have to go, then."

Melanie looked at her husband. "We should go get this over with before it gets much later."

Debbie said, "I'm going to stay here. Jim is at the hospital all night tonight anyway, and Emmie isn't going to leave under these circumstances, so I'm not going home alone. I'll clean up and get everyone settled. You go do your job." She put both arms around the two of them as they sat at the table and hugged them. Debbie's reaction to almost any action was a hug, but because it came from her most honest of hearts, it was always appreciated.

Telling Bud that his grandson was dead was the hardest thing to do, but it went as well as they could have expected. When they had approached the man's home, he met them at the door in his longjohns, with the pack of dogs barking and whining around his old, bent legs. He knew why they had come, and they sat with him for over an hour at the table, sipping on the syrupy coffee. He told them stories about his grandson before he had been taken away. He asked some questions involving the murder, the hostage incident, and the drowning. John answered them directly. A man like Bud Seeley demanded directness. He finally allowed Melanie to call his daughter so that he would have some family support. To Melanie's relief, the woman sounded reasonable, promising to come down in the morning.

At the end of their visit, Bud walked them to the door. "Come back in the spring," he said to Melanie. "I got some of them Mille Fleurs your uncle liked. I'll give ya a hen and chicks."

Melanie smiled though unshed tears and thanked him profusely.

Afterward, driving home, John and Melanie were silent, turning the whole dark episode over in their minds. John was the first one to speak as they came to the stop sign where the dirt road joined the main route. There were no cars coming, but he stayed stopped. The sky was beginning to lighten. He sighed. "You okay?"

Melanie shrugged. "Yeah. Sad, though, isn't it? I feel so badly for the old man. To have had that child and raised him until he was eight years old and lose him, and then lose him again." She shuddered. "I just don't like to think about it."

"You didn't get hurt getting pulled through the ceiling or anything?"

"Oh, no. John, you should have seen our children. They were a team. They're almost grown." He looked over at her. He could see tears in her eyes. "They rescued me." Now she began to really cry, softly, but her shoulders convulsed with the sobs she tried to repress.

John reached over and took his wife in his arms. They sat like that, watching the sky go from velvety purple to pale lavender with the first light of day. He kissed the top of her head. "Let's go home and get some sleep."

She nodded and slid back into her seat. They turned south onto the main road.

Chapter Twenty-Seven

It was Saturday night, and the Giamo entourage was backstage at the Ragged Rainbow concert in the hockey rink in Hanover, New Hampshire. Present were the Giamo family; the Cohen family, this time including the oft absent Dr. Jim Cohen; Steve Bruno and his wife; Jason Patterson; and Tim Cully. Becky Dearborne and her family had politely declined, their musical tastes seemingly incompatible with this genre.

The concert was set to start at nine, and they'd been there since seven. John had spent much of the first hour exchanging conversation with Hanover's police chief and some of the officers on duty. Then he turned his attention to the increased activity around him. The crew was setting up the stage. John had to admit it was fascinating to watch. It was a whole segment of society he had previously known nothing about. He watched them work on their instruments. He heard the backup singers complaining about the clothes they were supposed to wear. A skinny little man was darting back and forth shouting orders at everyone he met. John noticed his children were enthralled.

Gabriel approached them. He wore skintight jeans and a black T-shirt and had his guitar slung over his shoulders. He was ready to play.

"I'm glad you came." He smiled broadly and extended his hand to everyone. He hugged Melanie and Debbie. John watched the young man. Strand was in his element. This was his world. Melanie blushed as she returned his embrace, and John wrapped his arms around her, pulling her back against him.

"This is so great, Gabe," Mia said, reaching out with both hands to the musician. "Thank you so much for this. Thank you." She was really being nice, thought John. She had dropped her edge. He was happy to see her transcend the teenage girl defense and give in to honest enjoyment. She even took Cully's hand and dragged him out from behind her where he stood. "Do you know Tim Cully?" she asked.

"Yes," Gabriel said. "We've met. Good to see you here, Tim." No one who knew him called Cully "Tim," except perhaps his mother. It made John smile.

"Good to see you, Gabe," Cully said. "I'm glad everything worked out."

The musician's face changed then. He held the young officer's hand in mid-shake. Perhaps he had developed a healthier respect for cops, thought John. He nodded his head vigorously. "Me, too. I'm glad too. Thank you, thank you." There was a slightly awkward pause, and Gabriel said, "I've got to get going. We're on in two minutes. Enjoy yourselves, everyone."

The crowd was chanting. The musicians were taking their places.

"This is it," Gabriel said as he prepared to walk on stage.

"Break a leg," Melanie said.

Gabriel looked at her. Impulsively, he smiled, leaned over, and kissed her on the mouth. Then he walked out on stage, and the crowd noise surged.

"That took balls," Michael said, looking at his father.

"What the hell!" Peter said indignantly. "Mom!"

"Don't worry, guys," said their father, who was surprisingly jovial. "I can afford it."

"Stop talking, you guys!" Mia hissed. "They're on."

The show was fantastic. The music was good; the band was truly talented. Gabriel was full of energy, obviously revved by the crowd's adoration.

Melanie stood on tiptoe and whispered in her husband's ear. "I can smell the testosterone."

He laughed and whispered back, "Think the Cohens will have sex tonight?"

She winked at him. "I don't care about the Cohens, as long as we do. More of that crazy make-up sex."

John coughed.

"Are you blushing?" Melanie whispered, laughing.

He squeezed her hand in his.

There was an intermission as the set on stage was changed. The musicians tweaked their instruments, and the backup singers shed their costumes and appeared in T-shirts and jeans.

"They always play the real music in the second half of the show," Mia said.

"How would you know? You've never been to one of their shows," retorted Peter.

"Shut up for once, Peter!" Mia hissed back as Gabriel stepped up to the mike.

The crowd immediately hushed, on edge.

"This is where we always introduce our new song," Gabriel said. "Well, this song is special. For a special lady. I fell in love this week. I fell in love with a real lady, but it's not to be. She's married, and she loves her husband. Too bad for me, but she inspired me to write this song. Here it is. This song is dedicated to you, Melanie. I hope you like it."

Backstage, Melanie looked uncomfortable. The Cohens were staring at her. Her children were staring at her. Her husband stood behind her, his big arms wrapped around her. "He's overreacting," she muttered to her friends.

"I think it's wonderful!" Mia said. "Mom, Ragged Rainbow is doing a song about you. That's huge. Listen."

It was the wee hours of the morning. John and Melanie Giamo were climbing into bed.

"Well, what a surprise that was!" she said.

"You inspired him," John replied, crawling under the covers of the bed, naked. He loved to be in bed first so that he could watch her undress. He never tired of it. He thought she was the most beautiful woman he knew.

She unhooked her bra and let it slip to the floor. She didn't put on a nightgown, but slipped in beside him, naked too.

"Does this mean that we share in the royalties?" he asked.

"Ha," she laughed. "I doubt it."

"Well, he named the song after you. He said you were the inspiration."

"Who knew?" she quipped.

"You did," John said. "You knew very well, but I don't care. You're in bed with me."

"And that's right where I'll always want to be," she said, and then she switched off the light.

Acknowledgments

Many thanks to my Omnific Team — Elizabeth Harper, Coreen, Lisa, CJ, and Kim. Once again, many thanks to Cindy Campbell who did a wonderful job of unjumbling the complicated parts of this story and smoothing out the wrinkles along the way. Thank you to Traci Olsen for holding my hand when needed and coming up with some creative marketing. Thank you, also, to my children for providing me with constant inspiration, and a special salute to Rick Cloud, chief of police in my small town.

About the Author

Linda Cunningham grew up a small town country girl and it is here where she's still most comfortable. She has written steadily throughout the years, although usually other peoples' speeches, articles, and grants, primarily for medical and agricultural trade journals. Now that her three children are grown, Linda is writing full time and writing the stuff she loves—Romance!

Linda lives in a romantic stone house in the Green Mountain State of Vermont, surrounded by her gardens and animals which include horses, dogs, cats, chickens, sheep, a parakeet, goldfish and the wild visitors who tiptoe through on a regular basis. When time permits, she also enjoys cooking, sketching, and painting.

check out these titles from
OMNIFIC PUBLISHING

◄— ·····►Contemporary Romance◄····· —►

Boycotts & Barflies and *Trust in Advertising* by Victoria Michaels
Passion Fish by Alison Oburia and Jessica McQuinn
The Small Town Girl series: *Small Town Girl & Corporate Affair, Keeping the Peace*
by Linda Cunningham
Stitches and Scars by Elizabeth A. Vincent
Take the Cake by Sandra Wright
Pieces of Us by Hannah Downing
The Way That You Play It by BJ Thornton
The Poughkeepsie Brotherhood series: *Poughkeepsie & Return to Poughkeepsie*
by Debra Anastasia
Cocktails & Dreams and *The Art of Appreciation* by Autumn Markus
Recaptured Dreams and *All-American Girl* and *Until Next Time* by Justine Dell
Once Upon a Second Chance by Marian Vere
The Englishman by Nina Lewis
16 Marsden Place by Rachel Brimble
Sleepers, Awake by Eden Barber
The Runaway Year by Shani Struthers
Hydraulic Level Five by Sarah Latchaw
Fix You by Beck Anderson
Just Once by Julianna Keyes
The WORDS series: *The Weight of Words* by Georgina Guthrie
Theatricks by Eleanor Gwyn-Jones
The Sacrificial Lamb by Elle Fiore
The Plan by Qwen Salsbury
The Kiss Me series: *Kiss Me Goodnight* by Michele Zurlo
Saint Kate of the Cupcake: The Dangers of Lust and Baking by LC Fenton
Playing All the Angles by Nicole Lane

◄— ·····►New Adult Romance◄····· —►

Three Daves by Nicki Elson
Streamline by Jennifer Lane
The Shades series: *Shades of Atlantis & Shades of Avalon* by Carol Oates
The Heart series: *Beside Your Heart, Disclosure of the Heart & Forever Your Heart*
by Mary Whitney
Romancing the Bookworm by Kate Evangelista
Fighting Fate by Linda Kage
Flirting with Chaos by Kenya Wright
The Vice, Virtue & Video series: *Revealed & Captured* by Bianca Giovanni

Young Adult Romance

The Ember series: *Ember & Iridescent* by Carol Oates
Breaking Point by Jess Bowen
Life, Liberty, and Pursuit by Susan Kaye Quinn
The Embrace series: *Embrace & Hold Tight* by Cherie Colyer
Destiny's Fire by Trisha Wolfe
The Reaper series: *Reaping Me Softly & UnReap My Heart* by Kate Evangelista
The Legendary Saga: *Legendary* by LH Nicole
Fatal by T.A. Brock

Paranormal Romance

The Light series: *Seers of Light, Whisper of Light & Circle of Light* by Jennifer DeLucy
The Hanaford Park series: *Eve of Samhain & Pleasures Untold* by Lisa Sanchez
Immortal Awakening by KC Randall
The Seraphim series: *Crushed Seraphim & Bittersweet Seraphim* by Debra Anastasia
The Guardian's Wild Child by Feather Stone
Grave Refrain by Sarah M. Glover
Divinity by Patricia Leever
Blood Vine series: *Blood Vine, Blood Entangled & Blood Reunited* by Amber Belldene
Divine Temptation by Nicki Elson
Love in the Time of the Dead by Tera Shanley

Historical Romance

Cat O' Nine Tails by Patricia Leever
Burning Embers by Hannah Fielding
Good Ground by Tracy Winegar

Romantic Suspense

Whirlwind by Robin DeJarnett
The CONduct series: *With Good Behavior, Bad Behavior & On Best Behavior*
by Jennifer Lane
Indivisible by Jessica McQuinn
Between the Lies by Alison Oburia
Blind Man's Bargain by Tracy Winegar

Erotic Romance

The Keyhole series: *Becoming sage* (book 1) by Kasi Alexander
The Keyhole series: *Saving sunni* (book 2) by Kasi & Reggie Alexander
The Winemaker's Dinner: *Appetizers & Entrée* by Dr. Ivan Rusilko & Everly Drummond
The Winemaker's Dinner: *Dessert* by Dr. Ivan Rusilko
Client N° 5 by Joy Fulcher

Anthologies

A Valentine Anthology including short stories by
Alice Clayton ("With a Double Oven"),
Jennifer DeLucy ("Magnus of Pfelt, Conquering Viking Lord"),
Nicki Elson ("I Don't Do Valentine's Day"),
Jessica McQuinn ("Better Than One Dead Rose and a Monkey Card"),
Victoria Michaels ("Home to Jackson"), and
Alison Oburia ("The Bridge")

Singles and Novellas

It's Only Kinky the First Time (A Keyhole series single) by Kasi Alexander
Learning the Ropes (A Keyhole series single) by Kasi & Reggie Alexander
The Winemaker's Dinner: RSVP by Dr. Ivan Rusilko
The Winemaker's Dinner: No Reservations by Everly Drummond
Big Guns by Jessica McQuinn
Concessions by Robin DeJarnett
Starstruck by Lisa Sanchez
New Flame by BJ Thornton
Shackled by Debra Anastasia
Swim Recruit by Jennifer Lane
Sway by Nicki Elson
Full Speed Ahead by Susan Kaye Quinn
The Second Sunrise by Hannah Downing
The Summer Prince by Carol Oates
Whatever it Takes by Sarah M. Glover
Clarity (A *Divinity* prequel single) by Patricia Leever
A Christmas Wish (A *Cocktails & Dreams* single) by Autumn Markus
Late Night with Andres by Debra Anastasia
Poughkeepsie (enhanced iPad app collector's edition) by Debra Anastasia

coming soon from
OMNIFIC PUBLISHING